NECROPHOBIA
Book 1. Wake the Dead
By
Jack Hamlyn

COPYRIGHT © 2011 BY JACK HAMLYN
COPYRIGHT © 2011 BY SEVERED PRESS
WWW.SEVEREDPRESS.COM
ALL RIGHTS RESERVED. NO PART OF THIS BOOK MAY BE REPRODUCED OR TRANSMITTED IN ANY FORM OR BY ANY ELECTRONIC OR MECHANICAL MEANS, INCLUDING PHOTOCOPYING, RECORDING OR BY ANY INFORMATION AND RETRIEVAL SYSTEM, WITHOUT THE WRITTEN PERMISSION OF THE PUBLISHER AND AUTHOR, EXCEPT WHERE PERMITTED BY LAW.
THIS NOVEL IS A WORK OF FICTION. NAMES, CHARACTERS, PLACES AND INCIDENTS ARE THE PRODUCT OF THE AUTHOR'S IMAGINATION, OR ARE USED FICTITIOUSLY.
ANY RESEMBLANCE TO ACTUAL EVENTS, LOCALES OR PERSONS LIVING OR DEAD, IS PURELY COINCIDENTAL.

ISBN 978-0-9872400-0-2

ALL RIGHTS RESERVED

"Given the greater number of dead than living on this earth, a revolt of the dead against the living who had buried them would certainly end in defeat for the latter."

—Ornella Volta

CLOSING IN

It was the end of July and the air was hot and thick like boiled molasses. Ricki was in the kitchen whipping up some breakfast and I was in the living room, sweat running down my face as I tried to wire in the new air conditioner. I had just fished a Philips screwdriver from my red toolbox when I heard the screaming.

It went through me like a knife.

It was loud and cutting and absolutely shrill. It didn't even sound human. More like an animal being flayed alive. I stood there for maybe three or four seconds shocked into inaction, then I stepped out onto the porch.

By then, Ricki was at the screen door looking out. "What is it, Steve?"

"I don't know. I heard screaming."

"So did I."

But what I saw in the neighborhood was…nothing.

Absolutely ordinary. Old Lady Hazen was out tending to her flowerbeds. Jimmy LaRue was up on his roof, hammering. Cars were passing in the street. The mailman was walking up the sidewalk with his bag of letters, pausing now, maybe listening as well. Jimmy LaRue was pounding too goddamn loud, so he didn't hear anything. Mrs. Hazen…well, she couldn't hear cymbals crashing next to her ear let alone dogs barking.

I looked over to the mailman.

He had put his earbuds back in and went on his way.

The scream came again and it was wet and gurgling. By that time, people up and down the block were out on their porches wondering what in the Christ was happening.

"Should I call 911?" Ricki asked.

"I don't know. Maybe I better go look."

"Steve..."

"I'll be right back," I promised.

Then I ran up the sidewalk, listening for the scream, and it came again. Though this time it was weak and broken, more liquid than anything and I didn't care for that much. It was coming from Rommy Jacob's backyard. I was sure of it. Rommy was a widower. He lived for his garden. He made offerings to us each summer of tomatoes and cucumbers and snap peas. I jogged around the side of his house, almost tripped over a wheelbarrow full of black soil, and that's when I saw him.

He was lying on the ground, twisting and squirming. It looked like someone had painted his throat and face a bright, Technicolor shade of red. He saw me. He looked right at me and there was more than agony in his eyes, there was horror. Sheer horror. His red-stained fingers were at his throat and when he opened his mouth to speak, blood came out. It bubbled out of the side of his throat...which was missing, I saw, like a tiger had taken a bite out of it.

I just stood there.

My stomach rolled over and I got dizzy. The smell of blood was heavy, sweet, metallic in the air. I don't have a weak stomach. I spent a year in Iraq with a Stryker Brigade. I saw men die. I saw them die in numbers. I pulled pieces of them from Hummers when they caught IED flak. Yet...to see it here, in my neighborhood...it made it all that much more brutal and devastating and unreal. I had to force myself to move. Rommy was my friend, for godsake. But this was more than I could handle. He needed medical attention right away.

"Hang on, buddy," I told him, part of me wanting to run home for my cell to call 911 and another part telling me I should stay because Rommy wasn't going to make it until an ambulance showed and I didn't want him to die alone.

That's what was going through my head.

Then I heard something behind me and Rommy's eyes, which were beginning to get the glazed look of near-death, widened. I turned and there was a man standing there. His skin was horribly pale, mottled with gray patches, his eyes white, completely white. He was smiling at me: lips shriveled back from narrow teeth. It was no smile, it was a rictus grin. He came at me, snapping his teeth like a crocodile rising from a river, pushing a black wave of damp decay before him. It smelled hot, nauseating.

He opened his mouth to say something.

Rommy made a gurgling sound.

I took one step backward, shaking my head.

You see, that thing reaching out for me, I knew him. His name had been Bill DeForest. He'd been buried nearly a week before. Now he was back and he was no longer human.

"Bill…" I heard myself say, knowing it was ridiculous and pointless, but I couldn't help myself. Bill had been my next door neighbor. When Ricki and I moved into the neighborhood six years before, Bill was the first one to knock on the door to see if we needed anything. He came over with a six-pack and a strong back. His wife, Pearl, showed with fresh-baked cookies and a good heart. Bill helped me re-shingle the roof. He did wiring and windows for me. When I was in Iraq, he made damn sure that Ricki and Paul never went without.

Six days ago, we'd buried him. Heart attack.

I was one of the pallbearers.

Now he was back.

He went right for my throat with bared teeth. I tried to push him back, then he lunged. He almost put me down. He was trying to bite me, to get at my throat. He was wild and snarling and stinking of the grave. I shoved him away and he came right back at me. I had no choice. I hit him. I hit him hard. He staggered back and went down to one knee, staring up at me with a feral, fixed hatred. He didn't just want to kill me. He wanted to slaughter me. He wanted to gut me and lap up my blood.

He came again and I hit him.

He fell back again, but I knew full well we couldn't play this game all day. This wasn't Bill DeForest. Bill DeForest was dead. This was a dead thing that wanted to feed. There was only one way to stop it and I knew it. But I needed a weapon. That's when I saw the shovel leaning against the fence. I picked it up. I held it over my head, ready to swing. But if that would have had an effect on a sane mind, it meant nothing to Bill. He was a thing of hunger. He understood nothing but feeding.

When he came again, some kind of slime hanging from his mouth, I swung the shovel. The blade hit him square in the face. It opened up a gash from the bridge of his nose to the crown of his skull. But it did not stop him. It made him take a few foundering steps back and then he came again. I swung the shovel, putting all my strength and weight behind it. Bill's head split open like a ripe muskmelon. The impact drove him to his knees. He looked at me with those weird glassy eyes. A slop of brains had oozed down his face.

I swung it again and his head came apart.

He dropped face-first into the grass. He trembled, but did not move again.

I stood there, panting, the shovel in my hands, staring at the gore-spattered blade. None of it seemed real. Everything had taken on the dusky shades of a nightmare. I staggered back until I was in the alley. I stood there, just breathing, trying to get the world to stop spinning. When it did, I looked down the alley and the alley beyond that which terminated at the gates of Cedar Hill Cemetery.

I saw three, then four and five figures moving slowly, steadily in my direction. By the way they were walking with that loose-limbed sort of shuffling, I knew who they were and what they wanted.

There was no getting around it.

The dead were coming.

SHOCK TROOPS

When I stepped back in the yard, Dick Nickersen from across the street was standing there. Dick and I weren't real close. I didn't respect him or like him and I'm sure that went both ways. Dick was our neighborhood pain-in-the-ass. He knew all the city and municipal regulations and routinely reported people if their garages weren't up to code, if they forgot to cut their grass or rake their leaves in a timely manner or didn't keep their sidewalks ice-free in the winter time. He was fond of frivolous lawsuits. He had unsuccessfully sued Jimmy LaRue for allergies he'd suffered because of adverse reactions to smoke coming from Jimmy's backyard barbecue pit and he'd gone after Mitzy Streeter because the leaves from her maples clogged up his rain gutters and made his roof leak. He had motion lights strategically placed around his yard to halt vandals, but it never stopped the local kids from soaping his windows on Halloween or stealing his lawn ornaments.

Dick wasn't known as "Dick the Prick" or "Prick Dickersen" for nothing.

Right then he was staring at me.

He saw what his paranoid mind wanted to see: two badly-used bodies and me standing there with a shovel in my hand. I could see the fear on him: it made beads of sweat pop on his face. "What…what…what…"

Though I didn't want to touch it, I flipped Bill DeForest's body over so he could see it real good. "It's Bill," I said. "He came back. He killed Rommy. I hit him with the shovel."

It was obvious that he wasn't believing me. "Bill's dead," he said, immediately ascertaining the obvious as he always did.

"The dead are coming back," I said.

He shook his head from side to side. He didn't want to believe that. He preferred to think I was a nutbag who just did in two of my neighbors. "The dead…no, the dead are just dead."

Before I could stop myself, I said, "I saw it before, Dick. It happened in Iraq five years ago. Now it's happening here."

He looked at me like I was crazy. Maybe I was. As far as he was concerned, I was nothing but some fucked-up war vet. I was shell-shocked. I had PTSD. I wasn't in my right frame of mind. I wanted to grab him and shake him and tell him everything I knew about Necrovirus and what it could do and the assurances I'd been given in Mosul that it was all over with.

Instead, I dragged him right out into the alley and he looked like he was going to have a stroke. I turned him and faced him so he could see the others down the alley. There were not four or five now. There were a dozen of them and they were closing in fast.

Dick just stared.

Then he looked at me. His eyes were moist. "This...this has to be some kind of joke, Steve."

"It's not a joke, Dick. You better get home. You better lock your doors," I told him. "They're coming out of Cedar Hill."

"But, Steve..."

"Get home, Dick. When they come after you, they're insane."

"It's Halloween shit. Zombies. Nothing but Halloween—"

"Dick...go home."

But he couldn't leave. He came right up to me and put his hands on my shoulders as if he were trying to ground himself in my physical reality. "But this is Lincoln Park," he said, as if that made all the difference in the world. "This isn't Iraq. This is fucking Yonkers."

"Go home," I said again.

He turned and jogged away. It wasn't easy for him to take. I think, all things considered, he would have been far happier if I had killed him with the shovel. Dying knowing the dead stayed dead and God still made little green apples would have done his heart a world of good.

But I didn't have time to worry about that shit, the dead were coming and I had to protect my family. I cut back through Rommy's yard, thinking I should say something or do something but there simply wasn't any time. When I got around front, I heard screams in the distance. Then barking. A wild, frantic barking and yapping.

Old Man Castleberry's beagles.

Had to be. Castleberry was retired and had found a hobby: beagles. He raised them in a kennel in the backyard. Hunting dogs. Sold them for pretty good money. Problem was, when one started barking, they all joined in. And that could be at two in the afternoon or two in the morning.

But this was not your ordinary barking: this was the dogs going haywire, trying to alert any and all to a most unnatural threat.

The dead weren't just coming up the alley.

They were in the streets.

And they had found the mailman.

He was knocked on his ass. Letters were flying and drifting earthward like goose feathers. A corpse in a black burial suit was biting into the poor guy's arm. His blue uniform shirt was red with blood and he was screaming something terrible. I made to go to him and then two more zombies came through the shrubs, a teenage boy whose face was more skull than flesh and a little girl in filthy cerements. They both looked right at me with their graveyard eyes and then, passing me, they set on the mailman like hyenas on a fresh kill.

I had tossed the shovel so I had nothing to fight with.

The teenage boy was gnawing on the mailman's legs, the little girl was going for his throat. Poor guy was writhing and twisting, trying to beat them off, trying protect his face, screaming for help. The little girl seized one of his hands in her jaws and began to shake it like a chew toy. I could hear his finger bones snapping.

Shit!

Was anybody else seeing this?

I looked for a weapon, something, anything. The ice-chopper. It was on my porch. I still hadn't put it away and for once my incurable procrastination was going to come in handy. It was just a broomstick with a sturdy iron blade on the end, but it was better than nothing. I ran up and grabbed it. In the distance, I could hear screams rising to a fever pitch and I knew the dead were attacking the living. And not just here on Holly Street but all over town.

I made it far as the sidewalk with my ice-chopper.

That's when the little girl left the mailman to the others and turned on me. She wore a white dress gone gray with mildew. Her face was like wax melting off the bone below. She held her arms out to me like she wanted a hug. Her eyes were glowing hot and savage, teeth barred, tangles of saliva dangling from her mouth. I waited for her. When she got within three feet, I gave her a swift kick that sent her rolling in the grass.

She made a hissing sound and came right back.

She crawled through the grass, grinding her teeth.

She looked like some human insect.

When she came at me again, I swung the ice-chopper. The flat edge of the blade caught the top of her skull and there was a hollow, wet, cracking sound like a baseball bat striking a soft pumpkin. I hit her in the head again until her brains splashed down her face. She trembled in the grass and stopped moving.

Up and down the streets the dead were shambling about.

Some were up on porches pounding on doors and windows.

How could it have amplified so fast?

I ran for the mailman, the ice-chopper held up and ready to strike. A couple zombies shambled past me. They snapped their teeth at me. One of them—a woman wearing what looked like a hospital gown—reached out and I cracked her in the head with the chopper. It made no difference to her: she just shambled away. I might as well have hit a stump.

I reached the mailman about the same time as Jimmy LaRue.

Jimmy had brought a .22 semi-auto rifle with him. As I got into range, Jimmy shot the teenage boy through the head. He staggered comically back a few steps and then folded up, blood and brain matter leaking from a hole in his skull. Jimmy shot the man in the back, which did absolutely no good. He turned on us, his maw dyed red, feral as any wolf. He made a growling sound in his throat. As Jimmy took aim again, the dead man snatched one of the mailman's arms he had chewed free and tried to walk off. Jimmy cracked off two more shots. By luck or design, one of them went through the back of the zombie's knee. He hit the pavement, dragging himself forward in a slime trail of ooze and rot, refusing to drop the arm.

Jimmy popped him in the head and that was that.

"What the fuck's going on here, Steve?" he wanted to know. His eyes were wide and shocked, his face white as the hair on his head. "These aren't people...they're fucking corpses. Goddamn zombies like on the late show."

I was looking down at the gored remains of the mailman. "That's exactly what they are," I said.

The mailman's throat was torn out and his belly had been hollowed, his mangled viscera spilled over the sidewalk. Everywhere he was red and ripped and partially-eaten.

I turned away, my stomach rolling over.

Jimmy said, "I…called the police…there was no answer…"

I looked down Holly Street, dozens of other zombies were moving in our direction. They were making moaning sounds. An army of the dead had been set upon Lincoln Park.

Jimmy started shooting again, dropping three more of them with perfect head-shots.

It was insane.

But it was happening.

A bloated, naked woman whose flesh was mottled with green patches of mildew had Mrs. Hazen by the throat, was dragging her corpse off through all those carefully-tended azaleas, petunias, and morning glories. Her body flattened them as she was dragged into the backyard. I was going to go to Mrs. Hazen's rescue, but I could see she was already dead. A big, one-armed zombie with a face like a nest of black moss climbed up onto a porch and dove through the screen door. A car came winging down the road, hit the zombie of a young woman with a resounding thud that sent her rolling to the curb. A guy got out and two zombies took him down, began savagely biting at his face and throat. People came out on their porches and the dead went after them.

Everywhere now you could hear screaming and shouting and frantic pleas for help. Gunshots in the distance.

It was madness.

Shouting, sirens, gunfire.

A naked woman came strolling out between two houses. She was tall and leggy, flaxen-haired, and was probably very attractive in life. But in death she was a sheer horror and Jimmy shot her dead. I turned and a fat man greasy with rot and drainage came at me, jowls drawn away from teeth that were stained red. I went at him with the ice-chopper like a man possessed. I didn't even let Jimmy draw a bead on him. I charged in, swinging, like some bloodthirsty barbarian with drawn sword. I hit him six or seven times until he went down and I kept hitting him, landing that blade on his head, until he rolled over in the grass, from the neck up nothing but raw hamburger.

There were more coming.

Jimmy said, "Better get inside and get your guns out, Steve. I wouldn't open your door for no one."

Numbly, I staggered off towards my porch, still gripping the ice-chopper.

There were fifteen or twenty walking corpses in the street by then.

DOWN TIME

When I got in the house, Ricki was waiting there. Paul was with her. Her golden summer tan had gone pale and her blue eyes looked drained of color.

"Steve…what is this?" she said to me. "It's all over the TV. It's happening everywhere. They're declaring martial law."

She wanted to know what it was, but I didn't dare tell her what I suspected. I had never told her about what I had seen in Iraq. It was too weird, too painful, too unbelievable. She would have thought I was nuts. But what had happened over there in a small, isolated pocket had gone global now. It was everywhere. It was no longer murky, white-knuckled memories that would wake me up sweating at four in the morning. It was here and it was now.

"I'm not sure," I said.

"Well, they're not terrorists," Paul said. "That's for sure. They're goddamn zombies."

I felt it all start to boil out of me then. Normally, when your ten-year old son says something like that you tell him to watch his mouth. But I did not tell him that. Neither did Ricki. I had all I could do not to start laughing at the absurdity of it all. But I knew if I started laughing I would scare the hell out of them and they were plenty freaked out by then.

"There are no such things as zombies," Ricki said, just repeating by rote the things parents *have* to say. Even now, it was so ingrained in her she couldn't help herself.

"Oh yeah? Then what are they, mom?"

Neither of us had any answer to that.

"Spooks aren't real," she said, trying to believe it herself.

And isn't that what you tell your kids? Zombies and ghosts and all that crazy shit is just make-believe movie-stuff, comic book shit. There aren't really witches flying on broomsticks or ghosts in closets or things scratching under beds. Pure fantasy. Things dreamed up by superstitious people who were scared of the dark and confused by their world. The only reason any of that stuff survived was that people found a way to squeeze a buck out of it. First they did it to scare people and then to cater to teenage girls who thought ghouls were cute. That's how horrible bloodsucking monsters had become angst-ridden androgynous pretty boys who hung around smoothie bars and werewolves had become coiffed male models with waxed chests. Watered-down, romanticized, 100% non-threatening. But scary or effeminate, it was all bullshit and nobody with a modern, functioning brain took that crap seriously. And you made damn sure your kids didn't or they were headed for a future that included bi-weekly visits to the therapy couch.

But now this.

In the streets, the walking dead.

"Paul," I said. "Go upstairs and grab my cell. It's on the dresser."

"Okay," he said, taking off.

When he was gone, I took Ricki aside. I gripped her by the shoulders and said, "I don't know what's happening exactly, but this town is under siege and we better batten down the hatches and ride it out. Let the police clean it up."

Ricki still had that dazed look in her eyes. "They're dead. I watched them out the window. Those aren't people. They're dead."

"I know," I said.

"And you're okay with that?"

"It doesn't matter *what* I'm okay with, Ricki. It's happening so we deal with it."

I was trying to appeal to her practical streak. Inside, Ricki was tough. Maybe on the outside she was small and petite, but on the inside she was 110 pounds of attitude once she got going. And I needed her to get going right then.

"The best thing to do is hole up in the basement," she said, taking the bait, switching gears so fast it astounded me as always. "We've got a bathroom down there. A bedroom. A fold-out couch. The camping stuff and sleeping bags are down there. I'll bring some food down. Some water. We'll need some basic first-aid items."

She started sorting around in the kitchen.

Paul returned with my cell. I called a few people in the neighborhood and got no answer. I called Ricki's mom. Nothing. I didn't like it. I didn't like it at all.

"Did you get a hold of Carty?" Ricki called out to me.

"She's not answering. Neither is your mother."

She frowned. She dug her cell out of her purse. "I better call Diane."

When Ricki calls Diane, she means business. Diane's head wasn't much good from all the drugs she'd taken through the years. Let's just say that Diane's morals are loose, her ethics questionable, and her common sense negligible. Ricki called the apartment building where she lived—Diane did not have a cellphone, the FBI could track your movements with one—but there was no answer.

She sighed. "Where the hell is everyone?"

"You know Diane," I said.

We packed up stuff and brought it downstairs. There were still a few zombies in the streets but I was hearing gunfire, both near and far, and I knew people were fighting. That was good. As long as they kept fighting we could turn this around…however it had happened. I got out the only two guns I owned. One was a Remington 12-gauge pump. I loaded it with buckshot and gave it to Ricki.

"Use it if you have to," I said. "I don't think you'll need it, but let's err on the side of caution."

The basement was the best idea. The door leading down there was solid oak and it would take a tank to breach it. Once it was dead-bolted and locked, no one would get through it.

"Are you going out again, Dad?" Paul asked me.

Ricki stopped what she was doing and looked at me. Just for a moment. I knew without a doubt that she wanted to warn me against playing hero, but on the other hand we couldn't reach her mother or Carty, who was one of our best friends in the world. As much as I wanted to hide out with them—and as much as Ricki wanted that too—I couldn't abandon the people we loved. I had to check on them. There was no other way around it.

"Yes, son," I told him. "I'm going out to check on gramma."

"You need me as a backup?"

I didn't smile because he was serious. "No, stay here. Protect your mother."

"She's pretty tough. She doesn't need me."

Ricki was carrying another box down to the basement. She was out of earshot. "She needs you more than you'll ever know," I told him. "When I leave, you lock that door down there. Don't let anyone in."

"What about you?"

"Well, yeah, me," I said, noticing and maybe not for the first time the platinum highlights in his hair he had gotten from his mother.

"Zombies can't reason much, Dad. All they are is stupid eating machines," Paul explained to me, an expert on the subject from all the zombie comics and paperbacks he devoured. "We're going to need a password. They can't think. If you get zombified, you'll never remember it. That's how we'll know you're okay."

Kids are amazing. Absolutely amazing. I knew damn well that just about every adult (save the crazy ones) were scared shitless at that moment and I was, too…but kids, man, they reorient themselves so quickly it can be frightening. I was willing to bet that while most adults were ready to piss themselves, their kids were rising up to the challenge of the undead. Maybe that sounds silly, but I believed it. Kids are tougher and much more resourceful than adults. They are not so anchored to the physical reality of their world, they can adapt and improvise at the drop of a hat. You can spin their world 360° and they'll come up standing. We adults would be thrown on our asses.

"What do you suggest?"

He scratched his tawny head. "Hmm. Didn't you guys use passwords in Iraq?"

"Yeah, sometimes." I thought it over. "Zulu Foxtrot."

"I like that!"

I explained it was military phonetics for Z and F, in other words, Zombie Free.

"Okay," he said. "Watch it out there. Aim for the head."

I gave him a hug which he did not appreciate—there's no tougher soldier than a ten-year old fighting man—and went over to Ricki. I gave her a kiss and, surprisingly, she slipped her tongue in my mouth. "Give you a good reason to hurry back," she said.

Paul had the TV going. "I'm setting up the comm center, Dad," he said.

"I'll keep in touch with my cell. I should be back in half an hour," I told them.

"Then what, Steve?" Ricki wanted to know.

"Then we hold out until this is sorted out."

I wanted badly to tell her about what I'd seen in Iraq. But there wasn't time and I didn't want Paul knowing about it for some reason. Though, again, being a kid he would have probably just shrugged and said, "Gotta start somewhere, I guess."

"Please be careful," she said.

Then the door was closed and locked.

I wondered if I'd ever see them again.

I went up the steps and got my gun and went out into the world of the dead.

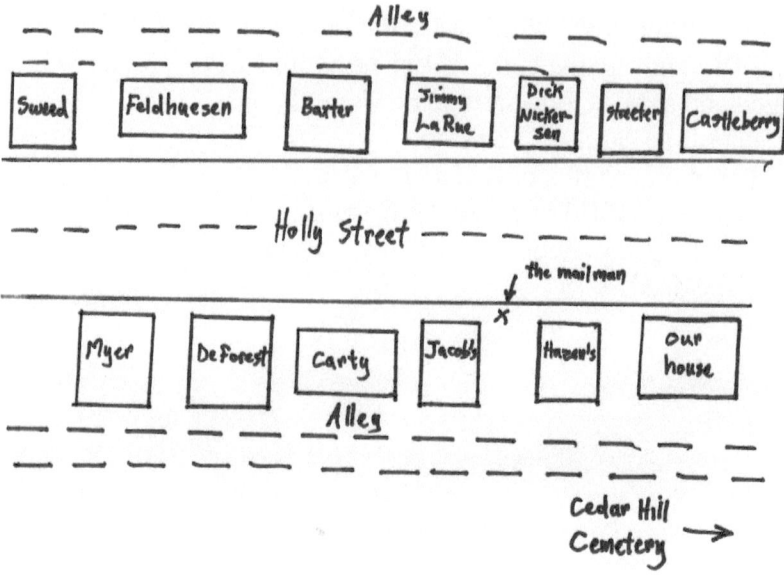

IMMEDIATE THREAT

In the thirty or so minutes I'd been in the house, the war—if that's what you can call it—had not slowed down nor even taken a breath. In the distance I could hear gunfire, sirens, people shouting, and even a few thumping concussions like some real firepower was being used. The sound of it brought back memories of the war. I saw no zombies in the streets. Maybe they had pushed on. Not that it gave me much hope, because what I saw was devastation, minor maybe, but ugly for America. There were bodies everywhere. Bodies of zombies. A couple half-eaten dogs. Cars were stalled in the middle of the avenue, doors opened. Their drivers were nowhere to be seen.

What else was nowhere to be seen was the body of the mailman.

All I found was a single blood-spattered shoe which was being investigated by a couple flies.

Could he have risen so fast?

I scanned around looking for trouble.

I had my old man's gun, a Browning Hi-Power he had carried in Vietnam. I hadn't used it in a couple of years and then only for target practice. But it would do the trick. As I moved up the sidewalk, I heard someone clear their throat.

"Where you going, Steve?" Jimmy LaRue asked. He was hanging out of a second story window with his .22.

I looked up at him. "I'm going to check on Carty."

"You need me?"

"No, I can handle it," I told him. "I got Ricki and Paul barricaded in the basement. Keep an eye on my house, will you?"

"You got it. I'll cover you."

Jesus, it was insane. In a matter of hours our peaceful neighborhood was like something out of Fallujah. Here I was patrolling the streets with a sniper above keeping an eye out for unfriendlies. Hour by hour the entire thing was becoming more and more surreal. And scary. My natural paranoia was whispering in the back of my head and it kept saying things like: *What if this situation is not containable? What if this zombie plague keeps rolling until there are no people left?* I had to force that stuff from my head. When I was in the war, we'd go out on these mounted patrols to see if we could draw fire from insurgents so we could hunt them down and kick their asses. The Army called it "Pacification" but the bullet-eaters and grunts on the ground called it "pussification". *Pussifying* the enemy. Our officers called it "movement to contact" and what it consisted of, basically, was exposing your ass to fire. Creep around in Stryker vehicles and see if any RPKs or RPGs opened up on us. Baiting, that's all it was. Like hanging your dick in a piranha tank and seeing if you got any nibbles.

And that's what it felt like I was doing right then: baiting the dead.

Like I was a hooker or something, trolling my wares and seeing if any righteous zombies wanted to take a bite.

It was insane, yes, but it was only the beginning of the madness. Just a delirium fever compared to where it was all going.

I made it over to Carty's house. She lived next to Rommy Jacob, whom I knew was dead. I did a quick reconnoiter of Carty's yard, made sure no bad boys were hanging around out by the garage or under the shade of the sour apple tree picking maggots from their teeth. There was nothing. That was good. But what was bad is that Carty's back door was wide open.

Carty wouldn't allow that.

Carty hated flies.

Swallowing, I entered the house silently.

Like a mouse into a shoe, I moved with stealth and silence. My throat was dry. It felt like it had been powdered down with beach sand. My heart was hammering, my knuckles white on the grip of the Browning.

Carty was laid up after knee surgery which was one of the reasons I thought I better check on her.

Years back Carty owned a saloon, but had sold it off after her husband died. In her eighties, she was very spry, full of wit, off-color jokes and salty metaphors. She could cuss like a sailor and took her bourbon in a water glass. She had an ongoing battle with old Mrs. Hazen and her goddamn flowers—*her and her goddamn flowers, Steve, you know how fucking sick I am of hearing about those pissing flowers of hers? Bitch called the cops for chrissake because my leaves blew into her flowerbeds last fall, you believe that shit? You don't hear Rommy bitching about it. Green goddamned thumb...I'd like to stick it so far up her ass she'd get a tickle in her throat*—yeah, that was Carty.

I loved her like a mother.

She, along with Bill DeForest and his wife, had sort of adopted us when we moved into the neighborhood. I could remember the day we moved in. Bill and his wife had come over. Not to be undone, Mrs. Hazen had followed suit and brought us an apple pie. Very nice, I thought. But as I'd gotten to know her I realized the only reason for the kindness was to get a look at us so she could make some rash judgments as to the sort of people we were. Carty had brought no pies. She'd invited me in for a few fingers of Jim Beam. Told me if she were forty years younger, Ricki would have been in trouble, big trouble, because she would have stolen me away.

I felt tears well in my eyes.

Because I knew what I was going to find.

Soon as I got in the living room, I smelled it. That heady, metallic, almost savage stink of human blood. The living room was a mess—lamps knocked over, magazines scattered, end tables overturned.

Carty had two Chihuahuas. Nice dogs. Liked to bark a lot, but they were harmless creatures. Pathetic, really. Shivering and shaking, prone to colds and infections of all sorts. Bred by man to be pretty much shit useless in the real world. Mimi and Momo. When I got into the living room, I called out to them. The very fact that they had not barked told me all I really needed to know about their fate.

I found them first.

I could never tell them apart and less so in death. One of them was mangled in a red-stained heap in the corner. There was a bloody splatter mark about three feet up as if somebody had picked the poor thing up and hurled it with serious velocity at the wall. I found the other one lying at the foot of Carty's rocking chair. It was nearly bitten in half.

"Carty?" I called out, just sick to my stomach.

Nothing.

I pressed my fingers against the kitchen door. Pushed it open.

Carty was sprawled on the floor in jogging pants and a collegiate sweatshirt that read UBP, and beneath that, UNIVERSITY OF BIG PECKERS. Something had been at her and she'd been bitten repeatedly in the face, the throat, the wrists, the belly. She was almost unrecognizable such was the severity of the attacks. Her face was a bleeding, livid bruise.

An ocean of blood had spread around her corpse.

It was nearly dry. That made me think that Carty had been one of the first.

I can't say that she was eaten exactly. It was more like whoever had done it just kept biting her until she bled out. It seemed inconceivable, but if somebody had asked me what had happened to her I would have had to tell them she had been *bitten* to death.

There was nothing more to see.

I turned away and went back in the living room. I pulled out my cell and called Ricki. "Carty's gone," I said. "There's nothing I can do."

And it was as I stuck the cell back in the pocket of my carpenter jeans that I heard something. A noise from behind me that made a cold chill run up my spine and play down my arms: a wet, sticky sort of sound. Like somebody peeling up a rag that had been stuck to the floor.

That's what I heard.

As I turned, the Browning shaking in my fist, the kitchen door swung open and Carty was standing there. Her left eye was that same glossy white as I'd seen in the other walking corpses, her right eye glazed and staring off at the wall. Beneath the bruising and the bloodstains, her face was a cool porcelain white. The left side of her mouth was hitched-up in a cadaverous grin, all teeth and gums.

"Carty," I said.

A couple flies buzzed about her face. She paid them no mind. Things like that no longer bothered her. She was driven now by forces that knew only appetite.

She shuffled forward, her hands coming up like she wanted to caress me.

"Please, Carty," I said. "Just go away."

I tried backing towards the door but she followed me like my own shadow. I told myself this wasn't Carty any more than that dead thing in Rommy Jacob's backyard had been Bill DeForest. She came at me. Her mouth was open. Her lips had pulled back from the gums. Her teeth looked almost unnaturally long and white.

But what made me bring up the Browning was that she was drooling.

She was drooling for my flesh.

Biting down on my lower lip, I sighted in on her forehead. "I'm sorry, Carty," I said, and squeezed the trigger. The round was neat, efficient. It popped a nickel-sized hole dead-center of her forehead. Something sprayed out of the back of her skull. She dropped and hit the floor like a stunned steer, legs bicycling for a moment and then she stiffened up and was dead again. I felt a wave of remorse wash through me. But I had no business feeling anything: it wasn't Carty. It was walking meat. It was an abomination. Yet, my eyes were wet when I walked out of her house. It felt like something was stuck in my throat.

Outside, I had to sit on the porch a moment and catch my breath.

The streets were silent.

I heard plenty of commotion, but there on Holly Street, the hub of my little world, there was nothing.

I didn't waste any time. I went back home.

Browning Hi-Power
Type: 9mm Semi-Auto
Kill Range: 150 feet
Magazine: 13 rounds

INHUMAN WAVE ATTACK

Twenty minutes later, I was driving.

I was in my pick-up heading up to Dunwoodie to check on Ricki's mom. I figured if I found her—or didn't—that would be it for the day. I'd hole up in the basement, see if Jimmy LaRue wanted to join us. What I saw as I drove was pretty much what I was seeing in my own neighborhood: cars abandoned in the middle of streets, bodies in yards. I saw a burning house and two zombies on a street corner feeding on a corpse, pulling entrails from its belly and stuffing themselves with them. No one was trying to stop them. I saw two teenagers running. I saw a naked woman with autopsy stitching running up her torso in a Y just walking up the sidewalk. She paid me no mind. She just kept walking.

I saw three or four others.

It was unbelievable. Yonkers was being overrun by the living dead. I wondered what it was like in New York City which was just a few miles south of us. I thought of all the cemeteries there. The funeral homes. The morgues. The mortuaries. I thought of all the people there who had been bitten and were now waking up. It would be like some kind of insane geometric progression. If it wasn't brought under control and fast…

I called Ricki and pulled to a stop before her mother's house.

I stepped out with the Browning Hi-Power in my hand. Just up the block, hidden behind a delivery van there was a police car. Carefully, I went over there. I saw no one about, but I could feel eyes watching me and I didn't think it was my imagination. Like a lot of the other cars I'd seen, the driver's side door was open. There was blood on the seats. On the dashboard. Sprayed up onto the windshield. The police radio was still working and there was a steady chatter between dispatchers and mobile units. Some of the voices were hysterical and shouting.

I could hear gunfire in the distance. A lot of it. I didn't like that at all. There was a steady stream of traffic out on Central Ave and, realistically, it didn't look much different than any other day. But it *was* different. It was different now in just about every way.

I went over to Ricki's mom's house.

It was a trim little brick ranch with a flowering wall of white and pink tea roses. They were beautiful. Even I had to admit that. Ricki and I had stood before them and had our engagement picture snapped by her mom. The photo was up on the mantle at home. Thinking that, I felt something twist in my belly. I put it out of my head and went up to the door. I knocked three times, then I just went in.

A TV was playing away.

"Della?" I called out. "It's me, Steve. We've been trying to get a hold of you."

No response.

Nothing but the blare of the TV. I tracked the sound and went into the bedroom. Della wasn't in there, but I knew her well enough to know that she would not turn the TV on and just leave. She was frugal as all hell. Della was manic about turning off lights if you weren't in the room and turning down the heat in the wintertime to the point where you'd be shivering. She did not waste electricity.

So where was she?

The feel of the house told me it was empty. It had that cavernous, deserted feeling that empty houses have. I detected no unpleasant smells that would have told me something awful had happened. There was nothing. It smelled like Della's house always did: flowery, fresh, a distant trace odor of something like baked bread and pots of soup. A good smell. The kind that made you feel at home. Made you want to kick off your shoes and curl up in a LA-Z-Boy.

I turned towards the TV to shut it off.

CNN was on and they were following stories about military containment operations in the continental U.S. I flipped to the BBC to see scenes of the British Army patrolling streets in armored vehicles. They looked like Panthers. I kept clicking and found FOX. One look at the screen told me all I wanted to know: DEATH VIRUS? I shook my head and turned the TV off. *Death virus.* Maybe that was a good name for it, but it sounded like tabloid shit. Typical FOX. When they weren't stroking the Right Wing they were ladling out the bullshit in great steaming heaps.

But none of that found Della.

And I was worried. Della, for all intents and purposes, could take care of herself. She grew up hard in the South Bronx and, despite just celebrating her sixty-fifth year, you didn't want to piss her off. But all that aside, she was kind. She treated me like a son and she was the one who'd given us the down payment on our house. Despite having deep pockets from when her husband (Ricki's father) died on the railroad, you wouldn't have known it. She still did most of her shopping at flea markets and rummage sales.

"Della...where are you?" I said under my breath.

With the TV off, I could hear the almost claustrophobic silence of the house. I heard more shooting in the distance. I looked everywhere and saw nothing. Everything was in its place. I had no reason to suspect anything weird had happened...that was, until I peered out into the backyard and saw all the sheets flapping on the line.

I went outside.

I found a house slipper in the grass. Nothing else. No blood, no nothing.

I called Ricki. "I don't know where she is," I told her, leaving the slipper and TV out of it. "Everything looks fine. Maybe she's out."

Ricki was not convinced and I didn't blame her. But I'd done my bit and now it was time to leave. As much as I cared for Della, I didn't like the idea of leaving Ricki and Paul alone any longer than necessary. As I was getting ready to leave, I heard that gunfire again. And it was closer. Real close now. I went outside to my pick-up and stopped right on the sidewalk.

The dead were coming.

And not just the dead but the men fighting them.

It was an awful cacophony of rifle fire and screams, vehicles squealing their brakes and men shouting on bullhorns. Overhead, a chopper buzzed the neighborhood.

Driver ants, is what I thought.

I'd seen a program on TV. South American driver ants cutting a killing swath through the jungle. Trees and bushes stripped, animals eaten down to bones. Nothing escaped them, not even men who were stupid enough to get in their way.

The dead were coming on in much the same way.

They were coming from the direction of Downtown.

If I had to reduce it to military terms, I would have said the walking dead I had thus far seen were reconnaissance units and now here was the main force. There were literally hundreds of zombies pushing forward, a huge and voracious machine of destruction. They overflowed the street, they filled lawns and sidewalks and boulevards. People—*normal* people—were pushed before the wave of the dead, screaming and crying out as the hissing army bore down on them. I saw zombies eating people. I saw zombies eating each other. I saw two women who were running ahead of them fall and disappear amongst a flurry of clutching hands and swarming bodies. Blood was flowing and gathering in a heaving, stinking mist over the streets. And still the killing and atrocities continued.

Out on the Avenue, people tried to run cars right through the crowds of zombies, to blast through their numbers. But that was a mess. They smashed into one another, into zombies, popping curbs and slamming into houses. The dead were caught in the traffic pile-up, their own crushed—but still animate—bodies becoming ramparts until that forced the traffic to stop. And then, of course, it got worse as cars and trucks backed-up, trying to escape the snafu and bashing into one another, tangling things up worse. The zombies were the sharks in the confusion and chaos, of course. Like some reaction force of the living dead, they thronged in, throwing themselves against windshields. Battering themselves bloody, thrashing and biting and forcing their way into cars, feeding on flesh and burying screaming people in their masses.

A jacked-up four-wheel drive Chevy Blazer with balloon tires came screeching in, smashing zombies to pulp. In the cab and in the bed, men with shotguns and hunting rifles kept shooting into the legions of blood-maddened ghouls. There was so much confusion and screaming and dogs barking you could barely hear the reports of their guns. Zombies were dropping, but never enough. It was like some pipe had burst and Dunwoodie was being drowned in an ocean of the undead.

Finally, even the four-wheeler was overrun as zombies got into the cab. The driver and his shotgunner were yanked out and offered to biting mouths and tearing fingers.

The zombies got up into the bed, too, and the men dove for freedom and were instantly inundated, shrieking as they were dismembered and torn to shreds.

One of the zombie hunters escaped the crushing swarm. He had produced a machete and was frantically chopping at the dead, but, he too, was overwhelmed. I saw a man stumble free. A zombie that was nearly split in half hung from his belly by its teeth.

I wanted to help, but there was nothing I could do. There were too many and they were pouring forward in a tide. If selfishness is the key to survival, then I was selfish. I went to my pick-up, refusing to watch the slaughter any longer, my guts shriveling like fruit in a drought. This was it, I thought. This was really it. Civilization was falling. The dead were rising. They were gutting society, making more and more of themselves. And if it was this bad here, I didn't want to think of the slaughterhouses that Manhattan and Los Angles and Chicago had become...or the Bronx, which was just minutes away.

For one frantic insane moment, I couldn't find my keys.

They weren't in my pockets.

They weren't in the truck.

I had left them in the house.

Jesus.

It was a habit of mine built up by many years of repetition. I always set my keys on the table in the foyer of Della's house. I ran inside and they were right where I'd left them. As I got outside, the dead were converging. They were no more than fifty feet away. I could smell their putrescent stink which was hot and seething. My heart banged against my ribs as I dashed for the pick-up and came around the side and two zombies were waiting for me.

The first was a heavy woman in a flowered bathrobe.

The other was a priest. He still had his Roman collar on, his eyes fixed and glaring, his mouth open like that of a rattlesnake ready to strike. They both came at me simultaneously, moving with slow and economical strides, but persistent, endlessly persistent.

I didn't have time to aim.

I put two rounds into the woman to drive her back and I turned and fired twice right into the priest's face. The bullets split him from chin to scalp and his face literally fell off. Somehow, the bullets had not punctured his brain. Maybe they were deflected by the skull itself and maybe my aim was poor (it was).

His mold-speckled fingers brushed against my shirt and I jammed the muzzle of the Browning right up to his left eye and jerked the trigger. His skull blew apart with a grisly splashing sound…then the woman grabbed me. I spun from her grip seconds before she would have bitten into my shoulder. I cracked her in the face with the butt of the Browning which made her stumble back a few steps. Then I jumped up and drop-kicked her, slamming one foot into her sternum and driving her to the pavement. It was a wild and insane thing to do—something from a fucking Chuck Norris movie—but it was the first thing that entered my mind.

I threw myself in the cab of the pick-up and turned it over.

It jumped in my mind at that point—the wall of zombies was twenty feet away—that this was the part in every cheap-ass horror movie I'd ever seen that the car or truck won't turn over. I felt a white blossom of fear in my chest at the very idea. But she cranked and I threw her into reverse just as five or six zombies that stumbled along in front of the pack reached the truck.

They slammed their hands against the windows.

Two of them climbed up on the hood.

I stomped on the accelerator and squealed out into the street, hitting a parked Volvo and throwing my riders.

I heard their fingers fumbling at the door handles just as I threw the locks. Then one of them with a face of septic rot became more enterprising: he smashed his head into the passenger side window like a hammer, his skull coming apart like a juicy, rotten plum and spraying the window with gore until it spider-webbed out with cracks and fell in.

I threw the truck into drive just as the undead army were seconds from converging.

But my other rider wasn't letting go. He was forcing himself in through the window and I pulled the Browning and drilled three slugs into the mush of his face until his head exploded in a spray of gray matter, bone chips, and strands of coarse hair.

Another had climbed into the bed and I jammed on the brakes, throwing him up against the cab. I stomped the accelerator and he was thrown back, flipping over the tailgate and into the street.

And then I was driving.

Driving like a bat out of hell, shaking and sweating.

HOMEWARD BOUND

I was half out of my mind as I drove back to Lincoln Park. What was chewing away at what was left of my sanity was not the walking dead, but the fact that I couldn't raise Ricki on my cell. She just wasn't answering. On any other day that would have been no big deal—our cellular provider, name deleted, was notorious for dropping calls and losing signals and just being unavailable in general. But what I feared was not those things. It was something of a much darker variety.

I kept calling.

I had four bars.

I should have been getting through.

I wanted to put the pedal to the metal but I didn't dare because there were so many cars abandoned in the streets. Some were driven into trees and right up onto lawns. The walking dead were everywhere, it seemed. I saw them standing in driveways and up on porches banging on doors, looking in windows. I almost ran down a guy that darted out from between two parked cars. He kept running and I soon saw why: there were zombies coming after him. Seven or eight of them. They walked across the road, oblivious to me. They had tunnel vision, it seemed. Once they had locked onto their targets, they had no interest in anything else. That was something I planned on remembering. It might come in handy.

About two blocks from our house I saw someone walking up the street.

Someone familiar.

She turned when she heard me coming. It was Diane, Ricki's sister. Though I hate to admit it, I was tempted to keep on going. I couldn't do that, of course, but I was tempted.

"Hey, Steve," she said when she climbed in, bushing glass from the seat. "What's happening?"

I was kind of at a loss for words. *Oh, not much. Just out sightseeing zombies. How 'bout you?* "I'm heading home," I finally said.

"Cool. I was coming to see you guys. What happened to your window?"

"I had a run-in with some…ah…*people.*"

"The dead ones? Man, they're everywhere," Diane said. "I mean, it's not like I didn't suspect something like this. I woke and I knew today was going to be freaky. You ever have those days?"

"Sure." I shook my head. "You shouldn't be out in the streets, you know."

"Oh, well you just have to be careful. They're not real fast. Just don't let 'em box you in, man. That's the secret."

"I guess," I said.

Diane had a fanny pack with her and nothing else. She unzipped it. "Got some good stuff in my pharmacy here. You wanna get high?"

I was at a loss for words again. The city was under siege by the living dead and she wanted to burn a joint. Unbelievable.

"No, I'm good."

She shrugged and zipped her pharmacy shut.

We drove on and I thought about Diane waiting it out with us in the basement. Good God, I didn't know if I could handle it. Ricki and she had a way of getting on each other's nerves and I didn't feel much like playing referee. Ricki didn't like Diane around Paul for obvious reasons. Paul was fascinated by her, probably because she represented a world that was foreign to him. Honestly, though, I think it was more than that. Diane was not an unattractive woman. She had long dishwater blonde hair, big blue eyes—very dazed-looking eyes, you understand—and a rough, tough, albeit very sexy aura about her. She was dangerous, I suppose, and Paul was a boy and he was not immune to it. Besides, Diane had a pretty good body and she wasn't above showing it off. Right then, she had on crotch-high blue jean cut-offs, her long legs crossed, her ample cleavage spilling out of a spaghetti-strap top.

I pretended not to look.

I pulled into our driveway and nothing looked much different. I saw a couple undead at the end of the block, just standing around on the street corner like they were waiting for the bus. I made note of that, too. I remembered Paul telling me they were nothing but stupid eating machines. Maybe he had something there. Maybe unless they had some food in their sights, they lacked direction or purpose.

"Man, looks you guys fought a good one here," Diane said, staring at the bodies on the lawns and in the streets.

"We had some trouble," I said.

I unlocked the front door and in we went. When I got Diane inside, I locked the door behind us. The very fact that the doors weren't torn off their hinges or no windows were broken was a good sign. Diane plopped herself down in my recliner and lit a cigarette. Christ, Ricki would have a bird. She didn't allow smoking in the house and she had ridden me pretty hard until I quit the damn things two years before.

"Where's the wife and kid?" Diane asked.

"Downstairs," I said.

"Cool."

But Diane and her habit were hardly my problem.

I went downstairs and the door was still locked from the inside. I knocked.

"Who's there?" I heard Ricki say.

Her voice filled me with calm. I could feel my guts unwinding knot by knot.

"What's the password?" Paul asked.

I almost started laughing. "Zulu Foxtrot!" I shouted.

Locks were freed and the door opened. Ricki pretty much fell in my arms and I held her tight.

"It's been quiet," Paul said. "No activity."

Ricki looked over at him and sighed. "He's running this like a military operation," she said. "He's already worked out a strict rationing system."

Paul beamed at me.

I smiled back. I was getting the feeling that he was enjoying this. But it was only a matter of time before the novelty wore off. Summer camp was always fun at first, but you got sick of it soon enough and especially one where things wanted to eat you.

Ricki was sniffing the air. "I smell smoke," she said. "You're not smoking again…"

"No…not me."

Diane came down the steps with a cigarette in her mouth. "Hey, little sister, what's up?"

At that precise moment I couldn't have said whether Ricki was pleased to see her sister or annoyed at her very presence. It was really hard to tell. Paul, on the other hand, was *very* pleased to see her. I could see it in his eyes: he was completely smitten with his aunt. She was the hot, wild woman of every boy's fantasy.

"No smoking," Ricki told her.

"Relax, Polyanna," Diane said. "I'm almost done."

Ricki glared at her and Diane just laughed. "The Glare" usually worked with me, but it was powerless with Diane. Ricki thought her older sister was pretty much a dirtbag and Diane thought her younger sister was wound too tight. I did not look forward to having them together in the close confines of the basement.

Diane finished her cigarette and crushed it out on the steps.

Ricki blanched.

Paul grinned.

I led Ricki away into the rec room which looked something like a barracks with all the stuff piled around in there—canned and dried food, jugs of water, boxes of clothes, flashlights, candles, batteries, etc. etc. etc. Ricki being Ricki had apparently been in the process of making one of her detailed lists of provisions. Paul had been handling the security and rationing.

"Where in the hell did you find her?" Ricki asked me.

"She was walking up the street. I picked her up."

"She was just out walking?" Ricki rolled her eyes.

"How typical. Well, I guess we're stuck with her."

"Well, she is your sister."

"Don't remind me."

Diane sat on the couch with her arm around Paul while he detailed how we were going to survive the zombie menace. I stood there, having one of those moments of unreality. You wake up in the morning and everything is fine and within a matter of hours you and yours are hiding out in the basement like some 1950's nuclear family fearing the atomic menace of the Communists. And, dear God, if that's all we had to worry about. It was not only unreal it was insane. I had to take a moment and breathe in and out to calm myself. I had to fight the nasty urge to start laughing uncontrollably and have a nervous breakdown.

It was unbelievable.

But that was the reality of our situation.

The world, *our* world, had shifted on its axis and we were stuck with it, for better or worse.

DOMESTICS

"You want some more SpaghettiO's, Pauly?"

"No, I'm good, Aunt Diane. I'm stuffed."

Diane turned from the hot plate. "Ricki? Steve?"

We both grunted that we were fine. Funny, as I wired the air conditioner earlier that morning I had been thinking it was a nice summer day, a great day to grill a couple sirloins out in the backyard. I had it all envisioned in my mind. The steaks sizzling over a bed of hot charcoal, the cold Budweiser in my hand. Maybe a game of Jarts with Paul after supper, then a good, mindless action movie before bed. A typically suburban sort of day. Instead I was eating SpaghettiO's in the basement rec room on paper plates and living out some outtake from a George Romero movie. Just goes to show how much your day can change from the time you get up to the time you go to bed.

"You should get the kind with the little wieners in it," Diane was saying, her discourse on the joys of SpaghettiO's going on for nearly twenty minutes by that point. "You know they're my favorite."

"I know," Ricki said.

"My favorite, too," Paul said.

"Since when?" Ricki wanted to know.

He just shrugged. Diane sat next to him and put her arm around him, pulling him close. He wasn't minding that at all. He was falling completely under her spell and Ricki was feeling threatened as she always did by Diane's presence. We were about to witness an escalation of hostilities and I knew it. I could already feel a tension headache knocking on the back of my skull.

"I like 'em best," Diane continued on. "The kind with the little wieners, I mean."

"They're great," Paul chimed in.

I wanted to slap him. I really did. Don't get me wrong: I never hit him. I didn't believe in that sort of thing. But the more he clung to Diane's side the more pissy Ricki was going to get. Ricki doted on him the way mothers always dote on their sons, particularly when they only have one. And when Paul started siding with Diane, that was an insult to Ricki. It was all childish as hell and I knew it, but sometimes the relationships between sisters can be very complex (and dangerous).

"Yes." Ricki maintained her composure, though she was tensing and I could see it. "I guess the last time I went grocery shopping I wasn't using my head."

Diane shrugged. "We all make mistakes."

Ricki chewed her lip. "Yes, don't we? I guess I should have foreseen a future when we were all trapped in the basement because of walking dead people and my sister would demand a pasta product with little wieners in it."

Diane giggled, elbowing Paul who giggled, too. "You're mom's getting sarcastic with me," she said.

Ricki gave her a forced grin. "What gives you that idea?"

"Chill it, Ricki. I was just saying I like SpaghettiO's with the little wieners in it best. That's all."

"Yes, Diane. We got that part. I know you like the kind with the little wieners in it best. You've told us about fifteen times now. We get it. *I* get it. Enough okay?"

"Oooo, Ricki's getting miffed. Look out," Diane said.

"Just shut up, okay?"

Diane rolled her eyes. "Your mom's been like this ever since she was a kid, Pauly. See, gramma always paid more attention to me and it drove your mom nuts so she overcompensated by getting straight A's and being Little Miss Goody Two-Shoes. I never really cared about all the attention because I was always, like, so what? But your mom craved it."

"That'll do, Diane," Ricki said, starting to boil.

"Don't wig out, Ricki. I mean, *damn*. Don't be so touchy."

"I am not touchy!"

Diane laughed. "It's okay, baby sister. You have a fragile ego. It's not uncommon in younger siblings. That's why you can't handle criticism or people poking fun at you."

See, this is what I was worried about. Those two always got under each other's skin. Perfectly innocent conversations about

SpaghettiO's with little wieners escalated into ugly cage matches at the drop of a hat. And it didn't have to be canned pasta products. It could be the color of the sky or the mole on Diane's ankle or the tires on my truck. And you never knew when it would start. Blood was always in the offing with those two and sometimes I got very exhausted just trying to steer conversations in lighter directions.

"Why don't you just be quiet?" Ricki said hoping to have the last word. "I'm sick to death of listening to you."

No dice. Diane laughed again. She looked over at her sister, wrinkled up her face, made her fingers into cat's claws and said, "*MEEEEEOOOWWW!* Somebody want to get my sister a saucer of milk?"

"THAT'S ENOUGH!" Ricki cried out, on her feet. "I HAD TO PUT UP WITH YOUR SHIT GROWING UP BUT I SURE AS HELL WILL NOT IN MY OWN HOUSE!"

"Whoa," Diane said. "Talking about somebody needing a little wiener. Steve, see what you can do about that."

"That'll do," Ricki said, trying desperately to control her temper and barely succeeding.

"It's cool, Polyanna. Lighten up, man. Everybody needs a little wiener now and then."

Ricki walked away into the back bedroom. It was the smart thing to do. The adult thing. Diane did not know when to shut her mouth and every time we had her over, which was seldom, it turned out like this. It was tough being diplomatic with the both of them sometimes. Believe me, I very often wanted to grab both of them by the scruffs of their necks and crack their heads together. *You're sisters! Act like it!* But that wouldn't do. I had to take the long view on this. True, Diane did not know when to shut her mouth. She often said things that were silly, stupid, or hurtful. But I don't think she *meant* to be hurtful. It was just her way. She thought everything was a joke. She took nothing seriously. Ricki, on the other hand, took *everything* seriously. What was needed was a little diplomacy. A little give and take: Diane had to think before she opened her mouth and Ricki had to thicken her skin a bit.

But, then again, the politics of sibling rivalry were very complicated.

I went into the bedroom and Ricki smiled thinly at me.

"I guess I lost it," she said. "I'm sorry."

"It's nothing."

"She drives me crazy."

"I know. Just don't let her push your buttons."

Ricki nodded. "I try…but she knows exactly what buttons to push."

I told her I understood completely because I did. "Let's just be easy right now. I'm just worried about Paul. He doesn't need to see any of that. He's taking all this pretty well, but he needs to see a unified front."

"She takes control of him so easily."

"He's just a normal male," I told her.

"I suppose. But it irks me to see my son smitten with the Crab Queen of Greater Yonkers."

We had a good laugh over that.

I left Ricki sorting through blankets and sleeping bags and went out into the rec room. Diane, true to form, was telling Paul about her ex-boyfriend who only had one ball. He'd gotten the other caught in a chain link fence when he was eluding the police and it had to be surgically removed. "After that," Diane said, "we called him *Sterile Daryl.*" Good old Diane. I think that was yet another reason why Paul loved his aunt: she did not talk down to him. She treated him like an equal and did not insulate him like Ricki and I did (or any adult for that matter). There was something very refreshing about that and, at the same time, very disturbing from a parental point of view.

"I'm going upstairs for a minute," I told them. "I want to get the rest of my shotgun shells and take one last look and make sure everything's locked down before dark."

"I'll join you," Diane said.

"Me, too," Paul piped up.

"You're staying," I told him.

"Oh, Dad."

"Stay. Man the door, mister."

"Aye, aye."

I went upstairs and Diane followed me, lighting a cigarette. I checked all the doors and windows. Across the street, Jimmy LaRue was still posted at the window with his rifle. I saw nothing out there moving, either of the living or dead variety. But what worried me was that mob of zombies up in Dunwoodie. They were moving south which meant they'd be cutting right through Lincoln Park and possibly our neighborhood. That scared me. I didn't know where they had all come from but in my mind I saw them crawling out of graves and leaving morgues and walking out of mortuaries, gathering into a funeral procession of the living dead, a voracious eating machine that would take down anything in its path.

That scared me.

I stared out the window and Diane came right up behind me. I could feel her breath on the back of my neck and her breasts pushing into my shoulders.

"Anything out there?" she said.

"Nothing." I cocked an ear towards the window. "You hear that? Still a lot of shooting."

"Yeah." She pressed her breasts harder against my back. "I smell something burning, too. Like campfires. Must be houses burning out there. A lot of them by the smell."

I kept looking and I saw somebody come walking up the sidewalk in the distance making for Orient Street. It was Rommy Jacob. I had no doubt of it. He had reanimated and was out on the prowl, stumbling along mindlessly looking for something (or some*one*) to bite.

I extricated myself from Diane and she followed me around, smoking her cigarette. I don't know what she was doing with the ashes and I really didn't want to know.

"We better get back downstairs," I said.

She extinguished her cigarette butt under the faucet. "Okay. I like do to what I'm told. I'm easy."

Good old Diane.

THE AWAKENING

Moments, it seemed, after sundown Jimmy LaRue called on his cellphone. "You people locked down good over there?"

"Sure, Jimmy. Got room if you want to join us."

"No, shit, I'm fine. Just called to warn you."

I tensed. "About what?"

"The dead ones," he said. "I got a call from my sister up on Crotty. She says there's hundreds of 'em moving down Belmont Ave. They're coming this way."

"Okay, we're ready."

"Keep your head down, Steve. She's says they're tearing apart everything in their path."

"Will do."

That's when the waiting started. I had been hoping for a quiet night. I thought it might let everyone breathe a little easier and wind down. But it wasn't going to be like that. I explained the situation to everyone. I had no idea what we might expect. I had seventeen rounds for the Browning Hi-Power and fifteen shells for the Remington. It wasn't a lot but I hoped it would be enough if it came down to it. Even if the dead broke through the doors upstairs I couldn't imagine them breaching the basement door. It would have taken a truck to break through it…but, then again, I remember what I had seen up in Dunwoodie. The sheer numbers.

We settled in because it was all we could do.

The city was still functioning as such because we had power and water. I was grateful for that. We watched TV and it was nothing but despair, doom and gloom. It was disturbing to watch the national news and hear them talking about the dead rising. It was happening everywhere, all over the country, and we saw scenes from Denver, Chicago, Atlanta, and Houston—throngs of the living dead in the streets. The National Guard and Army were out in strength putting the dead back in their graves and running major decontamination operations but they were seriously outnumbered. According to what was being said, it wasn't just the dead they had to contend with but looters and rioting and open insurrection in the streets. It was absolute chaos and it was getting worse by the hour. There were so many subversive groups out there that had just been waiting for a collapse of social order to start kicking up their heels and they wasted no time in making a nuisance of themselves.

We saw a few scenes from Manhattan that showed the Theater District and Times Square completely empty of people. Oh, the neon was still going but there was no one there to enjoy it. The financial district was overrun with zombies. There were unconfirmed reports that the Air National Guard had hit certain sections of Brooklyn with cluster bombs. Rumor had it that Bed-Sty was burning and Flatbush was nearly entirely zombified (to borrow Paul's word). Supposedly, Los Angeles had been so besieged by the dead that there had been napalm strikes in the San Fernando Valley and the resultant firestorms were sweeping neighborhood to neighborhood. It hadn't rained in southern California in over a month and things were tinder dry. The hot Santa Ana winds were pushing the fires into Beverly Hills and West Hollywood. The freeways were jammed bumper-to-bumper with the resultant exodus. It was a real mess. CNN claimed that the napalm strikes were ordered by an Air Force officer who had no authority to do so.

It was a fucking mess.

The President would address the nation in the morning.

Martial Law had already been declared nationwide and the police and Guard were putting down riots in Southside Chicago with extreme force, opening up on looting mobs with machine guns. Another unconfirmed report said that the President had ordered a full withdrawal of American forces from overseas stations and theaters. The CDC was flashing 1-800 numbers on just about every station concerning an outbreak of infectious disease being spread by the walking dead. Nobody was saying it yet, but I knew pretty much what was happening: anybody bitten by the zombies was dying and returning *as* a zombie.

It was all being collectively known as The Awakening.

It was bad in the US, but absolute hell in other places. In the Middle East, governments already weakened by mass uprisings of the civilian population were teetering as the dead swarmed the streets. Rumor had it that Iran was using chemical weapons against its own people. Tensions had risen to new levels between Pakistan and India. The North Koreans were blaming the United States for it all and promising "retribution of an unprecedented scale". For once, they were being taken seriously and the Navy had positioned guided missile cruisers in the Yellow Sea which were armed with nuclear warheads.

At first, Paul had been real excited about the images of zombies in the streets. One of his comic books had finally come to life. But it wasn't long before he grew quiet, clinging to Diane. I held hands with Ricki. I never thought I'd live to see the end of the world but it seemed to be happening. We were on the verge of international social collapse and ensuing chaos. Everything man had built up in the past 5,000 years of civilization was starting to unravel.

After awhile, I turned the channel to Nickelodeon.

We watched *Spongebob* and even managed to laugh a little bit.

I wondered if we would have anything to laugh about a week from then.

PANIC LIST

Okay. As far as I know here's how things are looking for the neighborhood:
1. Rommy Jacob is dead, but zombified.
2. Bill DeForest, dead
3. Carty, dead
4. Mrs. Hazen, dead but possibly zombified
5. Mitzy Streeter, unknown
6. The Castleberrys, unknown
7. Same for the Feldhuesens, Myers, Sweeds, Baxters
8. I don't know the other people on Holly St.
9. From what I saw upstairs (other than Rommy), the street looks empty. But is everyone hiding? Have they left? There's supposed to be National Guard camps set up or being set up—did they go there?
10. I think we're safe in the basement (for now)

11. I wish Jimmy LaRue would join us
12. Food, water, general supply status is good
13. I'm worried about Ricki and Paul, I have to keep them safe
14. I will kill if I have to, I will not let them come to harm
15. Pessimistic thought for the day: <u>What happens if one of them gets the germ? Will I be able to do what I did with Carty and Bill?</u>

THE NIGHT BRIGADE

It started just before eleven.

Jimmy LaRue called and said: *"Here they come."*

And really, he didn't have to warn me because we all heard them: the drumming, marching sound of hundreds and hundreds of feet. I heard people screaming and crying out. The dead were assaulting the living, seeking them out, pulling them from their hiding places and feeding on them. We were trapped in the basement and there was nothing we could do. We shut the TV off and turned out all the lights. I didn't know if lights would draw them in but I wasn't taking any chances. There were two windows in the basement. Both were far too small for anyone to fit through. My insurance company wouldn't even let me call the bedroom down there a bedroom because it lacked a window large enough for egress and escape in the case of a fire. For the last couple years I'd been planning on putting bigger windows down there and now I was glad that I hadn't.

We cowered in the darkness while the dead laid waste to the neighborhood.

It was absolute anarchy out there and we could hear people shooting, people screaming, the continual thud of marching feet, windows breaking, thudding noises and smashing sounds. I couldn't take it anymore. I had to see. I had to know the nature of the enemy. I crept up to one of the windows and pulled the curtain aside. In the glow of the streetlights I saw, all right. Hundreds and hundreds of them, packs and gangs and swarms of the dead. They were forcing their way into houses. They were pushing through doors by sheer volume and strength of their numbers, they were going right through windows. I heard old man Castleberry's beagles barking and yipping in a mad rage…and then the squealing sounds as they were devoured.

And then they found our house.

I heard windows shatter and the doors up there come off their hinges as the night things battered into them again and again. Then they were upstairs. They were pounding on walls, tipping over cabinets, overturning furniture. I heard our plasma TV get ripped off the wall and shatter on the floor. The sound of dishes being smashed underfoot, cupboards looted through. The refrigerator—I thought it was the refrigerator—went over with a resounding boom and with such force it seemed like it was going to come right through the floor.

It went on and on.

Ricki was gripping my hand so tightly by then I thought she was going to crush it. She was scared. We were all scared. But I really thought it was more than that with her. This was her house. She had put together everything up there lovingly for our care and comfort and now these ghouls were destroying it all, tearing down everything she had built up. Each crash from above made her jerk as if she'd been hit herself. She was scared, yes, but I think she was angry, too. In fact, I knew she was. She was pissed off and she had all she could do not to charge up there with guns blazing to put down the things that were desecrating her home, violating it and fouling it.

Even above all the clamor you could hear them up there.

I can't say they were voices as such but more like animal sounds: hissing and growling, shrieking and moaning. It was hard to say whether they were sounds of hunger or sounds of agony and maybe they were both. Regardless, it seemed to go on and on and on. They weren't finding any fucking prey, I thought, so why weren't they moving on?

Those voices…yammering/shrilling/hissing, it had risen up into a constant, nerve-jangling droning that went right through my skull. Not people, dear God, not people but insects. Human insects swarming. Like millions of locusts stripping orchards and fields. That's what they were. Not remotely intelligent: just things that were driven by the stupid need to feed and feed and feed. The most basic of survival instincts had been perverted in them into a mindless, slobbering ravening. Just the sound of them up there, that wall of almost insectile piping and screeching and gurgling. It thrummed in my bones and made my molars ache. It was deafening and ceaseless, a yelping, howling barrage of minds driven insane by insatiable hunger.

Then, just about the time it seemed to quiet down up there, I heard a worse sound.

The very sound I did not want to hear.

I heard bare feet slapping down the stairs.

I heard one of them standing beyond the door, just breathing with a phlegmy, liquid sound.

Then hands began to slap at the door.

The knob was rattled.

More feet on the stairs, then more and more and I could hear them gathered in the stairwell. They were pounding on the door, not knocking as you or I would, but hammering at it, beating on it, clawing and slapping it, hitting it with fists and maybe smashing their heads against it. All the while that awful animal gurgling and groaning, slurping, and slobbering sounds echoing up the stairwell.

I was starting to doubt whether the door would hold.

If they breached it…I could kill a lot of them but there was no way we could hold out against the sheer numbers of them driven by that voracious, mindless hunger to get at us. There was no other way out of the basement. It would be a goddamn buffet down there, a slaughterhouse and there was no way I could let something like that happen.

"Quick," I whispered. "Help me with the floor freezer."

Using flashlights we went into the junk room, as we called it, where we stored everything from Xmas decorations to old clothes and toys and appliances. It was also where the hot water heater and furnace were located. Stuck away in a corner gathering dust was a huge aluminum floor freezer that had belonged to Ricki's Uncle Charlie who had run a very lucrative hamburger stand in Palisades Park in Jersey before it was closed down and the real estate parasites put up condos and ruined everyone's childhood memories. The freezer was huge and it could hold four-hundred pounds of meat. It weighed a ton. With all four of us working at it we got it into the rec room, puffing and straining and sweating. We could only move it three feet at a time because it weighed so much. But eventually we got it in front of the door and wedged it up against it.

Between the door and that freezer, it was going to take some unbelievably determined zombies to get us.

They kept up the racket at the door. I positioned myself nearby with both guns and a flashlight. I was ready to do some killing. I was ready to do whatever it took to protect my family.

Then I heard a shattering sound.

Ricki screamed.

Paul cried out and Diane shushed him.

What seemed like a dozen hands were reaching through the windows, I saw in the flashlight beam. Pallid, rotting hands with bloated fingers and strips of flesh hanging from them like ribbons. They were clawing and grabbing, trying to seize on anything they could get. The curtains were torn away. The molding was stripped free. I saw one puffy white hand with a shard of glass impaled right through it.

Everyone was panicking and I didn't blame them.

"STEVE!" Ricki called out, her nerve gone. "DO SOMETHING!"

The only thing I could do was to go over there with my shotgun and blast a few rounds into the mutiny of hands. I did it at one window and then the other. I pulverized several hands into fragments of white pulp and foul-smelling gray juice that ran down the walls. But I was doing it mostly for effect. The windows were too small for any of them to get through and they were so greedy in their hunger that they were all trying to get through at once.

"They can't get in," I told everyone. "We just have to wait it out."

We huddled together on the couch and did just that.

The zombies kept battering the door and reaching through the windows, but they did not get in. It was a very long night. By about three a.m. they had pretty much given up and moved on to better pickings. There were a few stragglers. I could hear them from time to time upstairs or out in the streets, but the siege was over.

I heard a few gunshots close by now and again and I figured it was Jimmy across the street.

About five a.m. my cell rang. It was Jimmy, all right. "You people still in one piece over there?" he asked.

I told him we were.

"Man, it was like a blitzkrieg, wasn't it?" Jimmy said. "They tore apart my house same as yours. I don't know if my barricade can take another assault like that."

"I'm thinking of moving on to somewhere better," I said. "You with me?"

"Damn straight," Jimmy said. "I'll start throwing some things together. Be like a camp out. I haven't done any Boy Scouting in fifty years, Steve, but I'm game."

"First light, we'll come up with a plan."

Diane and Paul had drifted off by then and Ricki was sleeping fitfully, closing her eyes for ten minutes then coming wide awake in a panic.

I waited for daylight.

I began to know what it must have been like for my primitive ancestors, the terror night must have brought.

I waited and thought of where we could go next.

DEVASTATION

Around eight a.m. when it was full light out and I spied no deadheads wondering in the streets, I had the others help me move the floor freezer. To my surprise—and horror—the freezer had slid about three inches away from the door and that was because the door itself was coming off its hinges. I was amazed. Shocked. But there was no doubt in my mind: we had to abandon the house. We couldn't handle another assault like that. It was time to move, time to get gone. There was no joy here.

But to where?

Jimmy called and said he was packed-up, ready to leave. Being a widower, he didn't have much. I almost got the feeling he was getting a kick out of this. But since his wife passed three years before, there wasn't much for him but home improvement. Maybe the excitement gave him a reason to live. Just like it scared the shit out of me.

Ricki and Diane—working together surprisingly—and Paul got most of our stuff organized. Clothes. Food. Sleeping bags. Blankets. Flashlights. Batteries. Essential stuff, really. Our problem was that Ricki's car was a little VW Jetta and there was no way we'd all fit into it, especially not with our gear. My pick-up was the same. You can't fit five people in the cab of a pick-up. I didn't like the idea of trying to make a run with two different cars.

I called Jimmy and he had been out on a recon through the neighborhood.

"Saw three dead ones, Steve, but I avoided them. I went house to house and I hate to say it, but I think we're the last living people in the neighborhood."

It was grim, but no worse than I suspected.

Jimmy was taking a big chance going around knocking on doors. I suspected that many of our neighbors were now zombies and the ones that weren't might shoot first and ask questions later.

I told Jimmy about our problem with vehicles. "Yeah, we'll never fit in my truck either."

"I don't like the idea of too many vehicles," I told him. "Too easy to get separated."

"Castleberry's got that big Suburban," Jimmy said. "We could all ride in high style in that baby."

It was a good idea.

I had Ricki lock the door after me and I went to meet Jimmy out in the street. What I saw upstairs pretty much took my breath away. The house was trashed. I knew it would be, of course, but to see it was something else again. Furniture was flipped over, some of it broken to kindling. Pictures were yanked off the walls, the plasma TV shattered into pieces, the computer desk broken. The hard drive had been thrown through a window. All of Ricki's plants were scattered about with the remains of their pots, black soil tracked from one end of the house to the other. Both back and front doors were bashed-in, screen doors completely torn off. It was just a mess of dirt and broken dishes and shards of glass all powdered down with flour and sugar and just about everything else that had been in the dry goods cupboards.

It broke my heart seeing it.

It would devastate Ricki.

But I had no time for that sort of thing. I met Jimmy in the street and we had just started discussing our options when a dead one—not from the neighborhood—came out of Mrs. Hazen's side yard. I had smelled something fusty and rotten, but that odor was on the breeze. It was now the rule rather than the exception so it didn't give me too much pause for concern.

Then that stink went from bad to sickening.

It became almost hot and feverish.

That's when the dead one showed. A woman in a business skirt. Her blouse was torn wide open. There were crusty stains of gore and slime all down her chest and over her breasts. Looking at her, I knew she hadn't come from any graveyard or morgue. They didn't generally bury women in business wear. Her face was clown-white, kind of swollen and cracking open in places. I noticed that she had no lips. No lips at all. There was just the bloody hole of her mouth with pink-stained teeth jutting from it. She had wide bleached eyes with tiny black pinprick pupils.

She came at us with no hesitation, dragging one leg behind her as if it were damaged.

Jimmy had his .22 up. "You can always walk away, miss," he said.

To that, her face screwed-up into a sort of psychopathic leer, her mouth opening and teeth gnashing. She made some sound. I don't think it was speech exactly, more like a rough animal growling. Gouts of black blood oozed down her chin.

Jimmy pulled the trigger.

The .22 slug caught her right between the eyes and popped an exit wound out the back of her head that sprayed Mrs. Hazen's bushes with gore. The impact spun the zombie woman in a complete circle. She started walking again in the opposite direction…for about three steps, that is, before she fell into the Azaleas, twitching.

Jimmy and I wasted no more time.

We went over to the Castleberrys.

We cut around the side through the alley and immediately regretted our decision. That's where Castleberry kept the cages for his beagles. I remember how many times they'd annoyed me with their barking and yipping, but they wouldn't annoy anyone anymore. The doors to the cages were torn open and there were the remains of dogs strewn up and down the alley. There were dried pools of blood smeared and splashed everywhere. I saw a set of bloody prints moving on down the alley. They looked like the footprints of a child and I had this awful image in my head of some zombie kid gnawing on a beagle carcass as he or she or *it* shambled off.

"Don't think about," Jimmy told me, as if reading my mind.

The back door was smashed-in. We went through it with guns drawn like a couple TV cops. There was wreckage everywhere. We found neither Castleberry nor his wife, Myrna. What we did find was blood sprayed over the walls. A smeared trail of it led to the front door which was wide open. It looked like somebody had been bleeding profusely, dragging themselves along the wall, then dove through the screen door and continued crawling down the steps and into the grass. The most telling thing we found was a discarded mailbag. The rest we could put together.

We found the keys on a pegboard and jumped in Castleberry's big maroon Suburban. We were beginning to make some progress, I hoped.

THE GRAVEYARD

The Suburban had a full tank of gas which was a plus. We drove it over to Jimmy's and loaded his things. Nothing much. A sleeping bag and a couple duffel bags.

Then we went over to my house and backed in the driveway.

While Jimmy stood guard, we loaded up our stuff and climbed in. Jimmy took the wheel and I rode shotgun. Paul was in the back between Ricki and Diane. Both of them were oddly quiet and I had the feeling they'd got into another one while I was gone.

"Where we going?" Jimmy said. "Any idea?"

"Let's take a ride through town, see what we see."

"Good enough."

As we drove, Jimmy kept casting glances back at Paul, who was uncharacteristically silent. Jimmy was always real good to Paul. He was practically like a grandfather to him. Jimmy had no kids of his own, so he'd never had the pleasure of being a grandpa. When I was busy working or off in the war, Jimmy had been there going to Little League games with Ricki, teaching my boy how to throw and how to hit a ball. He'd taken them camping while I was in Iraq. Always brought over birthday presents and Christmas presents for the boy. Between Bill DeForest and Jimmy, we'd had it damn good. I started thinking about the neighborhood. I was going to miss it. I started to get pissed off at the damn zombies.

"This is going to be an adventure, eh, Skip?" Jimmy said. He always called Paul *Skip* for reasons unknown.

"Sure will, Jimmy. It'll be like going to war or something. You were in the war, weren't you?"

Jimmy nodded. "Yes, many years ago."

"What did you do?"

"I was in the Navy, Skip. I was a gunner on a PBR."

"What's a PBR?"

"That's Navy talk—Patrol Boat, River. We gave the Cong hell in the Delta. Sometime, you remind me, I'll tell you about those PBRs. They were something."

"Vietnam," Diane said. "Legendary weed."

Jimmy started laughing.

He pulled away down Holly Street towards St. John's Ave, heading North. We hadn't even made the end of the block when somebody came charging out at us. They were running so I didn't figure it was a zombie.

It wasn't.

It was worse.

It was Dick Nickersen, the scourge of the neighborhood. The one guy I was hoping to never see again.

"Request permission to run his ass down," Jimmy said.

"Stop!" Ricki said. "You have to help him!"

Diane shook her head. "So says Polyanna."

"He's kind of a creep," Paul said.

Ricki told him that wasn't polite and Jimmy slowed the Suburban down and rolled it to a stop. Dick came right up to my window, slapping his hands against it. His face was streaked with dirt, his polo shirt torn. There was dried blood on his arms and leaves in his hair.

"HELP ME!" he shouted. "OH PLEASE DEAR GOD HELP ME!"

As I unrolled my window, Diane said, "You know they're saying a virus might be responsible. He don't look so good."

"You never mind," Ricki told her.

"Excuse me," Diane said, "but I don't like exposing Pauly to a deadly disease. Maybe it's just me."

As soon as I got the window open, Dick grabbed me by the arm. He was crying and spitting and just about out of his mind: *"Oh Steve, oh Jesus Christ, they're everywhere...those things are everywhere...they got Elena! Last night they got into our house! We fought them off! But they bit her...they bit her arm...they bit her hand!"* He looked frantically around to see if they were coming for him. Wiping drool and grime from his mouth, he went on: *"There were so many of 'em! They tore our house apart! We hid in the attic! I nailed the hatch shut and they stood there...those things...those monsters...scratching at the hatch for hours.*

Elena...oh God...my wife...my wife...she started acting funny! She she she she—"

"Calm down, Dick. You have to calm down...all right?"

He leaned against the Suburban breathing in and out deeply. "Yes, yes, yes, yes, yes...I...I must be calm. I must be rational."

He kept breathing hard and I waited while Jimmy and the others kept an eye peeled for *visitors*. After a time, Dick relaxed a bit and started to make some sense. Just after dark, Elena started complaining that she was sick to her stomach, that her muscles ached any time she moved, and that the bites were burning, just burning. She spiked a fever, wiping at her runny nose, talking to people who weren't there. Getting weird and violent. She went into convulsions and started chewing her own lips until her mouth was a bloody hole. Dick held her down, did the best he could. She started screaming, crying out that she could feel the poison in her blood making its way into her brain. *"The infection! The infection! It's eating me alive!"* is how Dick put it. Then she lapsed into a coma.

By three in the morning she was dead.

No heartbeat.

No breathing that he noticed.

She grew cold. Then, just before dawn, she woke up.

Her eyes opened and she looked at Dick, her mouth making chewing motions.

He stared at me as he told that part, his eyes like two windows looking into hell. "She was *dead*...she was cold and dead...she came at me...she wouldn't speak...*she just kept crawling at me,*" he said in a high, broken voice. "I...I had to do it, didn't I?"

"Do what?"

"I had to take the hammer...I had to beat her head in. I had to keep swinging it until she stopped moving." He looked at his hands like he wondered if they were capable of such a thing. "I had to...didn't I?"

"Course you did, Dick," Jimmy told him.

"Now listen to me," I told him. "Listen good, Dick: did Elena bite you? Did she scratch you?"

He shook his head. "I wouldn't let her...get that close. I hit her with the hammer. But I had to. Didn't I have to?"

I got out and helped Dick in-between Jimmy and I. I thought he was in shock. He certainly acted like it. Once inside, he clammed up and just stared. Nothing more.

"I got some Percocet in my pharmacy," Diane said. "Some Vicodin. Maybe it'd help."

"Let's just leave him be for now," I said.

So, like it or not, we had another member of our little club.

Jimmy drove on and we saw the sights.

In twenty-four hours the world had changed immensely. We came upon neighborhoods where half-devoured corpses were sprawled in yards, houses were burning, cars were smashed in the streets and up on curbs and flipped right over. I noticed quite a few were riddled with bullet holes. We saw a few armed bands of civilians that watched us warily. We saw zombies, too. We saw them everywhere, walking, always walking, driven in a constant forward momentum for prey. At St. John's and Nile Street, one of them—a woman—stepped right out in front of us and Jimmy jammed on the accelerator and ran her down.

"Good God," Ricki said.

"Harden your heart, honey," Jimmy told her. "Gonna get worse than that."

He was right. Oh, how right he was.

Behind us, the zombie lady lay broken in the street, inching along like a slug.

"I wonder if this is like the biblical Rapture," Diane said, as if it were no big deal if it were, she was just mentioning the fact.

The farther North we pushed the more of it we saw. Not one or two zombies, but dozens of them patrolling through neighborhoods that were absolutely deserted. Lots of evidence that they had once been populated—bullet holes in the sides of houses, wrecked cars, bodies in the streets stripped like wolf packs had been gnawing on them, not enough left to rise up. But nothing living but the trees and grass. Just those hollow-eyed corpses mindlessly walking, some standing in yards, others on porches. If you slowed down, they'd all begin to converge like seagulls when you tossed a French fry out the window. But if you kept cruising right along they seemed disinterested.

"Man," Paul said. "There's zombies everywhere. I mean, *everywhere.*"

"Thicker'n flies on shat," Diane said.

"Or ticks on scat," Jimmy said.

"Zombies," Dick said like it was something he had not considered before.

Ricki wanted to say something. The wheels in her head were turning and turning, throwing a lot of sparks, but not grabbing on anything like cogs without teeth. How did you frame this with positive parental reinforcement? You didn't. That stuff was all part of polite society and there was nothing polite out there now.

Diane lit a cigarette and Ricki didn't even comment on it.

Jimmy turned on the radio because he said it was time for the President's speech. "Let's see the old Prez put a spin on this one."

The Prez didn't bother. He was fresh out of spin and pretty much milked of hope. "Good morning," he said. "I speak to you now on a matter of not only national security but *international* urgency. Due to the outbreak of a viral agent known as Necrophage I have been forced to not only declare nationwide martial law but to call our fighting forces back home from every corner of the globe to better contain the threat that faces each and every one of us. You have no doubt by this point heard a great many things on TV and the internet. The more unfortunate among you have *seen* them. I stand before you now, not only awed but hesitant about what I must say. Now, according to our best minds that have been working on this problem since its first occurrence early yesterday morning, the Necrophage virus is extremely dangerous. It's too early to tell for sure, but we are estimating a communicability factor of something like 80% and a mortality factor of nearly 100%. Believe me when I say I share your fears and anxieties. The virus appears to be not only airborne but transmitted by the bites of those infected. The origin of the virus is unknown at this time. But those infected exhibit flu-like symptoms followed by coma that lasts anywhere from two to six hours. Upon awakening, the infected are irrational and violent, often clawing and biting anyone that gets within close proximity. This is a time of great peril for our nation. As medical experts confront this issue, I ask each and every American to avoid gathering in crowds, to stay home when possible, and to cooperate with civil authorities in their task of restoring order. Following this address, there will be an announcement by Homeland Security detailing quarantine procedures and ongoing containment operations. Stay tuned to your local radio and TV stations for Civil

Defense information and the location of the nearest shelter where food, medical aid, and protection may be found..."

"Notice how he didn't mention the word *zombie,*" Jimmy pointed out. "Hell, he ain't even admitting they're dead people. Just *irrational* and *violent.* Now ain't that a kicker?"

The President went on to assure the country that all available resources had been activated and the outbreak would be contained. Maybe he was right, but from what I was seeing it seemed unlikely. *Necrophage.* That was apparently the new name for the virus. In Iraq, the spooks had called it *necrovirus.* I wondered if the Prez would ever publicly admit that this had not been the first outbreak. I doubted it.

"He never mentioned the Rapture," Diane said.

"What's that?" Paul asked.

"Never mind," Ricki told him.

When we reached Yonkers Ave we ran into a roadblock enforced by the National Guard. When we got up there a soldier came right up to the car. He was in full combat kit with his M-4 carbine held in a ready position.

"This road is closed to civilian traffic," he said. "I need to ask you to turn around and return to your homes."

"Shit," Jimmy said.

I leaned over. "Hell, they letting you play with live ammo, troop?"

The soldier took off his shades. "Ha! Hey, Sarge! Get this shit, eh? Two months back from dancing with the dune coons in Af*crap*istan and I pull this. Fucking-A! You believe it? Just like you used to say in Iraq: if you're horny, join the Army and you'll get fucked every day."

Jimmy burst out laughing. So did Diane. I saw Ricki glaring at me in the rearview. I guess I had quite a mouth on me when I was in combat.

The soldier's name was Tony Russo. We'd both been part of the 2nd Platoon, 1st Stryker Cavalry Brigade, one of only two National Guard units in the country that used the Stryker vehicle. We'd seen a lot of shit together.

"They call you back up yet, Sarge?"

"Hell no. I been out five years."

"Don't matter. They're going to be calling up guys out for six and seven."

I had a nasty suspicion something like that might happen. "Any chance you letting us through?"

"You sure you want to? It's bad up ahead. Lots of wrecks and pile-ups."

"We need to get somewhere."

Tony looked around. "Yeah, just for you, Sarge. You were always good to us, man. Anybody stops you, tell 'em you're doctors or some shit."

He waved us through and we got out on the Avenue and Tony was right: it was bad out there. There were wrecks everywhere, Guard units and police and ambulances. There were choppers buzzing overhead. I saw Guardsmen dragging off bodies and throwing them in the backs of trucks. I had the feeling they had not been living people when they were put down. From the Avenue we could see great sections of the city were burning.

"Can I ask where in the hell it is we're going?" Jimmy said.

"Get us on Sprain Brook," I told him. "We need to make the Taconic Parkway."

"Oh boy," Ricki said.

"Oh boy what?" Paul asked her.

"You ask your father. I have a nasty feeling I know where we're going."

I looked at her in the review and she said, "Tucker?"

I only smiled.

When things get bad you need help from someone who's just a little bit badder. We needed somewhere to go. Somewhere safe. Somewhere we could lay low and not have to worry about the walking dead coming to take a bite out of us. We needed to seek the aid of someone who would protect us. And if that someone just happened to be a little crazy…what of it?

We were going to see Tucker.

TUCKER THE GREAT AND TERRIBLE

A word about Tucker will probably be necessary.

I never mentioned what it is I did for a living. I was a bricklayer, a union guy, and I generally jobbed from one construction site to the next. The hours were long but the pay was good. And after my Guard unit was mobilized to Iraq, I never again complained about my aching back. After a few runs down the IED Highway, even Manhattan rush hour is doable.

Although I had worked construction in various capacities through the years—cement guy, sandwich guy, coffee guy, ditch guy, shovel guy, flag guy, dump truck guy—it wasn't until I got back from Iraq that I joined the OPCMIA and started making good money. The OPCMIA—Operative Plasters' and Cement Masons' International Association—had its union hall on Laconia Avenue in the Bronx. The first two meetings I attended were uneventful, just the usual union business, gripes, grievances, pissing and moaning that is lock, stock, and barrel for the working man.

The third monthly meeting was where I first saw Tucker, or "Sixty-Five" as some of the old hands called him.

When he walked into the meeting ten minutes late nobody dared mention the fact.

The guy next to me, Tommy Shills from Brooklyn, elbowed me and whispered, "There he is, old Tuck the Great and Terrible."

And you know what? It wasn't sarcasm. This guy *was* great and terrible. He stood about 6'3, had to go in at a sharply-chiseled 250 pounds. He was bald as cue ball and had a steel-gray ZZ Top beard hanging to his chest that gave him the look of an outlaw biker. He had massive squared-off shoulders, a barrel chest, and arms like dock pilings. There were tattoos on those arms and not the vanity art you see on so many wannabes these days, but the real thing: the one on his left forearm was a skull-and-crossbones and said USMC beneath it. An old, rugged jarhead by the looks of him.

But no ordinary rugged jarhead.

Tuck came in with a six-pack of Black Label and a fiddle, of all things.

While most of the boys refrained from making eye-contact with him, yours truly was staring. He caught my eyes and stared back. And smiled. It was a warm, friendly sort of smile that just seemed out of place on that mug of his that looked like it was chipped granite.

As union business was discussed, Tuck swallowed one beer after the other. Then when one of the boys from Queens was bitching about some Dominican scabs working a site up in Jackson Heights and how the union had best intercede before things were handled in the time-honored way (and some Dominicans ended up in the hospital), Tuck let out this massive belch that rattled the windows.

Sammy Argante, the business rep, said, "Easy, Sixty-Five."

At which point, Tuck pulled out his fiddle and started knocking out licks from the Charlie Daniels Band which got stone silence from some members and uncontrollable laughter from others. When the meeting was ended, Tuck went on his merry way, fiddle in tow, without saying a word. I learned in successive meetings that Tuck very rarely spoke. That when people asked him questions he often knocked off a few chord progressions with his long bow in lieu of speech. The absolutely fucking insane thing was that the union guys not only accepted this as a reply but seemed to *understand* it like a language.

"Call for vote on the Astoria situation," Sammy would say.

Hands would go up, there'd be some arguing. Then one of the boys would say, "Tuck? You been around the block, what do you think of us combining with #603?"

Tuck would scrape the strings of his fiddle.

"Yeah, you're probably right," the guy would admit.

Then somebody else would say, "Tuck brings up a good point. #603 didn't fine those shitheads for crossing the picket line. What kind of shit is that?"

It was all lost on me. Then…as the meetings proceeded…I began to *understand* it myself. You could read into the tone and know if he was okay with things or pissed off, just clowning around or drawing a line in the sand. Then one day I ended up on a site with Tuck putting up a foundation. I went right up to Sammy the day before and said, "He don't carry that fiddle on the job, does he?"

"No, Sixty-Five just likes to toy his union brothers with it."

"Why do some of you call him Sixty-Five?"

Sammy lit a cigarette and said, "Tuck was Marine Recon in Vietnam. He pulled three tours and killed more men than fucking cancer. Got medals like I got freckles. He's a good guy, loyal as hell, but don't go pissing him off. He's sixty-years old and he's in better shape than any five twenty-year olds. Let's put it this way. We were working a site up in Bed-Sty. We popped into a local tavern for a cold one on our break. Jamaican bar. Not a single white boy in the place. These three Jamaicans start getting tough. Tuck took 'em outside by himself. He was the only one who walked back through that door."

"But why Sixty-Five?" I said.

"Oh, that," Sammy said, blowing out a cloud of smoke. "They were up North somewhere in 'Nam. Tuck's platoon got wiped out. When the Marine reaction force got in there, they found sixty-five confirmed kills laying around in the bush. Only about thirty of them had been shot, the others were cut, slashed, chopped. They found Tuck there with a machete and a Marine K-Bar knife, blood right up to his elbows. The VC wanted him alive and they paid the price."

I knew about Marine Recon. Marine Force Recon, as they were technically known, were Marine Corps special operations. They were involved in things like long-range reconnaissance, demolitions, commando-style raids, intelligence operations like snatching enemy officers or guerrillas/terrorists, and assassinating the same. They were badass and I knew it. Some of the Marine Recon hunter/killer teams in Vietnam were legendary. During the war, I was stationed for a time at FOB McKenzie in Samarra and there were lots of crazy stories making the rounds about things the special ops people were doing. There was one going around about a Marine Force Recon unit known as the Nightcrawlers that supposedly went out after terror cells in the dead of the night.

They'd locate them, then go in and kill everyone on site. I figured it was just another wild tale, then one night I glimpsed a group of men wearing black fatigues and black bandannas that were armed to the teeth climbing into a chopper. When I asked an Air Force Combat Controller who the hell those guys were, he said, "Those are the Nightcrawlers. Now forget you ever saw 'em."

Now, I'd had combat training. I'd been an infantryman, more specifically a Truck Commander, TC, a .50-cal gunner on a Stryker vehicle. But I was nowhere in the league with a guy like Tuck. He was the real thing. He'd even been interviewed for books on Vietnam special ops. He knew his shit. If we were going to survive the zombie plague (if it can be called that), then we were going to need someone to whom survival was second nature.

And that person was Tuck.

We became good friends working sites together. Ricki, of course, didn't exactly approve of him. But he was all right. I liked him. Being war vets, we always had a lot to talk about. Tuck had built himself a stone tower just off the Taconic Parkway on a farm he'd inherited from some uncle of his. Tuck was a survivalist. He'd loaded his tower with weapons and provisions so he, as he liked to say, "could fiddle about at the end while the rest were slitting each other's throats for crusts of bread."

Tuck believed in being ready.

And he was.

Of course, his neighbors were all rich Westchester County horse breeders and they hated him and his tower and had tried numerous times to buy him out and force him out. But never to his face, of course. They wanted the crazy bricklayer and his tower gone. It was hurting property values and insulting the aesthetics of the countryside. So far it hadn't happened. But they kept trying, as he told me, and he kept resisting simply because it was pissing them off and that gave him great satisfaction. Rich or not, they were learning what the North Vietnamese had learned in the war: Tuck doesn't leave until he's good and goddamned ready.

THE TOWER

You could see it half a mile away.

It looked like the battlement of some Medieval castle. Tuck had twenty acres of farmland, a silo, an old barn, a ratty-looking farmhouse...and the tower. It was built atop a hill in the center of his property. The hill had long ago been hollowed out and turned into a potato crib by his uncle who'd been something of a tater baron following World War II. Tuck re-bricked it, reinforced it, then built a stone tower block by block atop it...then installed a state-of-the-art security system. He was a guy who took no chances and that was exactly what I was counting on. The tower rose forty feet above the hill and had a fenced widow's walk circling around the top of it which gave you a clear view straight to Manhattan. Half-way down like a wreath of garland there was a barbwire encirclement so nobody could climb their way up to the walkway.

It was something all right.

"Jesus H. Christ," Jimmy said when he got his first look at Tuck's compound, because calling it a *farm* was like calling a Surface-to-Air Missile a firecracker. "He expecting World War Three or what?"

"You might say that," I said.

I'd already told them about Tuck. As much as I could, I guess. The rest they'd find out themselves. All they needed to know and all I really cared about was that Tuck was your best friend in the world or your worst enemy, depending on which side of the fence you stood on. His survivalism, I knew, was an outgrowth from his war years when security and carefully-orchestrated defense were the difference between life and death. Had he carried it to an extreme in civilian life? Absolutely. Was he paranoid? Yes and no. He'd once told me that his philosophy of life could be summed-up in the following: "They'll never take me alive because I'll be waiting for 'em every time."

"Is that a lighthouse?" Paul asked when I cut off the road and pulled up at the gates that sealed off the drive going in.

"More like a watch tower," Diane told him. "Pretty effing sweet. Very…very phallic, isn't?"

"Looks like something from *Monty Python and the Holy Grail,*" Ricki said with her usual deadpan humor.

"What's phallic?" Paul said.

Jimmy and I grinned at each other like a couple schoolboys who'd just peeked into the girl's shower room.

Tuck's property was enclosed by a high chain-link fence topped by double coils of military-grade razor wire. About twenty feet inside from the fence there was a perimeter ditch dug all the way around. It looked to be about fifteen feet wide and at least that in depth. If you got over the fence you'd have to deal with the ditch and I could just about guess there were surprises in that ditch you didn't want to know about.

There was a big padlock on the gates. We weren't getting in unless Tuck wanted us to. There was a sign that read DANGER! ELECTRIFIED FENCE so I wasn't about to get too close to it. I had a pretty good feeling he'd already spotted us. I tried my cell but I wasn't getting anything.

"This don't look like a real friendly sort of place," Jimmy said.

Seeing no deadheads about, I jumped out and walked over near the gates. In the distance I could see someone up on the widow's walk. I caught a shine of chrome and then the first shot rang out. It landed just inside the gate, medium-caliber, maybe a .30-30. I knew that the shooter in question could drop me anytime he wanted. I dialed-up Tuck's number again and it was answered right away.

"You can stop shooting anytime," I told him.

"Booky? That you out there?" he asked. "Hang tight, I'll be down to get you. Shit! I was hoping somebody decent would come calling!"

Tuck called me *Booky* because I was always reading on my lunch break at the sites we worked. He got a kick out of that. Seeing a blue collar schlub like me reading Hemingway and Proust. It sent him into gales of laughter. But it was no stranger than a crusty old jarhead scraping a fiddle.

"Are you okay?" Ricki said when I got in the Suburban.

"Fine," I told her.

"Hell of a way to greet a man," Jimmy said.

"Well, you can't say that Tuck's place isn't secure," I told him.

Paul was getting excited and I could see that. The tower. The crazy guy I'd told him about. He was expecting something out of a comic book and I was pretty sure he would not be disappointed. About two minutes later I heard a dirt bike roar to life and here came Tuck roaring in our direction. He jumped off it and opened the lock, swinging the gates in for us.

"Hell, you people out on picnic?" he asked. "Well, you're all welcome to the last redoubt. This is where mankind makes its final stand. Shit, yes!"

He was dressed in camouflage fatigue pants, scuffed combat boots, and a black sleeveless Tee that had a pot leaf on it. It read: LEGALIZE THE SEED AND I'LL MAKE THE WEED. Maybe I left that part out: Tuck was also a firm believer in the power of the sweet leaf and was something of a dope farmer. His security measures had something to do with that, too, I imagine. He stood there, appraising us, a 9mm Sig-Sauer hanging on the web belt at his waist, a knife in his boot.

Nobody was too sure what to make of him as I gave a quick round of introductions. Ricki was intimated by him. Jimmy was unsure. Paul was in love. Diane just smiled, looking at his shirt. "I think I'm going to like this guy," she said.

I pulled the Suburban down the road to the tower and, after locking us in and reactivating the voltage in the fence via his Blackberry, Tuck joined us. Since I'd been out there last, something like six or seven months, he'd made a lot of changes. The silo and farmhouse were gone, two sheet metal pole buildings were in their place over near the barn and a variety of security technology had been installed, hemming the tower in.

"C'mon, let's get inside," Tuck said.

You got into the tower by entering a metal security door set into the hillside. It had an electronic entry keypad and Tuck punched us in. Inside, the old vault-like potato crib had been turned into something like a storeroom in a fallout shelter. Tuck showed us locked cages that were stocked with olive drab Army packing cases of MREs, medical gear, sealed bottles of pure drinking water, Army/Navy surplus fatigues and boots and jackets. You name it, he had it. There were also three Suzuki dirt bikes and drums of gasoline and oil.

"I got like three-hundred gallons of hi-test out in the barn," he said.

He keyed us through another metal door and we climbed a circular staircase (very lighthouse-like) up to the first level which was more storage. The second level held bedrooms, small but functional, military cots lined up in rows along with blankets and pillows. The third level was Tuck's living room and kitchen. It's where the bathroom was located. There were three windows looking out set with steel bars that were just above the garland of barbwire, I noticed. We climbed to the upper story and it was some kind of panic room or control center, call it what you will.

"God*damn!*" Paul said when he saw it.

"Watch your mouth," Ricki warned him.

"Awesome," was Diane's comment.

Both Paul and Diane were right, though: it really was something.

Tuck had a tech board set up with video screens and infrared monitors, motion detectors…the works. It was all tied into his laptop. He could access all of it remotely with his Blackberry. He took us over to a sliding steel door in the wall. He keyed it open and it led to the walkway. We stepped out there and you literally could see for miles and miles, just like in that old song by The Who.

"You've made some improvements since I was here last," I said.

"Lots of 'em."

"This must've put you back some," Jimmy said.

"I dropped every cent that Crazy Joe left me into it," he told us.

"Crazy Joe?" Ricki said.

"That's my uncle," Tuck explained. "They used to call him *Crazy Joe the Potato Ho*. He left me this farm and a pile of cash. I put it to good use, don't you think?"

She just nodded.

Dick was out there with us, still staring. I figured he was seeing something other than what the rest of us were seeing. He looked positively haunted and with good reason, I suppose.

"This is wicked!" Paul said. "I mean this is so sick I can't believe it!"

Tuck laughed and ruffled his hair. Then he put his arm around Ricki and held her close. "See now, baby, this is the place for you and your son. Defensible. Impregnable. The dead want to get up and walk? Let 'em, I say. They ain't gonna breach my defenses. Let the world go to shit and you and me and your boy, why, we'll just be cozy as two peas in a pod. Hell, cozier than turds in a blanket. You know what I'm saying?"

Ricki just stared at me wide-eyed.

Funny thing was that Tuck…out of all of us he could have taken a shine to…he had a real gleam in his eye for Ricki, the last person who probably would warm to him. But maybe that was why. I wasn't sure if I should have felt threatened or laughed at the absurdity of it.

Towing her around with him like a prize kewpie doll he'd won at a carnival pitching booth, he said, "Let me lay it out for you, sugar. Now like I said, this tower is impregnable. I got food and water stocked that could last us over a year. I got medical. I got transport—got three hardass SUVs reinforced with steel plating—plenty of fuel, weapons and ammo, everything." He gave her a squeeze. "What if somebody tried to attack? you say. Well, I got high-res CCTV with pan/tilt/zoom and night vision that monitors the fence, the grounds, the outbuildings. We can see right where they are, day or night. That fence is fifteen feet high. It's unclimbable and electrified. I've got Passive Infrared sensors just inside the fence and around the tower. They pick up body heat. Problem with that, of course, is that the dead don't throw off much in the way of a heat signature. But I'm guessing that in the days to come the living might prove just as much of a problem. In conjunction with the PIR we got microwave motion detectors as a failsafe. If they both detect intruders, my board lights up and motion lights flood the compound."

"What if it's just a woodchuck nosing around out there?" Jimmy asked.

"Not a problem," Tuck said. "I have a software recognition package. It can differentiate between animal and human signatures." He gave Ricki another squeeze. "But say the bad boys break through my fence. Say the voltage don't deter them. Then what? See that ditch all along the inside perimeter?" He pointed down towards it. "I got 50,000 gallons of fuel oil hooked to a gravity feed system. I touch the button, it floods the trenches. I fire an incendiary into it and you've got a curtain of fire that will burn for hours and hours. But you ask, well, Tuck, what if *that* is breached? Well, that's what I'm working on now. See, I got me a friend with connections. He got me a bulk of surplus AP mines— that's anti-personnel. Me and your husband are going to be mining this place. We're going to be ringing in our tower with M18 Claymores. When we're done, hell, 1st Marines couldn't breach this place."

Good old Tuck. Landmines, of all things. I didn't want to know how much illegal stuff he had. I was just glad that he had it. Just buying some of that stuff could have put him in a federal prison for decades especially since the Patriot Act.

Jimmy said, "But if they were to get through even all that...hell, up here, sitting pretty with a rifle and scope it would be turkey shoot."

"You got that, man."

For the first time in the past twenty-four hours, I felt somewhat relaxed. I think we all did...though it was hard to tell if Diane had ever really been concerned because she lived on her own private planet. Dick still wasn't saying anything and Tuck was watching him very intently.

"He lost his wife," I told him, filling him in on the situation.

Tuck stared at me. "He didn't get bit, did he?"

"No."

"You're sure? I wouldn't care for it if you brought the infection in here."

"No. I wouldn't do that."

"All right, Booky. That's cool then."

We went down into his living quarters and all fell into comfortable chairs and let out one long collective sigh. Tuck clicked on his widescreen and it was doom city on every channel. Things we (the world population, I mean) had feared for a long time were coming to fruition. We were standing at the very edge of World War III, and at a time when we all desperately needed to quit pointing fingers and work together to defeat Necrophage and the damage it was creating. But instead of unilateral cooperation, it was bipartisan dirty politics as usual between the Liberals and Conservatives in the U.S. Worldwide, it was even worse: death on a spit, particularly in Asia, Africa, and the Middle East. Things had gotten so bad they were calling airstrikes on their own cities. India and Pakistan were inching closer to a nuclear confrontation. China was pissing that the West had loosed Necrophage to destroy the economic might of the Chinese people. Meanwhile, the worse-case scenario became a reality on the Korean Peninsula. The KPA, Korean People's Army, had surged towards the South Korean border en masse and tactical nukes had been used against them. It was being said that the KPA had lost 80% of its armed forces in fifteen minutes. Pyongyang and the crazy midget, Kim Jong-Il, responded by hitting the outskirts of Seoul with a ballistic missile carrying a nuclear warhead. Deaths were climbing well into the millions. U.S. and South Korean forces were currently responding by decimating the North Korean infrastructure with a surgical bombing campaign. Two-thirds of the country, apparently, were now without water or electricity and people were dying by the droves.

And, as you might guess, the more people that died, the more Necrophage amplified itself in a lethal chain of transmission. Aerial reconnaissance by unmanned drones showed the countryside and burning cities literally swarming with the walking dead (which was a term now being used by the media even if our own government and most of those of the world were still referring to them as "irrational and violent" mobs.) It was pretty much the same over much of Asia. A microbiologist on CNN said that if the virus was not eradicated or at least halted in its transmission, that it was reasonable to assume that Asia, Africa, and the Middle East would soon be a graveyard in the literal sense.

Southern and Eastern Europe were the hardest hit by the pandemic, but it was making itself known in Scandinavia and Russia, too. The Third World in general was absolutely devastated and dozens of countries were on the verge of immediate collapse. They were begging NATO and the U.S. for assistance but there wasn't any to be had.

Over here it wasn't exactly peaches-and-cream either. According to CNN the Army was fighting zombies and militias in Dallas, Atlanta, and Cleveland. Helicopter gunships had attacked armed bands in Manhattan and the Bronx as well as veritable armies of zombies in the other boroughs. There were rumors that napalm had been used in Chicago, and Detroit had been targeted with cluster bombs. Half of Los Angeles was burning. Riots in Baltimore, Houston, and Miami had resulted in an absolute bloodbath as thousands were gunned down in the streets by Army and Marine units...and that wouldn't last much longer because not only were individual soldiers deserting but entire companies.

It was chaos.

And this within like thirty-six hours.

What would a week or a month bring?

And how had that damn virus spread everywhere practically overnight? What possible common vector could explain it?

After a time, content that the world was going to shit as he'd long expected, Tuck turned off the TV and put on some bluegrass music.

That was what our first day at the tower was like.

Everything was going to hell, but we were alive and we were safe and we really couldn't hope for much more.

PANIC LIST

1. Thank God for Tuck, a.k.a. J.J. Tucker (don't know what the Js are for)
2. We seem safe here
3. The world is going to shit
4. Social order is collapsing around us
5. Necrophage is everywhere—how long before one of us gets it???
6. Think positively!
7. The above, not so easy
8. <u>Here's my anxieties:</u> the zombies scare me, Necrophage terrifies me, and the idea of nukes with resultant fallout sweeping over our position here fills me with horror. I was never this freaked out in the war, but back then I didn't have to worry about Paul and Ricki.
9. On the above: the fallout. If nukes <u>were</u> used on New York City, the fallout would reach us. We're too close. Even a tactical will fry us if the wind is right. I've been through most of Tuck's supplies by this point and I see

no NBC protection, no biohazard suits, radiation gear, or anything.
10. I've been something of a confirmed atheist for years (though I never mention the fact), but lately I've been praying. I feel like a hypocrite.
11. I just want us to survive this if that's at all possible
12. Pessimistic thought for the day: Tuck is like a father-figure to us. He will not let anything happen to us…but he watches everyone very closely. He's at war. If one of us picks up the virus, I'm afraid what he might do.

LIFE ON THE FARM

Over the next week or so as the world continued to split the collective seam of its pants, we settled in at the tower which was, for all intents and purposes, our home away from home. Ricki, Paul, Diane, and I shared the biggest room on the second level. Dick and Jimmy were in the one next door. I'd never seen Paul quite as happy. Each day he got closer with Tuck, much to the chagrin of Ricki who still did not entirely approve of our benefactor. At least, that's what she liked to say. But I think she was taken with him, too, she just wouldn't admit it. Jimmy and Tuck got along fine as I knew they would. They liked to spend their evening in a couple lawn chairs out on the walkway, talking about 'Nam, about the '60's, reliving their younger days.

Diane was really something.

I had to finally admit it.

All these years I thought she was just a free-living, slutty stoner and now I had to wonder how much of that was true and how much was general middle class judgment and how much was just the impression she liked to create for her own amusement. During that week I learned things I already knew (she worshipped good pot and pot culture in general) and things I never suspected (she had a green thumb and was an absolute natural working Tuck's crops). She never complained or griped and she generally went out of her way to avoid Ricki's wrath...though her natural sarcasm often slipped through. One thing about Diane, she's always content wherever she is. And on Tuck's farm, she was very, very content. She would rise early and always be the first one outside to start working.

Tuck, of course, wasn't crazy about that.

Despite his security system he did not like anyone going out on their own. The way he had it set-up was that when we went outside to work, one of us was always posted as a sentry. He wanted somebody on the ground keeping an eye out for trouble and another up on the walkway scanning with binoculars. He could get a little confrontational when someone disobeyed his orders as Diane always did.

"I ain't trying to turn this into a fucking prison or anything," he told her. "But we gotta have rules. We gotta live by 'em. If we follow 'em and respect 'em, they'll keep us alive."

"I'm cool with that," Diane told him.

Of course, the next morning she'd break them and go outside anyway and Tuck would get miffed but he'd get over it. I started to wonder if, as good as Diane was, maybe she lived the life she did simply because she *couldn't* follow rules. Maybe it was something genetic. A short in her hardwiring.

Ricki turned into a very good lookout up on the walkway or "catwalk" as she liked to call it. Being down on ground level made her nervous. We were all traumatized by what we had seen, but with Ricki it was almost a physical thing: leaving the tower for any reason made her nearly physically ill. She didn't like me going out but she knew I had to. Paul tagging along with Tuck and I or Jimmy scared her.

Dick was proving day by day to be trouble.

He was unhinged by what had happened in his attic with Elena. I think we all sympathized with that, yet him wandering around with that blank-eyed (I hate to say it) zombie-stare was enough to give you the creeps. You had to practically force him to eat and then he just nibbled. He would stand there staring into space, his mouth moving but no words coming out. Twice Tuck had caught him wandering about in the dead of night. I myself had caught him trying to get into the gun locker. Tuck wouldn't have liked that much; he was real particular about his collection of weapons. He made all of us wear 9mm Sig-Sauer's like his own when we were out in the compound or out in the fields (the sentry carried a .30-06 with a scope) except for Paul, of course, but he did not want Dick anywhere near a gun because he was convinced he was going to snap any day. In the gun locker, Tuck had quite an armory, lots of semi-auto weapons and riot guns, but also fully automatic CAR-15s that were illegal as hell and were identical to the M4 carbine I carried in the war. He also had a vintage Walther MPK submachine gun, an M-14 sniper rifle, and a MAC-10 that no one, absolutely no one, was allowed to touch.

We just didn't know what to do about Dick.

He would rarely speak and when he did it made absolutely no sense. I had the best luck with him and then he'd usually say something along the order of what he'd said that day we picked him up on Holly Street: *"She was alive, Steve, then she was dead...I didn't want her to be dead...but she was dead and then she was alive...she was crawling at me...she wanted to bite me...she wanted to kill me so I was like her...I had to hit her with the hammer, didn't I? I had to do that, didn't I?"*

Even Ricki, who was one of the most sympathetic and mothering sort of people I'd ever known, was reaching her limit. One night as we lay in bed and Diane had crashed-out (soon as her head hit the pillow usually) and Paul had finally wound down from talking about all the things Tuck was teaching him (good and bad), I pulled Ricki into my arms and said, "Are you okay?"

"I'm fine," she said. "Worried. Stressed. Concerned. Other than that I'm fine."

"I think we'll be okay."

"How about six months from now? A year?"

She liked to think ahead and our new life made that really hard for her. "We just take it day by day. Sooner or later, people are going to get the upper hand out there. It's got to happen."

I didn't think she believed me anymore than I believed myself, but she sighed and said, "I suppose you're right. What about Dick, though?"

"What about him?"

"I'm starting to wonder if Tuck isn't right," she said. "That he might just flip out one day. I worry about it. He needs some kind of help, Steve. Only we don't have that sort available."

She was right, but what could we do about it but watch him and take care of him and hope for the best?

Tuck had quite a "garden" out there if such a term really applies to what was more or less a working farm. He had rows of sweet corn, squash, carrots, three kinds of tomatoes, onions, parsnips, rutabagas, and potatoes. Lots of potatoes. He also had a dozen apple trees, another dozen cherry and peach trees. It had been raining off and on and the days had been hot and sunny, so the crops were bursting with leaf and fruit. I realized how dependent we were going to become on those crops like people back in the old days—one good season of blight and we'd be starving.

Diane and Paul and Jimmy spent a lot of time tending fruits and veggies while Tuck and I continued securing the place. Outside the perimeter ditch we laid down seventy or eighty AP mines. They wouldn't blow anyone to fragments or anything. Their purpose in a war was to create disabling injuries, blow off toes and mangle feet, take an enemy combatant out of action. And when he was unable to walk, a couple others would have to help him, thereby tying up more of the enemy. More of a nuisance sort of thing. We decided against wiring the Claymores in a perimeter around the tower until we actually needed them. Nobody liked the idea of being out there with the business end of a Claymore staring down at them.

"We can wire 'em in about ten, fifteen minutes if the need arises," Tuck said. "We used to do it in 'Nam for our NDF, Night Defensive Position. We'll set 'em out, wire 'em to a single clacker or in pods of twos and threes. Nothing will get through 'em. *Nothing.* "

I'd seen them used a few times in Iraq. One time, a group of Johnny Jihads at our FOB in Samarra tried to run the perimeter and the grunts drew them in real close and then fired their Claymores. There'd been maybe forty Johnnies out there, but after the Claymores there was nothing but a lot of gore and body parts for about 200 feet. The Claymore fires some 700 steel pellets that literally vaporize the enemy.

They work. Trust me, they work.

The third night we were there, cell service went down and Tuck was pissed because he couldn't run his security from his Blackberry anymore. One provider after the other bit the dust that night. The fourth day we lost satellite TV and all we had was the radio and internet, though I feared the latter wouldn't last too much longer.

In the world at large, things were approaching critical mass.

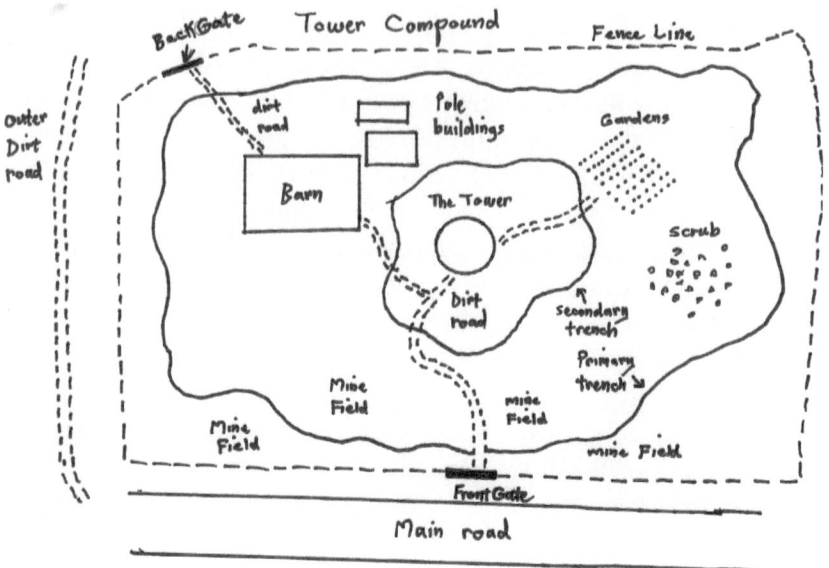

THE WATCHERS

The next night, after a long day working out in the compound—we were digging a secondary trench system with Tuck's backhoe, me being the shovel guy, of course—we were just beat. Jimmy, Tuck, and me sat out on the walkway after the others crashed for the night. We sampled some of Tuck's bourbon, chatting and having a few laughs. I remember thinking it was almost like all the badness out there was going on in some other world that we were isolated from. Then Jimmy stood up and went to the railing, "Lookit that, will ya?" he said.

Tuck and I were at the railing and we saw: the lights of Yonkers were going out. Section by section the city was plunged into blackness.

"Grid's failing," Tuck said. "I was hoping it would last another week or so."

Not an hour later, we watched as the lights of the Bronx and Manhattan which lit up the horizon followed suit. There was blackness creeping in on us from all quarters and it was very sobering. I couldn't imagine what it must have been like in those places. Like being in a Medieval city under siege. We listened to the radio, grabbing a station from Jersey, and the gloomy-sounding DJ said that the power was failing all across the northeast and that most of New England was blacked-out. It was all very sobering.

And frightening.

"Now it's going to get ugly out there," Tuck said.

The announcer said that Europe was pretty much blacked-out, too, and there had been no word coming out of Eastern Europe in over twenty-four hours now. China, for all intents and purposes, had fallen and the rest of Asia had already followed suit. Satellite imagery showed that Africa really was the dark continent and news out of there was very sporadic. There had been nothing out of Mexico in forty-eight hours. Same for most of the Midwest where Necrophage had, for some reason, spread like wildfire. Before we lost satellite, there had been video on CNN of literally thousands of the undead flooding the streets of Chicago. It looked like the noon rush in Midtown Manhattan.

On the BBC we'd seen similar images from London and Manchester, Liverpool and Cardiff. All of which was minor in comparison to what was going on in India. According to estimations the dead outnumbered the living 800 to 1 in Calcutta and in China and Southeast Asia it was something like *fives* times that. I wasn't about to say the war was lost before it began, but it wasn't exactly promising. The CDC, State Department, Department of Homeland Security, and the White House continued to broadcast emergency bulletins over the airwaves as well as state and local agencies, but the latter were getting a bit spotty.

I didn't want to imagine a world that was an open grave from sea to shining sea, where the cities were ruined sepulchers and the rivers ran black with mortuary run-off, the sky blown gray from crematoria ash…but I thought that's where it was all going. If we did not get the upper hand and soon, the human race would be nothing but one immense smoldering bone-pile.

As we watched the darkness out there which was thick and unbroken save for an occasional flash of light from the direction of Yonkers and the Bronx, probably an explosion, I looked over at Tuck and said, "What's your long-range plans? We're safe for now, but—"

"But we can't hide like rats in our hole forever?"

"I guess."

He thought about it, sipping his bourbon. "We lay low for a few weeks, maybe a month or so. We let the dust settle. Then we go out there on recon missions, scope it out, find out where the dead are."

"And then?"

"Then we start taking it back house by house, block by block, city by city. It'll be ugly. But this world wasn't tamed the first time around without blood, sacrifice, and hardship. We'll do it again." He had our attention and he kept going: "If this Necrophage thing follows the course of most pandemics, man, then in six months it'll have peaked. What I mean is, most of those who are going to get infected and die by the virus will have died and risen back up. The people still around by then will have developed immunities. And when that happens, when the human population has flat-lined and stabilized, then it's all-out war. I don't know about you guys, but I'm not about to raise the white flag here. I'll be damned if I'll let a bunch of worm-brained shit-eaters take my world and make me hide under a bed."

"Hear, hear," Jimmy said.

Tuck refreshed our drinks and we toasted his words which were not only optimistic, I thought, but rock-bottom practical. I think when our glasses touched that night a bond was formed, a blood oath: we would fight and we would keep fighting until Necrophage was a bad memory like the Spanish Flu epidemic of the First World War and every last zombie was burnt, blasted, broken, or buried back in the holes they crawled out of.

We would exterminate them.

And we would exterminate them because there simply was no alternative.

That night I fell into an uneasy sleep, fraught with nightmares where I saw the living dead marching in armies and the human race fighting a desperate guerrilla war tree to tree, tomb to tomb, and house to house. Then, around four in the morning, I woke in a panic as I was shaken awake.

It was Jimmy. "Dick," he said. "He's gone."

"Gone?" I said, still trying to make sense of it.

"I woke up and he'd not in his bed. We gotta find him."

"What is it?" Ricki said.

"Dick wandered off again," I said. "Go back to sleep."

We searched the tower from top to bottom, save Tuck's digs, and couldn't find him. That's when the alarms went off and I realized that Dick had gotten down into the crib at the base of the tower and had somehow keyed open the outside security door. He must have tripped the motion sensors outside the tower which were armed dusk to dawn.

Jimmy and I grabbed our guns and made for the stairs.

That's when Tuck showed. He had a short pistol-gripped pump shotgun in his hand that he must've kept under his pillow.

"It's Dick," I said. "He must've got outside."

"That motherfucker," he sighed. "Okay, go find him before he walks into the minefield. I'll kill the alarms and join you."

Jimmy and I hustled down the stairs, keying our way through the security doors that sealed off each level. When we got down into the crib, we grabbed flashlights and stormed outside. Lights were blazing everywhere. Jimmy was no kid so I told him to circle around the tower to see if he could catch a glimpse of Dick and I ran off down the road. Like I said, there were lots of lights but Tuck's farm was a damned big place so there were pockets of darkness everywhere. The lights threw my shadow before me.

"DICK!" I called out. "DICK!"

There was no answer, of course, and I knew there wouldn't be one but I had to try. About halfway down the winding dirt road I cut into the field, shining my light around. We had marked the perimeter of the minefields with red flags and we all knew to steer clear of them, but Dick, I was sure, was so out of it that he would have blundered right in there. In the back of mind, though I hate to admit it, some voice was saying, go ahead, let him get his ass blown away. It'll be one less worry. But I wasn't about to let that happen. I scanned the flags with my light. The minefields were like a belt that surrounded the tower and I began following the flags. Maybe he hadn't made it that far. Maybe he'd fallen into the new ditch we'd dug or curled up in the grass somewhere. There were an awful lot of maybes. I frightened a rabbit and it scampered off and nearly gave me a coronary.

Then I heard shouting.

I looked back towards the tower. The walkway was lit and I could see Ricki up there waving at me.

"HE'S IN THE ROAD!" she called out. "HE'S IN THE ROAD BY THE GATE!"

Dammit. He was quicker than I thought.

I got back to the road after tripping on a log and going face-down in the grass, grabbing my flashlight and realizing there was a big blacksnake about a foot from my face. He did not look pleased with me interrupting his nightly mouse hunt. He went one way and I went the other. If all we had to worry about were harmless farm snakes. On the road I ran at full speed and as I came around a bend in the road I saw Dick standing about a foot from the main gate.

I got up to about six feet from him when I realized he was talking.

On the other side of the gate there were seven or eight of the living dead—three adults and a group of kids, like some kind of extended undead family. They were not coming any closer, just standing back at the edge of the shadows about fifteen feet from the fence watching Dick. I couldn't see much beyond their shadowy forms and their glistening eyes, but I could smell the hot stink coming off them.

"Elena?" Dick said. "Is that you? Come closer so I can see you."

The zombies did not speak, of course. They just stood and watched and waited. Much like the blacksnake, they were creatures of opportunity driven by reptilian brains that understood only feeding.

"Dick," I said. "Come on. Elena's dead, dude. Come with me."

That's when Tuck arrived.

"I ought to fucking feed you to them," he said.

I put a finger to my lips and we both listened for a few seconds as Dick talked to the dead and it almost seemed like they were listening to him, maybe understanding him. I didn't think such a thing was possible, yet I couldn't deny what I was seeing.

I hooked Dick by the arm and Tuck did the same.

We led him away. The zombies watched us. But they did not approach the fence. Maybe they already had earlier and had gotten a shock. It was hard to say. The voltage was non-lethal, but it was enough to give you a good kick in the ass or to burn your hand if you grabbed hold of it. Still, I doubted they were smart enough to care: meat was meat to them.

When we got back to the tower, Jimmy led Dick inside and Tuck and I stood there a moment.

"What the hell did he think he was doing?" Tuck said, lighting a cigarette.

"He probably wasn't thinking at all."

Tuck blew smoke into the beam of a motion light. "It was weird, Booky, and you know it. He was fucking *talking* to them."

"Seemed like it."

"He was and you know it. I bet if you go down there and stand next to the fence, they'll rush it, they'll try to get at you. Or me. But not Dick. Why not? That's what I'd like to know: *why not?*"

Tuck was right: it *was* weird. But it didn't necessarily mean anything and I refused to jump to any conclusions or take any wild leaps of logic. Sometimes the human mind can be over-analytical and read too much into too little. Maybe something was going on, but if that were the case, I didn't know what so I refused to speculate.

"I'm going in," I said. "Coming?"

He shook his head. "Well, the dead know where we are now. Tomorrow night there'll be twice as many out there and the night after, twice as many again," Tuck said. "By this time next week we'll have hundreds. Like fucking moths at a streetlight. They'll keep circling until they find a way in. I just hope that way in isn't Dick."

INTO THE BREACH

Tuck, Diane, and I took a run over to Tuckahoe, partly to reconnoiter things and also to do some scavenging and lay in a few extra truck batteries, something Tuck admitted he should have done weeks ago. But then, who expects something like this?

We used the back gate because there were no zombies mulling around there and we'd already counted fifteen of them congregating by the main gate. Tuck was right: they'd found us and now they would keep coming. He said we'd give it a few days but if they kept massing we'd have to clean them out.

The vehicle we were using was a Jeep Wrangler with steel panels bolted over all the windows except the windshield which was impact-proof, bullet-resistant polycarbonate. It was ugly as hell, but Tuck had customized it for playing hard with Ram bumpers, a roll cage, and a mean 360 V-8 under the hood that could deliver all the juice you could want. It was about as close to a main battle tank as you could get in an SUV. There was even a locking sliding hatch on the roof that could be used for shooting.

Jimmy unlocked the back gate and we took off, Tuck bouncing Diane and me around as he drove through gullies and up over hills, fording a stream in a spray of water and spinning out on a secondary gravel road, doing a couple wild looping pissies and screaming out like a sixteen-year old in his brother's hot rod.

When we made the main road I had a few gray hairs and Diane was gripping my arm so hard her nails left ruts.

"Even when the world has gone to shit," Tuck said, "you gotta have your fun."

"You're way out of control, man," Diane told him.

"Don't I know it."

We passed by the front gate and the zombies stood and stared at us. None of them tried to get in our path but I knew from experience that they did not generally associate a speeding vehicle with prey, but if you slowed down it was a completely different story. As we made our way to Tuckahoe we saw very little in the way of human life. We saw a pile-up of six or seven cars that were burnt black that had not been cleared away, scorched corpses…or parts of them…hanging from windows.

"You know what that is?" Tuck said, jabbing his thumb at the pile-up.

I looked at him.

"To a zombie that's a barbecue."

Diane tittered but I said nothing, looking at a few near-devoured corpses sprawled in yards.

"Fast food," he pointed out.

A helicopter passed high overhead and in the distance I saw crows or buzzards circling in the sky meaning there was death somewhere and lots of it. Somebody took a shot at us once and a block later a naked man came running across the road. He was carrying a sack of potatoes over his shoulder.

It was disturbing, of course.

I knew everyone wasn't dead, dying, or crazy, but those people stayed indoors. The village of Tuckahoe which was really just part of Eastchester had been a pretty little town of well-maintained older homes, brick and clapboard, set on quiet leafy streets. Lots of historical buildings and the money to maintain them. As we drove on, I noticed that there were a lot of dogs running wild. I suppose that was to be expected. The houses all looked like crypts to me and I had the weird urge to jump out and go house-to-house, knocking on doors, just to see what might answer them. The air was redolent with the odor of burning wood and we all saw plumes of smoke rising over the trees. The farther we got into the town we could see that a fire had raged recently, consuming houses and stores and trendy shops. Most of them had burnt down to frames and nobody had come to put them out.

On the side of a white clapboard house somebody had painted the following:

THE RAPTUR IS HEAR NOW
CHRIST JESUS HAS GATHERD HIS FATEFUL
THEY SHALL BE WELCOMD TO THE BOSUM
THE SINNERS SHALL SUFFER
MEET NOW THY ABOMNATION

None of us commented on that. What was there to say? It was expected, spelling errors and all. What was going on would bring all the nut jobs and wackos out of the woodwork. Many of them were to be pitied. Others, those with guns and fatal visions, were to be feared.

We came up to a nice, well-manicured park and some guy came running out in the street. Not a zombie, of course, just a crazy. He was an old guy with white hair. He was barefoot. Tuck stopped and he ran right up to the front of the Jeep and slapped his hands on the hood. His face was covered with sores and his teeth were rotting out of his mouth. I got the feeling he probably made his home in an alley before all this happened.

"*BEWARE AND BE WARNED!*" he shrieked in his lunatic voice. "*THE MONSTERS ARE IN THE STREETS! THEY ARE HERE NOW! THEY WILL COME FOR YOU! THEY WILL FEED ON YOU! BE WARNED!*"

He stumbled off to spread the word and Tuck drove on. "Consider that our inspirational message for the day," he said.

Diane lit a cigarette. "I keep thinking what if it's only crazy ones like that who survive all this?" she said. "What then?"

"Then the world will look a lot like LA, like Hollywood Boulevard on a Friday night," Tuck said.

Never having been there, I decided to take his word on that.

He toured around the park and there were corpses everywhere. We saw the truly dead, well-picked by birds and dogs and unmoving, which had for some reason congregated there, as if some strange primal impulse had forced them to crawl out in the open to die. We also saw the sick, the near-dead. They were wandering around, some naked, some wearing pajamas and nightgowns. They weren't zombies. Not yet. A lot of them were delusional, chatting away and calling out to invisible friends. A few were on the ground, contorting and convulsing much the way Dick said Elena had right before she died. I saw dogs chewing on the cadavers, fighting over scraps. Ravens sat atop heads, picking at eyeballs and soft tissues. The stink of death was nauseating. Over near the ball field, the walking dead were putting in an appearance. They were marching in uneven rows, many of them holding their arms out before them like sleepwalkers. They did not move fast, but they kept coming and coming, shambling ever forward. Like the sick, they were in various stages of dress and undress. Some wore burial suits and dresses, others were naked from the mortuary slab, still others in hospital johnnies, and many more dressed in the trappings of the wealthy suburbanite.

"Gotta be a hundred or more," Diane pointed out.

"Good reason to get the hell out of here," Tuck said.

Sig-Sauer P226
Type: 9mm Semi-Auto
Kill Range: 130 feet
Magazine: 20 rounds, 9mm Parabellum

DAY OF THE LIVING DEAD

We wasted no more time.

Ten minutes later we pulled into the lot of Westchester Tractor which was just outside town. It was a big place with rows of agricultural tractors and harvesters, lawn tractors and compact excavators. There were a couple pick-ups in the parking lot but we were pretty sure their owners would not be about.

We took the safeties off our Sig-Sauers and left the Jeep.

We got inside easily enough because the front door was wide open.

"The batteries are back in the parts department," Tuck told us. "The cages will probably be locked so I'll have to shoot the locks off. You two stay out here, keep your eyes open."

He took off into the back with his shotgun and we waited there amongst the rows of shiny green tractor implements—aerators and cultivators, harrows and tillers.

"My whole building went to hell, man. "

"What?"

Diane looked through the plate glass windows at the parking lot. "The virus they were talking about. It spread through my whole building. That day you found me out walking…was that last week or the week before? I don't know. That's what I was getting away from. They were all infected. And I mean *infected.* That's what killed me about the whole thing, Steve. I mean, how could a virus move that fast? Think about it. How could it?"

I had been thinking about it and I had been tying it together with what I saw in Iraq, but it still made very little sense. A virus needed time to spread, it needed a vector to carry it person-to-person. That day last week when the dead started rising—The Awakening, as it was known—that was really the first that I had heard mention of a virus. But within hours, apparently, it was everywhere. Nobody in the government had actually admitted to isolating the bug. Yet, they were certain it *was* a virus. And were they basing that on scientific speculation or were they just assuming that this was the Necrovirus of Iraq going global? And with that in mind, had they suspected this might happen? Was the response we had seen since something that had been blueprinted years ago when it had first appeared in the Middle East?

I had too many questions and no answers.

But the entire thing *was* spooky and weird.

There was a common denominator, I knew that, and there were people in power who knew what it was, but we were not being told. I threw some of this at Diane, leaving out the Iraq stuff for the time being.

"Yeah, it *is* spooky, Steve. Traveling that fast. It's fucking mad." She shrugged. "We'll never have answers. Not good ones. The media are controlled by corporate interests and everything you hear has been carefully spun by their perception managers. The real truth of anything is kept from us. I mean, why do you think we're inundated with news stories—if you want to call them that—about the royal wedding and Kim fucking Kardashian and Charlie Sheen? It distracts attention from what's *really* going on. Keep 'em dumb, man, keep 'em dumb and uninformed."

Diane said it had all started during the Vietnam War when the media ran wild and free and started reporting the truth. That made the politicians and corporate mercenaries uneasy. The peace movement was a threat. And even those who didn't like hippies and the anti-war stuff were getting their noses rubbed in the grisly reality of war on a daily basis and it wasn't much like the John Wayne movies we'd been raised on. People were angry. American soldiers burning huts and exterminating villagers? That wasn't how Americans fought wars. That was the kind of shit Nazis and Russians and Third World despots indulged in...but not

Americans. The truth became a threat to the established power structure. Because if people kept getting more and more pissed off with the reality of war and the lies that were spun to pretty it all up, they were going to want change. They were going to want to tear down the house and build a new one and the politicians and their rich corporate backers would find themselves out on the street and out of the game, and the masses would demand a government that was *really* For the People and By the People.

"After the Vietnam thing, Steve, the corporations very quietly bought up the media so they could control them and further their own interests without fear of exposure," she went on. "There's an answer to all this, to what's going on now, but we'll never know what it is. Not unless some whistleblower spills the beans."

Wow. I never thought Diane was unintelligent, just dazed and unconcerned with the world at large. I stood corrected. She was watching all the time and she had cut right to the heart of the matter like a sharp knife. I had to agree with her and only because when I was in Iraq, what was being reported on CNN and FOX (especially FOX) and in the newspapers was not what was going on over there. It barely resembled the truth. We had a few embeds with us, but they were strictly controlled by the Army and the Pentagon. There were things they were allowed to say and things they were not. Which was bullshit. The fourth estate exists (we learned in school) to report the truth to the people, not carefully-sanitized, politically-correct spin. And the truth coming out of Iraq was no more factual than the propaganda spewed by newsmen during World War II: just as controlled, just as contrived.

"A lot of people don't want to believe what you believe," I said.

"They're scared. It threatens them. You can't blame 'em," she said. "When they hang their flag out they want to believe in what it stands for, they don't want to think that it's all been corrupted by greed and power plays. They don't want to admit to themselves that it's all a very carefully crafted façade, that it's synthetic and artificial. That what they've based their lives and beliefs upon has been a lie, that the wars their sons died in were unnecessary. Would you?"

"No," I said. "Sometimes it's easier to keep your blinders on."

She nodded. "And that's why we've become these spoon-fed, blank-eyed *zombies* who believe what we're told. You ever seen that movie *The Manchurian Candidate?*"

"Yeah."

"That's us on a national scale: brainwashed."

Up by the counter there were racks of junk food to seduce shoppers—chips and beef jerky and candy. Diane started loading as much of it as she could squeeze into plastic bags. I knew right then it wasn't for herself: it was for Paul.

She walked off and started nosing around in one of the offices and I followed her. There were some newspapers on a desk and she started leafing through them. I did the same. They were all a week out-of-date, but we read them anyway. I browsed through *The Journal News* from Yonkers. There was an interesting story about the nuclear power plants being in jeopardy with no one to run them, people falling sick left and right. The military supposedly had taken over quite a few but they weren't immune to Necrophage either. The debilitated state of the country put our nuclear resources in danger from terrorist attack. The AEC said there was nothing to worry about, but people *were* worried. They were worried about core meltdowns at Indian Point here in Westchester County, Haddam Neck, and Millstone Stations in Connecticut. There were nuclear power plants all over New England and the Northeast and nobody wanted a repetition of Chernobyl.

And then in black and white I found it: an open admission by a CDC source that preferred "not to be named" concerning the Necrophage virus. This person said it had not been isolated, but was acting in every way *like* a virus. Thus far, it was proving itself to be immune to antibiotics. It had multiple symptomology which pointed at viral. CBC blood tests and WBC counts confirmed this. The CDC were not completely ruling out a bacterium, but it seemed that "the offending invasive organism was most certainly a pathogenic virus."

"Check this out," Diane said.

She handed me a copy of the New York *Post*, which is probably the singularly most entertaining newspaper in the world now that the *Weekly World News* went balls-up. The *Post* didn't skimp on coverage of the infection and the zombies it produced. Lacking any good zombie photos, they just culled some creepy scenes from *Night of the Living Dead* and plastered them all over the cover. VIRAL DEATH SPREADS! BROOKLYN PLAGUE WARDS! NIGHTMARE IN NEW YORK CITY! Any other time I would have laughed shit like that off…but it was all very unfunny. There were more copies of the *Post,* the most recent being four days old. Apparently, getting shots of the living dead by that point was fairly easy (something I didn't doubt) because they had all kinds of them. One showed a dozen of them standing outside a house in Bensonhurst over in Brooklyn, another showed a little boy walking naked through Central Park dragging something behind him that could have been a very large doll but was probably the well-gnawed corpse of another child. Inside, there was a spread of blown-up full-color photos which were enough to put you off meat for a month: a group of the dead exiting a doorway above which clearly read STEIG FUNERAL HOME. All were naked except for one man in a suit. They were horrible, faces eaten down to the bone in some cases. One man was horribly bloated and a young woman was lacking her left arm. A particularly gruesome close-up showed an elderly woman with blank white eyes and clear evidence of maggots sprouting from a split chasm in her skull.

"What was that?" Diane said, stepping towards the doorway and pulling her gun.

I set my newspaper aside and went with her. I thought I'd heard something, too.

We stepped out into the immense showroom and started peering around. I didn't smell anything dead so I was pretty certain it was not the zombies. We stood there next to each other…then we heard running footsteps.

"I think they're kids," Diane said.

We split up and began touring amongst the various implements, both with our Sigs in our hands because we honestly did not know what to expect. I came around the side of an immense tiller and somebody ran off. It *was* a kid. A girl. She charged off back towards the parts department.

"Hey!" I said. "I won't hurt you!"

I saw Diane on a merry chase trying to catch a little boy who was agile as a monkey. Here, then gone. Ducking and darting through the implements, he left Diane in his dust. She circled around a display of garden tractors and the boy jumped over a few mowers, darted to the left and I grabbed him, holstering my gun. He was wild and dirty, frothing at the mouth and screeching at me.

"I WON'T HURT YOU!" I shouted in his face, shaking him.

He calmed down and just stood there, staring at me with wide eyes.

Then another voice said, "LEAVE MY BROTHER ALONE!"

The little girl came charging at me with a hammer held high and Diane stuck out her leg and tripped the kid. She hit the floor and started balling and I let the boy go to her. They held each other and stared at us, looking more like animals than children.

"We're normal," I told them. "You don't have to be afraid of us."

They looked unconvinced.

"Do you have anywhere to go?" I asked them.

They still stared.

"We have a safe place with food."

They continued staring.

"It's hopeless, man," Diane told me.

I figured she was right. Those kids were seeing us as a visible threat so we walked off towards the front of the showroom where we could watch the parking lot. And once we got there, we got an unpleasant surprise because there were eight or ten zombies coming through the lot. Most, I noticed, had been elderly when they died. It wasn't surprising, I suppose, since more elderly died daily than of any other age group. And they would be the ones that would probably die from the virus first: like any other predator, our mystery organism, Necrophage, would target the sick and the weak first.

"Shit," I said.

"They were following us," a voice said.

The boy and girl were standing not ten feet away. They were brother and sister, both with the same angular faces, shiny black hair, and huge dark eyes. And both dirty like they'd been sleeping under sheds and in ditches.

"They're not fast," the boy said. "They're slow. But they keep coming and coming. You can run away…but sooner or later you have to sleep. They don't."

The girl was still just watching us. She hadn't quite made up her mind.

"You can come with us where it's safe," I told him.

And he said: "It got our building. It got everyone."

As Diane watched the inexorable approach of the zombie corps, the boy told me his name was Davis and his little sister was Maria. He was nine-years old and she was seven. The infection hit their building five days before. It started in the morning and by afternoon it had spread everywhere. People were stumbling around in the hallways, delirious and screaming, some were convulsing. The man from next door was crawling around on his hands and knees and he was drenched with his own urine and vomit, soiled with his own feces. Davis and Maria stayed locked in their apartment while their mother got sicker and sicker. She was sweating and shaking, her eyes rolling back in her head. In a final moment of lucidity she told them to get out of Yonkers, to go to their Uncle Martin's farm (he had apple orchards). By late in the afternoon, she started screaming and thrashing and then she died. They packed up what they could in their school backpacks and not even an hour later their mother "woke up" (his words) and came after them. They ran away and barely got out of the building because there were zombies everywhere.

Even in the streets.

Diane said, "They're getting closer."

Tuck came back wheeling a cart with five big black batteries on it. "Where'd you find these scrubs?" he said.

"We got company," Diane told him.

Tuck saw. "Shit. We gotta fly."

I motioned to Davis and Maria. "I told them they could come with us."

Tuck just looked at me.

"Unless you want to leave them for the zombies," I said.

Maria ran right to him and wrapped herself around his legs. Tuck looked uncomfortable. "Hey," he said. "Hey."

"Please," Maria said. "Please take us away."

She had a sweet little voice that had probably melted many a heart in its time and Tuck just scowled. "Yeah. All right. Come on. Just do what you're told."

We started out of the building and Tuck raced over to the Jeep.

The dead were mere feet from it and he dropped three of them, smashed another in the face to drive it back, and got behind the wheel. He backed across the parking lot and I got the kids in the backseat and we loaded the batteries. Then we jumped in the front and Tuck stomped the accelerator. The zombies he had dropped were being fed on by most of the pack, but three others were coming for the Jeep. He floored it and smashed them out of the way. The Jeep with its reinforced bumper scattered them like nine pins. One of them thumped up over the hood and slid over the roof before falling away.

Out on the road, there were dozens of zombies in the fields, just walking and walking.

"Hey," Diane said when she spotted that Maria was terrified and close to tears. She dug in her plastic bag. "Who wants a peanut butter cup?"

She got two takers right away.

PANIC LIST

1. We've got a couple new faces: Maria and Davis, brother and sister.
2. Glad to have them, but they're kids. That gives me something else to worry about, I suppose.
3. I kind of wish they were adults, people who could fight with us.
4. We're in pretty good shape at the tower, thanks to Tuck.
5. Diane and Ricki have been kinda/sorta getting along
6. Dick remains a problem. I wish there was a way to snap him out of it before he does damage to himself or the rest of us.
7. Still seeing a few choppers from time to time.
8. New reports are conflicting. What's really going on?
9. Thus far, we have power and water. But for how long?

BACK AT THE FARM

Ricki and Diane took our guests out to the pond where we did most of our bathing and cleaned them up. When they got back they looked pretty much like kids and not much like animals at all. Still, though, in their eyes there was something that did not belong: fear, cold fear. Their eyes darted very quickly in their sockets, always on the move. Both of them reminded me of squirrels with their quick jerky movements. They continually cocked their heads, listening. They were prey animals and they acted like prey animals. It would take time to turn them back into children.

Paul was ecstatic, of course, to finally have some kids around. I thought it would be good for him to spend a little less time with Tuck and more with some kids his age. The way he was going it wouldn't be long before he became a foul-mouthed, hard-assed, blood-spitting Marine just like Tuck. Neither Ricki nor I cared for the idea of that.

Jimmy was good with the kids, of course, instantly reverting into his grandfatherly demeanor when he saw them. He showed them card tricks and played Snakes-and-Ladders with them on a board he'd made himself. They were good kids: both kind and very polite, raised-up right. Ricki took an instant shine to them. Tuck, however, just glared at them when they got too close to him, but Maria was fascinated by the gruff old Recon Marine. She was always following him around and asking where he was when he was gone and offering him food from her plate. She drew pictures of him and told him he was the toughest man in the world and told everyone that he would protect us like her daddy had protected them before he was killed by an Army patrol in the streets.

That did it.

Tuck melted.

He went from a bristling, hard-edged, jar-headed Marine to a soft, shapeless blob of warm butter. Maria wrapped him around her little finger and he was powerless. It wasn't long before her drawings were taped all over his board in the panic room (as I called it) and she was sitting on his lap and riding atop his shoulders. He played songs for her on his fiddle and told her stories I knew he made up on the spot. I don't want to sound too soppy, but it was pretty damn touching.

Things were going well.

Except for the world outside the fence.

Just like Tuck predicted, the dead were building up out there and at last count there were over fifty of them. That's when Tuck pulled me and Jimmy aside and said, "It's time to thin the herds."

My idea was to go out on the walkway and do a little sniping, but that wasn't practical because of the fence. Since the deadheads were clustering up quite near to it now, we'd have to shoot through the fence to hit them and that meant hitting the fence and we saw no reason in weakening the integrity of our barrier. Out also was Jimmy's idea of killing the juice on the fence and walking right up there and shooting through it. Tuck figured that was just asking for trouble—if we got close to it, they'd rush us and no sense risking an *in*human wave attack if we could possibly avoid it.

"Defense is great," Tuck said. "If we could hole up in here for the next couple years and never have to leave, it'd be great. But we can't do that. And we can't have the herds piling up outside the fence. That means we have to get out there and carry the fight to them."

"Sounds risky," Jimmy told him.

"It is. But we don't have a choice."

"What do you got in mind?" I told him.

"An ambush."

It was an interesting idea, but I wasn't convinced it was a good one. The ambush is a great military tactic to thin the numbers of the enemy. When they work—which is often—they can be devastating to enemy combatants. But when they fail, they can be just as devastating to your own people. I wasn't sure that using traditional soldiering techniques against a very non-traditional enemy was the best idea. And being out there, mixing it up with the walking dead wasn't something I much cared for.

"When I was in 'Nam and we're talking 1969/1970 here, my first tour over there," Tuck told us, "we had rules of engagement that stifled us and supported the assholes we were there to fight. The VC and NVA units would slip across the border from Cambodia and Laos, hit our units, then creep back across again. We weren't allowed to follow. Rules of engagement. The U.S. wasn't at war with Cambodia or Laos so we couldn't enter their territory. The North Viets weren't at war with them either, but they had no rules of engagement: they'd hit Army and Marine units then run over the border before they got their asses kicked. That's when battalion brought us in, Force Recon. Our job was to locate these border crossings, reconnoiter them, and when the Viets were safely within Vietnam again, call down precise air strikes and artillery bombardments on them. We did a lot of that. The Viets changed their infiltration routes a dozen times and we had to scout them out again and again.

"But reconnaissance was only one of our duties. Battalion wanted us to engage in serious H & I, Harassment and Interdiction. Which, for us, meant ambushes and sniping, mining their trails and setting out booby traps along their evasion routes. We got very good at it. We killed them in fucking numbers. I remember one particularly sweet ambush. A reinforced NVA/VC company was slipping across the border from Laos using a carefully-concealed high speed trail in the Que Son Mountains. They'd infiltrate to Da Nang, hit us, and retreat back into Laos. We watched them, studied them, followed their asses back and forth. Then we sprung the trap. How does a Recon platoon take on a company? Easy, man. By controlling the battlefield and preparing the killzone, tipping everything in our favor.

"We bottled them up in an open field surrounded by high ridgelines. There was a dirt road running through there with drainage ditches to either side. They sent out forward scouts and flanking guards and we took them out silently. When we had the main force where we wanted 'em, well, we opened up, firing for effect. We dropped twenty of them in the first exchange from our hides on the ridge. The rest did exactly what we wanted them to, what any infantry grunt would: they all jumped into the ditches for cover. Bad decision. We had the ditches mined with explosives. When they jumped in, we tied them down with machine gun and small arms fire, a few grenades to keep them bunched. Then we blew the ditches and took out over a hundred men in like ten seconds. Perfect ambush. Absolute clockwork."

"Sweet," I said. "But we're not dealing with soldiers. We're not even dealing with living men."

"Which makes it all that much easier," Jimmy said.

"Right," Tuck said. "See, these are deadheads. They only want one thing: meat. They have no sense of self-preservation or defense, no cunning, no nothing. They're stupid. They come in numbers. They only want meat. We prepare an ambush site, we tip the odds in our favor. We throw some bait at 'em to draw 'em in and then we close the lid on those motherfuckers."

I supposed it would work.

His plan was for the three of us and Diane to set up an ambush outside the fence. He had already selected the site. We would make it ready and then draw them in. Curtains.

"What's the bait?" I said. "Not Diane."

"Hell no!" Tuck said. "You think I got no sense of honor? No, not Diane. I got somebody better. Somebody big and juicy who can run fast. I got you."

Shit. I should have seen that coming.

But I supposed it made sense. I was much younger than Tuck or Jimmy. I had combat experience. I was still pretty fast and I had yet to see my fortieth birthday and wouldn't for another six years. Why not me? I was the logical candidate. So logical that I knew I could not tell Ricki about it or she'd have birds. She wouldn't like the bait idea at all. In fact, she would get downright ugly about me risking my life. She would (as she had in the past) point out that I was a husband and a father and I had responsibilities. Which was true, of course, except that now the game had changed: I had responsibilities to not only Paul and her but to our little community at large.

That night, we did not mention what the game was.

Tuck took Diane off to the side and explained things to her and she was all for it, of course. We were all kind of excited about it. For so long now we'd been running from those damn things and now we were about to turn the hunters into the hunted and we liked the idea. There were over forty zombies out at the gate that night (Ricki counted). Their numbers were swelling fast. It was time for a decisive punch. Later, I wondered if Tuck was not so much interested in thinning the herds as he was in keeping our morale up.

After three tours in 'Nam he knew a thing or two about morale. I figured he understood a lot more about the practical side of human psychology than he let on.

We set up a charcoal grill out on the walkway and had ourselves a wienie roast that night. The kids were really excited about it all. Tuck was big on hot dogs. He watched his diet very carefully, subsisting on a lot of green vegetables and very lean cuts of meat. He drove us all nuts with his morning round of push-ups, sit-ups, pull-ups, and isometrics. He had but one decadent unhealthy indulgence and that was hot dogs. He had four huge walk-in freezers and the sheer amount of hot dogs in them was frightening. We didn't have any hot dog buns and bakeries were pretty much cashed-in by that point, but being ever-resourceful Tuck made buns out of Indian flatbread that he then deep-fried. They were unbelievably good. We had a nice evening and Tuck even played a few songs for us on his fiddle.

Looking around at us sitting out there in lawn chairs I was struck by the fact that we were like some extended family now. Tuck was barely awake in his chair. Maria was curled-up on his lap with her arms around his neck, fast asleep. Diane and Paul and Davis were inside playing the only board game Tuck owned: *Monopoly*. Ricki and I were listening to Jimmy's tales of being a teenager in West Side Manhattan back in the 1950's and stealing apples from pushcart vendors. It was very nice. A very calm, easy sort of night. And that's the way I want to remember us: that night, everyone healthy and safe and relaxed in each other's company.

Things had been going too well for too long and I knew it was going to change. I could feel something gathering around us, call that bad luck or fate or a sense of impending doom. I don't know. But I could feel it and I knew there was trouble coming.

As it turned out, I was absolutely right.

AMBUSH

I remember back in infantry school at Fort Benning, our BC, Battalion Commander, telling us that in combat it was important to respect your enemy. Even if they were poorly-trained, poorly-organized, poorly-armed, and poorly-motivated. Because in every combat encounter or firefight there is the ugly element of chance that tips the odds away from you. That's when things happen. That's when you lose the advantage. That's when things go to hell and men die for no good reason. Just like they say in the NFL, "on any given Sunday…" Meaning, that even the most ragtag bunch of players can kick ass on the hottest team out there. It happens. Maybe that ragtag team in question has not won a game all year, but when you get arrogant and let your guard down you can be sure that they'll stomp you.

Respect your enemy.

Of course, we were in a pretty unique position being that our adversaries were zombies.

The thing was, what we knew about them we could have fit in a thimble. They were basically driven by hunger. They needed to bite and chew, to feed. They seemed to have no other primary motivation. They were not intelligent that I had ever seen or cunning or fast. But they were still scary. And what made them even scarier was that they came in numbers, in crowds, in mobs. I didn't believe there was any cohesion to those mobs, no organization: they were just mindless eating machines that grouped together because they all wanted to eat. Tuck said they had no true survival instinct or sense of self-preservation. I agreed. They would charge in to bite regardless of the firepower you displayed or how many of their zombie associates you put down.

But that didn't mean they would behave that way every time.

As far as I was concerned, they were unpredictable.

When you're dealing with a predator—any predator—you can never know how they'll react. That was the gray area we had to contend with the next day when we made our plans. We announced them to everyone, save Maria who was very sensitive about things and was out working in the gardens with Diane and Jimmy.

I thought Ricki would kick up a fuss. She did not.

"Their numbers have to be thinned," Tuck told them. "For our own safety."

That was practical and that made sense. Ricki understood it. Of course, we left out the part about me being bait.

About an hour later, the four of us went through the back gate in the armored Jeep and drove across the field to the ambush site that Tuck had chosen. It was basically a deep, rocky pit about three-hundred feet across and twice that in length. There was a trail leading down there. My job would be to draw the zombies in. Only problem with that being there was no other egress but that trail. Once I was down there with them I was in danger. I could probably climb out, but it would by risky with the sheer walls. Tuck said once I had drawn them down into the pit, he would throw me a rope and yank me out.

"Be on time," I told him and meant it.

"Don't worry, Booky. I have your best interests at heart."

"See that you do."

He smiled and stroked his beard. "Course…something were to happen to you, Ricki might just need a man in her life…"

We got down to it.

First things first. While Jimmy and Diane stood on guard with .30-30s, we went down into the pit and set out six Claymore mines which would waste the majority of the zombies. We daisy-chained them together and wired them to a single clacker above. My job would be to get on the other side of them before the zombies did.

Claymore Mine
Type: Anti-Personnel Device
Kill Range: 160 feet, optimum
Ordinance: C4 + Fragmentation munition=
Total annihilation of enemy

    Once the mines were set-up, Tuck went through the whole thing again and again with us. Once I was out, fire the mines. Then the four of us would pick off the stragglers one by one. The trail leading out would be a danger so Jimmy would station himself there with not only a .30-30 but a CAR-15 to put down a heavy volume of fire. We all carried CAR-15s in addition to our Sigs. Single shots to the head was what we had in mind, but if it came to it we'd cut them down any way we could.

    We got back in the Jeep and drove around towards the front of the fence. I opened the door and jumped out. Tuck handed me a Motorola walkie-talkie so we could coordinate things. Diane kissed me before I left and Jimmy shook my hand. Tuck just said, "Don't be a wimp."

    I stood there, watching the zombies in the distance as the Jeep pulled away and got out of visual. All righty then. Like I didn't have a care in the world, my CAR-15 slung over my shoulder and my Sig-Sauer hanging low on my hip, I sauntered down towards the front of the gate and one of the first things I noticed was that there were a hell of a lot more than forty of them. I was guessing sixty to seventy which I didn't care for at all. I had gotten pretty good at estimating the sizes of mobs in Iraq so I was figuring I wasn't far off.

    The zombies were just standing there like a bunch of extras waiting for the director's cue. They were facing the fence, but none of them came within ten feet of it. I walked on down there, whistling. I was within twenty feet before they saw me. That close I could smell them—God, like roadkill, hot and festering. Men, women, children. When one saw me, the others all seemed to see me, too. They turned almost simultaneously and looked over at me

They began to gnash their teeth.

They studied me with eyeballs that were blanched white with tiny black pinprick pupils that saw very well, apparently.

Then they started to move.

I got on the walkie-talkie. "I made contact," I said.

"Well don't dance with 'em," Tuck told me.

"Roger that."

One thing I knew was that I could not panic. If one of them started running at me, I fully intended to panic, but that didn't happen. They came at me slowly as was their way and I backed away one step at a time. I didn't know how good their vision was. I made sure I kept about twenty feet between us, but I never got any farther away than that because I didn't want them to lose interest.

I kept backing away.

They kept coming.

I don't know what happened then and don't ask me, but…I *stopped*. I just stopped and stood there as they came on. I was like a kid playing chicken with a knife. But something made me stop, made me look shivering death straight in the face. Made me stand there and watch it coming for me. Ruined faces watched me, dead-white eyeballs sized me up, teeth made ready to tear into me. The ones leading the pack had their hands raised to grab me. At such close range I could actually see the parasites living on and *in* them: worms, carrion beetles, burrowing insects. I could smell the hot fetid stench of their graveyard breath.

And I remember thinking: If you don't move, asshole, you're lunch.

That's what I thought and the most frightening thing was that for a moment there, one brief instant that is cold silver in my memory, I *couldn't*. I couldn't move. I was locked in place. I had seized up. I had never frozen like that in combat, not even my first firefight. But there I was, totally in control of the situation, and in no real danger if I kept moving…*and I froze.*

I watched them come on.

Fifteen feet.

Ten.

Five.

So close I could see the flesh of their reaching fingers hanging like confetti. And when those hands were but inches from my face, I let out a cry and backpedaled away. I fell down, got up, kept backing as fast I could until I put the requisite twenty feet between us. I had no idea what had happened. To this day I cannot figure it...but it was almost like I *wanted* them to get me. I'd seen guys do crazy things like that in Iraq, standing up in a firefight, strolling casually forward as AK-47s ripped up the ground all around them, pausing to light a cigarette as mortar shells exploded in every direction.

But I never thought it would happen to me.

But it had.

Some weird inexplicable trigger was pulled, some switch was thrown deep down in my psyche and it scared the shit out of me. I kept backing away, playing Pied Piper and leading my zombies away, still shaking about freezing up...and that's when I realized that not only had I locked up, but that I was not respecting my enemy. Because I heard dragging footsteps in the gravel behind me.

I turned and there were three of them closing in on me and what disturbed me most was that they were soldiers. They were dressed in desert camo BDUs, tanker helmets and goggles. What I could see of their faces was concurrent with what I had been seeing in a lot of them: their mouths were just ragged puckering holes like they'd chewed their own lips off like Dick said Elena had. They came at me, all teeth and gums, blank eyes glistening behind their goggles.

I brought up the CAR-15 and drilled some rounds into them to drive them back, pivoted, and did the same with the mob bearing down on me. Then I dropped one soldier with a round that drilled right through his goggles and I caught the second in the face with another round which drove him to one knee, his hands gripping his shattered jaw. The third was on me by then and I knew I had to fight like never before. I didn't have time to turn the CAR-15 on him. As I put down the second zombie, he was already on me. I felt his hot, rancid breath in my face and I swept the rifle stock around and hit him in the side of the head. Then I hit him again and again, pushing him back, getting those teeth away from me.

Then something grabbed my ankle.

The second deadhead was not so dead. I had caught him too low, just beneath the nose in the maxilla. The slug must have been deflected enough so that it didn't enter his brain. Gripping my leg, he dragged himself forward to bite and I put a three round burst right through his face. He relaxed his grip, shuddered, and did not move. The third one came again and I fired point-blank, blowing his chest apart, then I gave him three rounds in the eyes and he went over like a post.

By then, of course, the mob was nearly on me.

Tuck was shouting over the walkie-talkie but I didn't have time to answer.

I leaped over the bodies and ran full-out.

The mob followed, some of them dropping away to feed on the soldiers but the majority coming in my direction. They were moving no faster, I thought, but perhaps the smell of blood and meat had gotten them excited because they were all chomping their teeth. I moved along the fence until it ended and I heard the Jeep coming. Tuck must have heard the shooting and was coming to my aid.

"I'm all right," I said over the walkie-talkie.

"GODDAMMIT, BOOKY!" Tuck shouted. "I ALMOST SHIT MY PANTS OVER HERE!"

"Sorry. Three unexpected guests showed up."

I waved at the Jeep and Tuck pulled around and went back to the hide in the trees.

I led the undead through the grass out into the field where we would sort out their asses on a permanent basis. I wondered if Ricki was up on the walkway with her spotting scope watching the action. I really hoped not. Halfway across the field, I paused, letting the dead catch up to me and scanning in every direction to see if there were any more strays pushing in on me. I saw none. But that was part of the problem that we had with the field. The grasses were short in and around the pit, but not much farther on they grew high and wild, tall yellow sedge where it would have been real easy for dozens of the dead to hide.

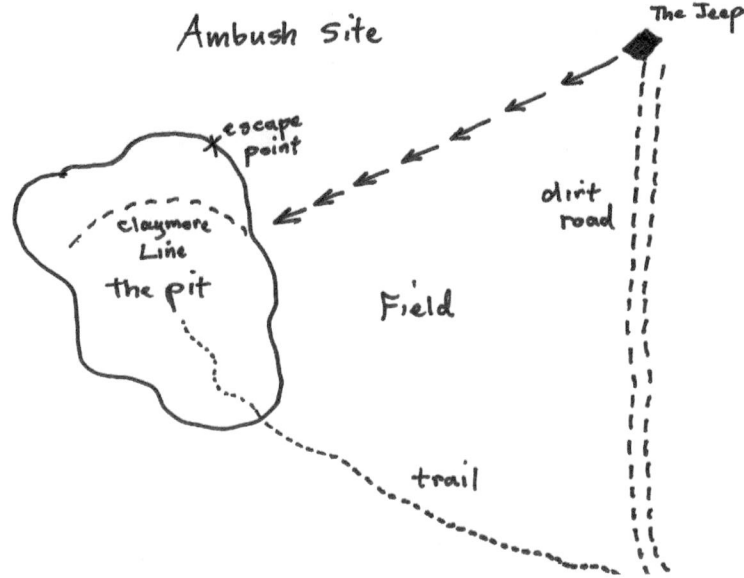

I made it to the pit and waited for the mob.

They came, spreading out now in a wall of enclosing death. I let them close ranks to about twenty feet again and I started down into the pit. The trail leading down canted at an easy thirty degree angle until it reached the bottom which was about twenty feet in depth. I got down there and waited, very much aware that I had Claymores at my back and zombies at my front. The dead began to ring in the sides of the pit and then, following one enterprising deadhead, they all started down the trail. They didn't move in single file. They were not orderly. They came in threes and fours, pushing forward, some of them falling and rolling, others pushing and fighting to get out in front. Just slavering pack animals, no cohesion, no unity. Just hunger.

I backed away towards the Claymores. I had to get them all down here, all bunched-in. As I was wondering if that was going to happen or how I would be able to do it, the problem was solved by the dead. They were so voracious to get at me that they literally flooded down the trail like some surging river of piranhas. They weren't much different really: just a swarm, a hungering school. They got down into the pit, congregating and bunching-up, stumbling forward.

I heard the Jeep racing to the pit.

"They're all down there with you," Tuck said. "Get in position."

When they were fifty feet from me, I got behind the Claymore line and went over to the sheer wall. The zombies came forward. They were all gnashing and chomping their teeth.

"How's about that rope?" I said over the walkie-talkie.

"Coming," was the response.

The zombies were massing, pressing in, filling the pit with their dark stink and darker intent. They were fifteen feet from the Claymores and closing. I looked up. I saw Diane up there. She was yelling at Tuck. Jimmy was there, too, he looked nervous. I didn't care for where this was going.

"You better get that rope down here or I'm fucking hamburger," I said over the walkie-talkie.

It dropped down behind me. Tuck had tied a loop in it and I worked it over my head and shoulders and tightened it under my armpits. He began pulling and I began climbing.

"There's no time!" Diane called down to me.

The zombies were ten feet from the Claymores.

"COVER YOUR HEAD!" Tuck shouted and I did just that.

The Claymores went off simultaneously with a thundering *THUMP-THUIMP-THUMP!* and when I looked back, the smoke clearing, I saw that the pit was a field of gore and body parts and trembling limbs. About 90% of them had been blasted to fragments but the others, undaunted, were coming for me. There were maybe a dozen left. As Tuck pulled me out, Jimmy and Diane started popping them one after the other. By the time I climbed up and over the edge, they were all dead down there.

"Just like clockwork," Tuck said. "Easy as pie."

I didn't necessarily agree with that, but things had worked out so I wasn't about to bitch about the close-calls I'd had.

"Gah," Diane said, turning away from the pit. "What a mess."

"That should clean 'em out for awhile," Jimmy said.

I was going to agree when Tuck said, "Shit."

As we had feared, the dead were coming through the grass. Not just a scattered few but thirty, forty, maybe fifty of them and they were all soldiers like the ones I put down. Somewhere very near to us, an entire unit had gotten infected. By the numbers I was seeing, I was guessing it had been a company strength unit, mechanized infantry or armor judging from the helmets. They came out of the grass, sighting us and closing in for the kill.

We opened up on them and dropped four, then five and six. We kept shooting until we tagged ten of them.

"INTO THE JEEP!" Tuck cried out.

We needed no coaxing.

We made it to the Jeep just as the main force converged. We barely got the doors shut and they were everywhere. Tuck threw the Jeep in drive and smashed five or six out of his way and rolled over several of them. He brought it around and as he did so I saw that the tall yellow grasses were thick with them like locusts. They were everywhere. And more seemed to be coming from every direction.

"We better make that gate before they do," Tuck said.

They were massing and we didn't bother with the side gate. Tuck pulled around front and we encountered a dozen more walking dead in two and threes. Diane went up through the hatch with her CAR-15 and thinned their numbers. But more were coming. We just got through the gate before they converged.

Barely.

NIGHT DEFENSIVE POSITION

After sundown, we watched the zombies massing out there with our NVDs, studying them at length in the green fields of our scopes. There were more than ever. I don't think I'm over-exaggerating when I say there were upwards of 100, possibly approaching the 150 mark. Most of them were soldiers, but there were plenty of civs out there mulling around with them. As before, they were keeping their distance from the fence but I wondered how long that would last. We were quickly approaching the sort of numbers that simple ambushes could not contend with, not unless we got our hands on some real firepower—a .50-cal machine gun or a minigun, some grenade launchers or mortars. We needed heavy squad weapons to disperse and annihilate a group like that.

And all we had were rifles, shotguns, and a few automatics.

"This is where you call in an airstrike," Jimmy said.

In my mind I could see an F-16 Falcon making a run at our friends and dropping clusterbombs and napalm. How easy that would have made things. I was beginning to wonder if there were any pilots left out there to fly them. Things were getting worse on the national and international scene. The internet was down now and radio traffic was sporadic. Everything was crashing and that didn't give me much hope that we were winning the war as such. According to what little we could glean from radio broadcasts, the Necrophage pandemic had been called a species-threatening event by several microbiologists, which meant that the old human race was teetering very close to the edge. Asia, Africa, the Middle East, Europe...there was no word coming out of any of those places. News from the UK was sketchy. Canada had sealed its border with the US and they were reporting something like 50% of the population were dead or dying from the infection. There was absolutely nothing coming out of Central or South America.

But we knew things were going on.

We were still seeing helicopters flying far overhead, many of them I could tell by their profile were Army AH-64 Apaches equipped with miniguns and rockets for direct fire support. I was guessing they were flying sorties into the Big Apple. We sure could have used their help. A couple runs by one of them and our problems would have been over with.

We watched the dead and they waited patiently.

Maybe they realized their numerical superiority was their edge and maybe they knew that in the end they would have us. I doubt it, though. But I suppose it's a very human sort of thing to grant things intelligence that have no real intelligence whatsoever.

Just after eleven that night, our power went out.

Everything went black and I saw the world as our Medieval ancestors must have—a threatening, forbidding place of clutching shadows and menacing night shapes. It was so unbelievably fucking black I really couldn't see my hand in front of my face. The only light came from the stars above and it was a hazy night so they weren't exactly bright. I could see the glowing ends of the cigarettes that Tuck and Diane were smoking, but nothing else.

I think we all sort of panicked.

I could almost feel the tension moving from body to body out on the walkway. But it was Ricki who gave it a voice: "THE LIGHTS! THE LIGHTS WENT OUT!"

"It's cool, lady," Tuck said. "The genny'll kick on in...five...four...three...two...one..."

We heard an engine kick on somewhere and I knew it was down in the cellar beneath the crib and the lights came on, nearly blinding us. They came on, dimmed, flickered, then held. Beyond the fence the zombies were still waiting. They had not moved.

"I'm surprised we had power this long," Diane said.

"Me too," Tuck said. "You ain't afraid of the dark are you, Ricki?"

"Of course not," she said.

But it was a lie. Ricki was high strung. That should come as no surprise, but she definitely was not fond of the dark and the battery of nightlights at our house could testify to that. Soon as the lights went out, she grabbed a hold of me and even when they came back on she was not letting go.

"Even with the juice out," Tuck told her, "they can't get in. No worries, okay?" He grinned. "Trust me, the only thing you got to worry about in the dark is me."

Ricki let out a nervous laugh. "Oh shut up."

And how I wished that were true.

Tuck broke into his bourbon stock and we all had a few sips, even Ricki who wasn't much of a drinker. It tasted good and it helped us all relax and unwind. We chatted about what we might do to thin the herds again and Tuck suggested the best thing would be to burn them out. How we might do that, he did not say.

After a period of silence, he said, "All right, Booky. Time to spill your guts. We all know you've had something on your mind since day one, so give."

Had it been that apparent? Ricki squeezed my hand as if to let me know it was okay to unburden myself. I looked around and they were all watching me and I felt like the victim of a conspiracy. Like I was the only one left out of some joke.

"All right," I said. "I'll tell you what I know."

So I told them about the sandbox.

THE SANDBOX

We were stationed at an FOB (Forward Operating Base) called Howard just outside of Samarra for much of the time I was in Iraq. Being the platoon sergeant, I was the first one Lieutenant Steakely would shake out of slumber when something was coming down. And one summer night, he did just that. O-dark-thirty and he's shaking me awake.

"We're rolling in an hour," he said. "We're taking out three Strykers to provide security for a raiding party up north. Get your squads ready."

The raiding party, as it turned out, was not a couple infantry platoons like usual but a shadowy group known as Task Force 121 who would be rolling in Hummers. Like the Marine Recon group known as the Nightcrawlers that I mentioned earlier, Task Force 121 was another of those spooky hunter/killer teams that generated lots of wild tales. The 121 boys were a group of hitters from Delta Force and the Navy SEALs, plus an assortment of spooks from the CIA's Special Activities Division (SAD). We were to provide an armed escort for them and direct fire support at a village about ten clicks to the north that was not given a name, only a map coordinate. When word got around that we were going out with an elite commando unit, the boys all got excited. This was big. This was the real thing. This was the kind of shit you told stories about when you were seventy years old hanging out with the other old timers. *Yep, I'll never forget that raid me and Delta and the SEALs were on. I saved their asses that day.* All my grunts were wired. They were carrying themselves with an erect bearing I hadn't seen in months. I knew that in every one of their heads they were playing out secret missions from every war movie they'd ever seen.

So was I.

We had strict orders that no matter what came down we were not allowed to leave the Strykers for any reason. We were to stay mounted to provide fire support for 121. They would direct fire.

We only had to shoot. That deflated a lot of my boys who thought they'd be kicking in doors with Delta and the SEALs.

"This sucks, man," Corporal Denning said. "I always wanted to be in Delta Force."

"Well, you can show us your shit today," I told him. "If you do good, they'll probably hire you on the spot."

"No shit?"

Denny, as we called him, was easy-going, funny, and loveable, but unbearably naïve. They were all so young. I think that's what bothered me the most. They were just kids. Hell, I wasn't yet thirty, but I'd already put in six years in the regular Army and four years in the Guards by that point. I'm not saying I was some well-seasoned sage, but compared to the eighteen- and nineteen-year olds I served with I was practically Father Time.

Anyway, we turned out in full battle kit and our OP orders were cut, so we rolled out of the motor pool and into the box, which is what we called the field. Two Hummers pulled out in front of us and led the way to the mystery village. It was easy rolling all the way. Sgt. Warez was on the M240 machine gun in the rear air-guard hatch of my vehicle. Denny was poking out of the hatch next to him with an M4 carbine in the AG position, Assistant Gunner. My driver was Ron Baker, a Spec 4 from Alabama. As vehicle commander, I was the gunner on the .50-cal. machine gun which I operated remotely so I didn't get my head blasted off if we got into the shit. My crew was tight and battle-tested. I didn't know what we were coming into, but if we took contact I knew we'd give better than we got.

In the back, we had three Army counterintel agents and a spooky NCO who was a real hardass. The counterintel guys didn't surprise me, not with Task Force 121 being involved, but the NCO had me concerned. He was a 74 Delta, a chemical and biological warfare specialist, an NBC guy. I didn't like that. What I liked even less was that he and the counterintel guys were wearing black Tyvek biohazard suits that were self-contained with Racal hoods, oxygen and blowers.

What the hell exactly were we going into?

I got on the comm with Lt. Steakely and told him my concerns. "Are we at risk of contamination, sir?"

"None. The teams are wearing biogear just as a precaution," he told me. "As long as we stay mounted and do what we're told we're in absolutely no danger."

I liked Steakely. For an officer he was okay. I wanted to trust him. I *had* to trust him, but I just wasn't comfortable with the set-up and neither were the rest of the boys. But, as they say, orders is orders, so on we went. We were moving north along the Tigris, up towards the apex of the Sunni Triangle. We passed through a few scrub villages with donkeys walking around, broken down rusted cars parked in front of dirty hovels, livestock in the streets. Same old, same old. After about two hours we approached the target, our AOA, Area of Operations.

"This is the shit even for Iraq," Denny said.

"Roger that," Baker said.

"Charlie Mike," Steakely said to them, meaning Continue Mission.

What we saw ahead of us was a narrow lane blown apart by immense bomb craters. The buildings to either side were riddled with bullet holes and shell impacts. Many of them were nothing but rubble. Shells casings winked in the headlights of the Strykers. There was debris everywhere, cars and trucks burnt and blasted, some of them flipped over or split right in half. There had been some serious action here at some point. We scanned our lights around and motes of dust drifted in them like deep-sea silt. There was a mosque at the turn of the avenue, but it looked mostly gutted like it had taken a direct hit from a rocket.

Nothing moved.

Nothing stirred.

There was no life here. This was a ghost town long-abandoned and I had to wonder why we had come all this way to look at an empty village. It was hot and we were sweating in our BDUs. There wasn't so much as a breeze. The lieutenant said that 121 wanted our Strykers in interlocking blocking positions so that nothing or nobody could make a run from the avenue.

"Who's gonna run from here?" Denny said. "Ghosts?"

I could hear Warez and him chatting over the intercom and I knew they were nervous. Baker and I were enclosed in the cab. We studied that dead city by video screen and periscope; we weren't hanging out the back end staring it in the face. I was receiving similar chatter from the other Strykers. The boys were spooked.

Using the thermal camera, I looked for heat signatures and got nothing.

I was going to mention that fact to the lieutenant, but that's when I got the word to drop the gate so the counterintel guys and that NBC sergeant could get out of the back. I saw them come around the front of the Strykers. They had their hoods on now and I could hear the hiss of their breathing apparatuses. The 121 guys joined them and they were similarly outfitted. They carried weapons of a sort I'd never seen before. And they all had stout tanks strapped to their backs with hoses that led to gun assemblies in their hands.

"Hell's that shit?" Baker said. "Flamethrower?"

"Don't look like it."

"You wanna let us in on this," I said to Lt. Steakely over the comm.

"You know what I do," he said.

So I waited and kept an eye out. It was getting hot in the Stryker and Baker kept pulling off his Kevlar CVC helmet to mop sweat from his head.

We watched the raiding party pick their way carefully down the street, the 121 guys moving out front with the sort of precision you only saw in the elite squads. They fanned out in a way that made me think they weren't worried about incoming because a good burst of machine gun fire could have dropped half of them in a single sweep. No, they weren't worried about shooters. But they were being very vigilant about *something*.

But what?

The counterintel people and the NCO hung back, waiting. They did not move an inch until the 121 troopers motioned them forward. Then they broke up into teams, four troopers and one counterintel guy per team. The NBC sergeant followed the lead group up the avenue and into the mosque.

Again, we waited.

"This is spooky," Denny said over the comm.

That was a good word for it. Waiting there was like waiting in a graveyard at the stroke of midnight to see what might come crawling out of the graves around you. Ten minutes passed, then fifteen. I was all for getting this over and out and done with. The avenue was crawling with shadows, they seemed to be everywhere. Sometimes, on the periscope I'd catch a glimpse of a manlike shape pulling back into the darkness. But it was my imagination. It had to be my imagination.

"I wish they'd get it done with," Warez said.

"Embrace the suck," Denny told him which means, basically, that the situation is bad and isn't going to get better so man up and deal with it.

As we approached the twenty minute mark, gunfire rang out.

I couldn't tell from where. Suddenly rounds were popping everywhere and I could see muzzle flashes from empty windows and doorways. The counterintel people came running out and the 121 boys were right behind them, shooting into open doors. They were capping rounds in every direction. I saw two of the troopers toss grenades behind them as they ran. The chatter over the comm got wild and frenetic.

"Get ready," the lieutenant told us.

For what?

I was scanning with the thermal camera but I was only picking up the heat signatures of the Task Force 121 people and their counterintel flunkies. The lead squad came bolting hell-for-leather from the mosque and that's when I saw eight or ten individuals come walking out after them. They put out no thermal signatures. It made no sense. They were dressed in black with red-checkered scarves over their faces which was about as close to a real uniform as the Jihadis had. They were hardcore extremists and I knew it…but something wasn't right.

In fact, something was extremely wrong.

The way they moved.

The way they acted.

They weren't running around shouting like your ordinary Johnny Jihads, emptying clips from their AKs at you. No, these Ali Babas had no guns. They were coming after the 121 elements with their bare fucking hands!

I saw three or four of them move in on a trooper.

He busted some caps into them to drive them back then he pulled up the gun that was hooked to the tank on his back. I expected to see a gout of fire come out of the end but it was like some kind of foam, white gushing foam.

I zeroed in on it with my periscope.

"What the fuck?" I heard Denny say.

The foam struck one of the unknown individuals—I wasn't ready at that point to call them ECs, Enemy Combatants—and what I saw then made my mouth hang open. The individual whirled around, clawing at himself...then he dropped to the ground, smoking and sizzling. I saw something rising from that foamy goo and steam: a polished white skeleton. There was something like acid in those tanks.

I watched three or four other 121 troopers lay down a defensive cordon of the stuff.

I watched the attacking individuals liquefy when they got trapped in it.

By then the counterintel people had run past our position and we lowered the gates and they climbed into the Strykers. The 121 troopers fought a rear guard action, pushing their attackers back and then running to beat hell. As one of them passed my Stryker, he shouted: "LIGHT 'EM UP! LIGHT 'EM UP! LIGHT THOSE MOTHERFUCKERS UP!"

I zeroed in on a group that came shambling forward, I put the crosshairs on them. They moved with a weird, jerky sort of gait like the way a puppet might walk. I opened up and cut them in half with the .50-cal. They went down...but they did not stop moving. Parts of them were trying to crawl away. I kept shooting, zeroing in packs of them and putting them down. But they just kept coming, pouring out of those buildings, swarming like ants, creeping ever forward to our position.

By then, of course, the .50s on the other Strykers were in action and there were tracer rounds flying like hail down the mouth of the avenue. The Assistant gunners were banging away with their M4s and the gunners were hosing down anything that moved with their M240s.

Right then, Lt. Steakely's vehicle let loose with a TOW missile that zipped right down the avenue and punched into the mosque. There was a resounding explosion, a flash of light that nearly blinded me in the darkness, and rubble was flying through the air.

"THEY'RE STILL COMING!" I heard Denny shouting. "THERE'S FUCKING HAJJIS EVERYWHERE! THEY'RE CLUSTERING! THEY AIN'T FUCKING DYING...DO YOU HEAR ME? THOSE HAJJIS AIN'T FUCKING DYING!"

And by then we all saw it.

We were ripping them apart with 7.62 from the 240s, .50-cal., and grenades, but it wasn't stopping them. We were cutting them down, slicing them like a little girl going after her paper dolls with a scissors, but it wasn't enough. Parts of them still moved. Torsos crept forward. Armless things slithered through the rubble. Men perforated with bullet holes pressed in at us. I kept rocking the fifty, putting them down again and again.

"THE HEADS YOU DUMB FUCKS!" one of the 121 guys screeched over the comm. "AIM FOR THE HEADS! BLOW THEIR FUCKING HEADS OFF!"

Sure, why not? We started doing just that and then they were going down and staying down. Another TOW missile took out the façade of a building and buried ten or fifteen of them alive (?) in a mountain of debris. We lit them up and greased them in numbers.

"COME ON, HAJJI!" Denny was shouting. "GET SOME! GET SOME! COME AND GET SOME, YOU FUCKING RAGHEADS!"

They kept coming and the lieutenant cut the order to pull back.

The Hummers were already pulling away and the Strykers followed. Mine was the last still in blocking position and we were still capping away. I was seeing our Johnny Jihads real close and personal by then. I saw the way they looked. I saw the bones sticking out of them. I saw their biting mouths and oozing, putrescent faces. I knew. I knew what they were. We *all* knew what they fucking were, but we weren't saying it.

As we pulled away I saw a figure come walking out of the stirred-up dust and debris and smoke: the NCO. I'd forgotten about him and so had everyone else. He came strolling out and I saw that he was wounded, his Tyvek suit ripped open from throat to crotch. His viscera was bulging out like pink snakes.

"Lieutenant!" I called over the comm. "That NCO...he's still back there! Request permission to evac his ass out of there!"

"Denied!"

"What?"

"DENIED!" and this time it wasn't Steakely but one of the 121 hitters. "YOU HEAR ME, TROOP? DENIED!"

"But he's wounded!"

"HE AIN'T FUCKING WOUNDED! HE'S DEAD! HE'S THE WALKING DEAD!" he ripped on me. "PUT HIM DOWN!

GREASE THAT MOTHERFUCKER! LIGHT HIM UP! LIGHT HIS ASS UP!"

As Baker pulled us away over the rubble, I was bounced all over the damn place and I had a hell of a time getting my crosshairs on him. No matter. Warez took his head off with sustained fire from the M240. *"WOOO-HOOOO!"* he kept screaming. *WOOOO-HOOOO!!!"*

He kept hosing the NCO down and keeping him on his feet, dancing like a puppet, until the barrel of his 240 melted from the heat and even then he was trying to shoot, just out of his fucking head. I came out of the hatch and it took both me and Denny to pry his fingers off the gun. Our Stryker joined up with the others which were redlining out of there as fast as they could travel. Denny and I almost got thrown free as we held onto Warez, trying to snap him out of it.

"YA-HAHAHAHA!" he shrieked. *"WOOO-HOOO! LIGHT 'EM UP, BROS! LIGHT THEM RAGHEAD ALI BABA HAJJI BABY-KILLING MOTHERFUCKERS UP! LIGHT...'EM...UUUUUPPPP!!!"*

Within about thirty seconds we found out why it was important to evac our asses out of there: a trio of F-15 Strike Eagles came screaming across the sky and dumped napalm on the village. They made run after run at it until the village was invisible, just engulfed in a cauldron of fire that lit up the horizon and reflected red on the low-hanging clouds.

What happened then?

We were debriefed, made to sign the Official Secrets Act, and told to keep our mouths shut because what we had seen was classified and one word of it could mean twenty years solitary confinement at a federal prison. So I never spoke of it. A few months later I received an email. I don't know who sent it and I wisely deleted it ASAP. It said, basically, that we had encountered a village that had been infected by something called *Necrovirus*. I can quote it from memory: *FYI: What you saw in Et Ukhbar that night was the result of something known as the Necrovirus. It is an infective organism that reanimates the dead and turns them cannibalistic. Its origin is unimportant. Thought you'd like to know. Don't bother replying to this for this address no longer exists. Delete this and forget it. Knowledge of the above will put you behind bars for a long time. Pleasant dreams.* That was it. Who sent it? I don't know. The 121 boys? I couldn't imagine SEALs or Delta Force or CIA/SAD operators spilling state secrets. One of the counterintel people? I don't know and I don't want to know.

I had trouble sleeping for many days following that night.

After a time I honestly believed it had never happened. I never spoke of it. And only on two occasions did we who were there mention it. I never saw anything like that again.

Not until it broke loose in Yonkers under a different name.

THE NIGHTWALKERS

We were running on straight genny after the power outage. The juice never came back on again. I told my story and got myself involved in a debate of sorts with the others as to what was going on, whether Necrophage was of natural origin or a biological weapon of foreign or (gulp) domestic design. I had no answers. And I didn't see where it really mattered. It was here. It was now. I got a preview of its hell in Iraq. But that was a privilege I could have lived without.

I haven't said much about Dick lately because there really wasn't much to tell. After his little episode out by the fence that night we really didn't have much trouble with him. Which was a good thing because Tuck was really out of patience with him and I was afraid what he might do if Dick caused any further trouble. But, like I said, he was quiet. He was totally withdrawn and he gave just about everyone the creeps standing around staring or mumbling to himself. He particularly freaked out Maria and Davis though Paul had pretty much forgotten he even existed. He was a stick of furniture. He was a marble bust in the corner. Something inanimate.

Ricki looked after him and Jimmy did some, too. I chipped in a bit when I could. Tuck just ignored him. Diane would talk to him but I don't think she really expected an answer.

Dick was just…Dick.

About two nights after my storytelling, Diane had a sleepover with the kids on the floor of the panic room. It was just something fun to do for them. Something different. Tuck wasn't sure about it at first but when Maria put the charm on him he melted like usual. Ricki and I took advantage of having the room to ourselves and made love for the first time in many weeks. It was nice, real nice. I think we connected in ways we hadn't for the past couple years. I'll never forget that night. We fell asleep in one another's arms.

Then, sometime in the dead of night, she woke me.

"What?" I said.

"It's quiet…it's so quiet."

At first I thought, c'mon, what a ridiculous reason to wake me…but then I knew what she meant. "The generator," I said.

We were both out of bed then, pulling our clothes on. Tuck had a few nightlights set out so you could navigate the stairs but they were out, of course. I rushed up the steps to the next level but the power was out so the keypad wasn't working. Tuck had a key that unlocked the doors manually.

I banged on the door and shouted his name until I heard him swearing.

"Power's out!" I called to him.

By then, Jimmy was awake and out there with us. "Hell's going on?" he asked.

"Generator's out."

Tuck unlocked the door and told Jimmy to go unlock the one leading up to the panic room. He gave him a spare key. Ricki was terrified and I could feel the dread running through her. I told her it would be okay and then I followed Tuck down to the crib. Using a flashlight, he opened the trapdoor to the cellar.

"The back-up should've kicked in," he said. "I don't get it."

But when we put the lights on the generators we both saw exactly how it had happened: the emergency stop buttons had been pressed on both the primary and the secondary. But who would have hit the E-stops?

"What the fuck is this shit?" Tuck said. "Who the hell would do this?"

I held the light while he went through the start-up procedure which he informed me would take about five minutes since the gennies had both been shut off two hours before.

That's when Jimmy peered down the hatch at us. "Dick is gone," he said.

Tuck started swearing. I thought he would start shouting but he didn't. He just looked over at me calmly and said. "You know he's gone too far now. When I catch him, he's going over the fence."

Off course, right away I wanted to tell him you couldn't do that, but when I tried to think of a good reason why not I couldn't come up with a thing. I mean, I like to think I'm as compassionate and tolerant as they come. I can handle a lot of shit before I crack or strike out. But in the final analysis, Tuck had saved all our asses. He mothered us all. He was our big brother who kept the bullies from us. He took us in when we had nowhere else to go. This was his place, his investment. Realistically, logically…could any of us stop him from throwing Dick to the wolves? Yes. No. Maybe. But did we have the right to?

"Steve, you and Jimmy track that fuck down and don't hurt him," he told me as he went through the generator system start-up. "You can leave that to me."

Sighing, I went up to join Jimmy.

When I got there, Jimmy had made a rather unpleasant discovery: the security door was open. Dick must have gone through it but left it ajar. Well, at least we knew where he was. We both had sidearms and flashlights so we repeated the procedure of the other night when Dick went roaming. Jimmy circled around the tower to see if he could find him and, flashlight in hand, I jogged down the road. Up on the walkway, I could see flashlight beams moving around. I didn't like this. With our security screen down, just about anything could happen.

I didn't bother searching around out in the field for him. I guess in the back of my head I was figuring, well, if he walks out into the minefield there's gonna be a big boom and we won't have to be doing this shit anymore. That sounds cold and I know it. But I had reached the point where I was sick of Dick endangering the rest of us.

I came around a clump of bushes and there was someone standing in the road.

I thought it was Paul.

But it wasn't Paul. Just a boy who had been around his age when he died. He stood there, stiff like a statue in a blue burial suit. His complexion was mottled gray. Yellow-green mildew had grown up from beneath his collar-line and spread over his cheeks like fuzz. His eyes were milky-white, his lips gone, nothing but chattering teeth behind that ragged mouth-hole.

He came at me.

I backpedaled and fell on my ass. He reached down and grabbed my wrist, my flashlight hand. I saw those teeth coming down to bite and I tore my hand from his grip. The skin of his palm came with it. I rolled away into the grass, hearing his thudding footsteps closing in. When I came up on my knees, still holding the flashlight, he was less than five feet from me. I pulled the Sig-Sauer and I did not aim. I busted three caps in him out of sheer adrenaline.

He stumbled back.

The next round I put in his head.

He took a step or two and fell into the grass, unmoving. In the back of my mind a few things occurred to me. Even if the voltage was off, that meant the boy zombie would have had to scale the fence to get in. I couldn't conceive of one of them having the reasoning or initiative to do something like that. To them, a barrier is a barrier. You can't get through it, you beat on it. So if he didn't climb the fence, that meant that—

Jesus.

I was running again. Two zombies came up the road at me and I dropped both of them with head-shots. It was pure luck. That's all it was. My hand was shaking like a leaf. In the distance I heard the roar of an engine and I knew it was the armored Jeep. I saw headlights come bouncing down the road. I kept pushing forward. Another zombie and another, both men, flanked by the third of a naked, obese woman with two bullet holes in her chest. I dropped one of the men, missed the second, corrected my aim and fired again. I caught him just above his right eye. The impact spun him around and dumped him into the woman. I thought she would follow the usual behavioral pattern and feed on him.

She didn't.

She threw him aside and came at me. She was an immense, bloated, livid thing with straw-dry red hair hanging down over her face. Her mouth looked huge. Her teeth looked sharp. I thought she would probably take out my throat in a single bite and suck my guts out.

I put three rounds into her face and one of them must have drilled into her brain because she fell at my feet.

Behind me.

Hands grabbed my throat. I whirled around and cracked another zombie in the face with my flashlight. I shot him in the belly. Then in the head. I spun around and the road was clear ahead of me. I caught sight of movement in the fields but I didn't have time for that. I came around the bend in the road, wondering how many rounds I had left.

The gates were wide open.

Dick was standing there. There were thirty or forty zombies facing him, seeming to listen to him as he babbled on in low tones. Why they didn't just take him down, I did not know. Whatever power he had over them, I was grateful for it. Very grateful. Because if they charged through him then I was a dead man and, believe me, I knew it. Though he had the majority bottled up out there and transfixed, there were still seven or eight wandering just inside the gate looking for a snack and I was it. They saw me and came walking in my direction.

Then the lights came back on.

An absolute explosion of brilliance. I took a few faltering steps back and the deadheads did the same. Even Dick stopped talking. I needed to get those gates closed. But with the numbers of the living dead out there, that seemed like an impossibility.

The zombies were coming again.

They were all snapping their teeth in anticipation of the feast.

That's when I realized that there were maybe a dozen more in the field to either side of the road and they were now converging. I fired repeatedly into the pack that was closing in on me until the Sig was empty. I dropped four or five of them but my final shot went low into the neck of a soldier and he kept on coming and then the Jeep was seconds away. Whoever was behind the wheel—Tuck, I figured—was a madman. The Jeep didn't even slow for me. I dove out of the way and it slammed right into the zombies coming at me and cast them aside. It plowed through and over them and Dick was so out of it he didn't even turn. The bumper hit Dick and threw him through the open gates and bashed into about fifteen of the dead, sending them flying into the others.

Then it backed-up and smashed three or four others down.

That's when I knew what the driver was doing.

This was the chance I'd been waiting for.

As the zombies outside the gates began to pull themselves up, I ran forward pushing the gate closed, glad the juice was turned off. But before I could get the chain and lock in place, they were pressing from the other side. Your average living, breathing human, I knew, was stronger than your average zombie, but there dozens and dozens of them out there and they were assaulting the gate, pushing it open and I couldn't stop them. I gave it everything but my feet had no purchase on that dirt road and as the gate swung in I swung with it, my boots leaving furrows on the road.

The Jeep revved again and the horn sounded.

I dove out of the way.

The Jeep hit the gate and swung it closed, throwing the zombies back with irresistible force. They stumbled and fell into each other and over each other as the Jeep held the gate closed. I took the chance and dove up on the hood as the zombies tried their might against that of the Jeep. But they weren't budging it. I got the latch in place and pulled the chain through the loops.

But where was the lock itself?

Zombies were coming from inside now—the ones the Jeep had knocked aside and others pushing in from the field. I had no bullets left. That's when the roof hatch of the Jeep opened and Diane emerged. She had a CAR-15 in her hands and as I watched, she dropped six or seven of them that were clustering together, spraying them in the heads on full auto. She dropped two more, turned, and three more zombies coming at me took head-shots and fell, gore spraying against the side of the Jeep. I had my cover. I jumped off the hood and looked around in the grass and found the lock where Dick must have dropped it.

It was a big heavy-duty Masterlock and I snapped into place.

Diane was putting down zombies left and right.

"GET IN!" she told me.

I heard her fire three or four more times. By then I was inside and so was she. She slid the hatch shut. I tried to slam my door, but three or four sets of hands took hold of it, pulling it from my grip. One of them pushed through the others to get at me. Without even a thought, I threw myself down, my head pretty much on Diane's lap, and brought both my feet up and kicked the zombie square in the chest. He flew back into the others and I got the door shut.

Then Diane threw the Jeep in reverse, knocking a few more to the earth. As she pulled away I saw all of them at the gate, pushing and beating on it. I saw something else, too. I saw Dick getting pulled apart in a red spray, a dozen mouths biting into him. They were pulling his limbs off like the wings of a fly, yanking things out of him and fighting over them. I looked no more as Diane brought the Jeep down the road to the tower, whipping around corners, flying over bumps, throwing me all over the damn place. She skidded to a halt at the tower.

"I owe you," I said.

"Hell, it's the most fun I've had in years, man," she said.

We climbed out and saw no zombies in the general area of the tower. Which was a good thing. What was bad is that we heard gunshots from inside. The outer security door was still wide open and I wondered why until we came through it and there were zombies standing there. Most of them were dead soldiers. A woman came at us and Diane dropped her with the CAR-15, firing on semi-auto now to save ammo. Three of the zombies were down on their hands and knees, prying the trapdoor open.

When they swung it up, one of them took a round in the head that threw it back and down.

Diane killed two more of them. "Tuck's still down there," she said. "We'll take care of this! Get upstairs!"

She tossed me her Sig-Sauer and off I went.

I heard two more gunshots and these came from higher up. When I made the second level, there were two dead women waiting for me. They dragged themselves at me, baring their teeth and I shot them both in the head. I keyed myself up to the third level and killed another. I keyed myself up to the fourth level and this is what I saw:

There were four dead zombies on the floor of the panic room, a fifth sprawled through the hatchway leading out to the walkway. Ricki was backed in a corner with a look of absolute shock on her face. She had Paul and Maria trapped behind her, the latter crying her eyes out. Jimmy was down on one knee. He had a crowbar in one hand, the claw end clotted with hair and gore. He had his Sig-Sauer in the other hand. His face was drawn and pale. He was having a hard time catching his breath. Davis was on the floor behind him, his arm was stained red.

"Jimmy killed them all," Ricki finally said.

Jimmy just looked up at me, sighing. He had fought a valiant guard action against the dead. He had shot them, beat their brains out with the crowbar. "I did everything I could," he said.

The tone of his voice implied that it hadn't been enough.

I went over to Davis. His face was stained with tears. "That lady came after me," he said. "She bit me."

CAR-15 Assault Rifle
Type: 5.56mm Full-Auto
Kill Range: 160 yards
Magazine: 30 rounds

THE INFECTED

In retrospect, I still had no idea what control Dick had over them. It made no sense regardless of which way I approached it. He was dead now and I supposed it didn't really matter. Still, it nagged at me. Dick had been out of it. Way out. Yet, he had not been as out of it as we had thought. He had enough going on to remember the key codes for the doors leading to the different levels. And he had enough going on to shut down the generators and get the key for the front gates. Maybe he had never been as incapacitated as we thought. Maybe he'd just been delusional. Maybe it really was all about Elena. Maybe he thought she was out there with the others.

The maybes could go on forever.

Tuck was a good medic and Diane was no slouch either. I'd had field training in first aid. Between the three of us we got Davis' arm cleaned up and we disinfected it and bandaged it. The bite bled a lot, but it wasn't too bad. Just a little painful for the kid. Tuck gave him a shot of antibiotics. We all knew that it would do no good against a virus, but it would kill any infection.

After that, we worked to clean the zombies out of the tower. The ones down in the crib would wait until full light, but the others from levels two, three, and four we threw off the walkway. Then we got hot water, scalding almost, and strong disinfectants (industrial strength) and cleaned up the gore sprayed about. We used plastic surgical gloves during all that just as we used them when we patched-up Davis. It took us about two hours to clean things back up to our own satisfaction. We talked very little during the process and that was because we were all worried sick.

We did not mention Davis.

Or what might be coming next.

I kept telling myself that he stood a good chance of survival. That the odds dictated that not everyone bitten would get infected. But I was just trying to convince myself of the fact. By dawn I started to feel fairly confident because Davis was his same old self. It was like a weight had been lifted off us all.

We relaxed an inch at a time.

And when Davis announced that he was hungry, I started to feel optimistic about things. We had eggs and bacon and toast. Tuck made his own bread and it was damned good. The eggs were powdered, but already he was making plans to raid the neighboring farms and bring back a truckload of chickens to make us that much more self-sustaining.

Just after nine, I sat down with Ricki out on the walkway now that Tuck had decided to take a nap after spending an hour or more out there with his .30-06 and scope, dropping upwards of two dozen of the dead. There were still more. But the bodies we'd thrown over the rail had drawn them in like bait piles and made the killing that much easier. There were still many crowded around the tower trying to find a way in, but that would wait for later since they were impossible to hit down there without hanging dangerously out over the railing.

Ricki said nothing for a time so I did. "What do you think?" I asked her. I suppose I was hoping her woman's intuition would tell me there was nothing to worry about.

"I think it could go either way," she said.

"Well, you're cheerful."

"What do you want me to say, Steve? You want me to lie to you?" She glared at me and then turned away. "I just don't know any more than you do. All we can do is hope, hope that the disinfecting took care of it. He seems fine. I like that. I guess if he's still okay in twenty-four hours we'll have reason to be optimistic. If there's nothing in forty-eight, then I would think it just didn't take and we'll all have reason to be thankful. Even you, Steve."

That last one was a barb, of course, at my lack of faith. Ricki believed in God and I never tried to talk her out of it. With me, faith came hard. I'd seen too much ugly shit in my life. There was so much suffering and evil in the world that the idea that it was all part of God's plan was ludicrous. What soured me further were the power plays, greed, and sex abuses of organized religion. It made me sick. When I combined all that with the millions that had died in the name of a higher power, there was no faith to be had. The well ran dry.

I thought, though, if Davis pulled through I might think differently.

I just wouldn't believe it until it happened. I guess I was a hard-headed realist and I had no patience with the invisible world, with things that you could not see, smell, hear, taste, or touch. Maybe I was a pessimistic idiot. And maybe I was the only rational one.

I kept an eye on Davis.

He sure seemed fine. I kept trying to find faith, I kept reaching my mind out to another that was bigger and omnipotent. I prayed. I hoped. I despaired. I was bitter. I was resigned. Circling around in the back of my mind was fear. Cold, irrepressible fear. I fought it off at every turn. I would not submit to it…yet, I could not exorcise it completely. It haunted me as I suspected it haunted all of us that day. I was worried sick about Davis. Have you ever had to deal with a sick kid? And I'm not talking about an outbreak of flu or a head cold or a broken leg. I'm talking life-threatening here. It happened to us the year before my Guard unit got activated and shipped to Iraq. Paul got very sick and ended up in the hospital for a month. It was a very long month. He was out of it, sweating and shaking, but mostly sleeping. They diagnosed him with a severe bacterial stomach infection that spread throughout his entire system. It got into his brain and he had convulsions and seizures. They doped him up so much that he barely woke day after day. They fed him intravenously. By the end of the second week, he improved. Then he got worse. Then he improved. Then he got worse again. It was like a bouncing ball and the ups and downs nearly destroyed us.

Finally, he improved dramatically.

A week later it was like he'd never been sick.

Three months later it was like one of those awful nightmares that faded through the day until you can't recall it. But I remember what it was like. I remember how angry and hopeless I felt. I thought he would die. I thought the call would come when I wasn't at his bedside and then it would be time for a funeral. My boy would never come home. I'd never hear him laugh or see him smile and I knew, oh yes, I knew that I would never be the same again, that something in me would die with him.

I guess what I'm trying to say here is that it's bad when an adult has a life-threatening illness. But when a child has one it's devastating. To see your kid in that hospital bed and you can't do a damn thing about it. You blame yourself. You blame the doctors and nurses. You get paranoid. A sick adult is minor in comparison and if you've never experienced it, consider yourself lucky. Because you may *think* you've suffered, you may *think* you've had it tough, but you're a virgin in a lofty castle in the sky. You have no idea what true violation of your soul is, what it's like to be dragged through the dirtiest, darkest gutter imaginable.

That's what I feared the most.

Feeling that way again.

True, Davis was not my kid. But I loved him. I think we all did. Maria and he were great kids. The best. To lose one of them was going to scar us badly. And to watch him slip off (as I'd watched Paul...or nearly) would be like a catalyst to all the horror and frustration we all were feeling.

But I wasn't going to let the anxiety and sickbed doldrums control me.

By noon he was still fine.

Then within the hour he spiked a fever.

I'm not going to go into a detailed analysis of what came next, I'll just touch upon the basics. It started when Davis claimed his stomach felt funny. He vomited. Then he spiked a fever, like I said. And it was like turning on a hot tap: sour-smelling perspiration beaded his face and within minutes he was soaking wet. We got him into bed. Ricki, Diane, and I watched over him. Jimmy took Maria and Paul up into the panic room. Tuck was there. The four of them played around. Tuck, I knew, wouldn't get within ten feet of Davis by that point. We did what we could for him. He was hot to the touch like his blood was boiling. His system was under attack by an invasive organism and it was throwing everything it had against it. He began thrashing in bed and we had to hold him down. He complained that his bite wound was burning. We gave him painkillers but they wouldn't touch it. His eyes rolled back in his head. His nose ran. He drooled and gnashed his teeth.

He screamed, he went into violent convulsions. And then he started doing the most horrible thing: he started chewing through his own lips. We got a tongue depressor in his mouth and he bit it in half. He shrieked. He raged. He screamed at us.

And then he went still.

While Ricki and Diane held him, he went limp and died in their arms.

What I did next I did not to play the macho man, but to spare them the horror that was coming. Diane took Ricki out of the room. I stayed in there by myself and waited. It was a wake. A vigil. Jimmy kept checking on me, peeking in every fifteen minutes without fail.

"Not yet," I'd tell him.

I waited an hour, then two, then…Davis began to tremble. I touched him. He was cold and dead. The feel of his flesh made me pull my hand away. His fingers began to wiggle. His back arched and he let out a low, throaty sighing that was more of a moaning. His ragged lips pulled back from his teeth. Then his eyes opened. There were perfectly white, the pupils like black dots. He looked at me and drool ran from his mouth.

I grabbed a pillow and pressed it down over his face.

He thrashed.

He made gurgling sounds.

His teeth chattered.

His hands clawed at me.

I put the barrel of the Sig-Sauer where I knew his forehead was and jerked the trigger. Then he was at peace. I walked from the room and Jimmy and Diane were standing there.

"It's done," I said.

Then I found a basin and threw-up.

THE SIEGE

We wrapped Davis up in his blankets and took him down to the crib. Jimmy and Tuck and Diane went out with CAR-15s and killed the zombies they found. There were about a dozen stragglers. Tuck said we should burn the body and we knew he was right. We built a pyre of sticks and logs then put the little blanket-shrouded form atop it. Tuck doused it with kerosene and lit it up. It was a huge blaze and it burned through the afternoon and into the evening. Even after dark it was still smoldering.

We weren't in very good shape after that.

Ricki and Diane explained it all to Maria (save for the shooting/burning part) and she accepted it easily. Too easily. An hour later she began to cry and she was inconsolable. The girls couldn't get her to calm down. We all felt so goddamn hopeless. The cure she needed we couldn't give to her, so she sought her own: she crawled into Tuck's lap and held onto him like she never wanted to let go. I heard him say, *"It's okay now. It'll be okay now. Hold on tight...just keep holding on. I'll never let you go. Never. SShhh."* There were tears in his eyes and I had to walk away.

I followed Diane out onto the dark walkway, my eyes running wet. She lit a cigarette and I bummed one off her. I hadn't smoked in years, save for a time in Iraq when the stress got the better of me. The first drag tasted like shit and made me cough. The second drag made me feel sick to my stomach as the nicotine mainlined. The third tasted wonderful and therein lays the horrible nature of addiction. I finished the cigarette and tossed it over the rail.

I had to keep it together.

Ricki joined us out there and I held her. Then Diane held the both of us. It was hard. It was all very hard.

The only thing that pulled us apart was the helicopter.

I'd told you that I'd seen them now and again, but at high altitude. This one wasn't much more than a few hundred feet off the ground. It buzzed over the tower and circled the compound with spotlights sweeping the ground beneath it. I think it was a Blackhawk. An unarmed scout chopper. It flew over the road outside, illuminating the zombies out there and probably targeting them. It was hard to know in the dark. I wondered what the pilot must have been thinking. Probably out on recon flight to find the dead and he finds the tower and the compound, security lights burning.

The chopper came and went quickly enough.

But its spots showed us that there were not just a few dozen of the dead out there or even forty or fifty, but what looked like hundreds milling about, an army of them. There was enough that it scared me, really scared me, because I could easily see them pushing their combined might against the fence and the gate coming right off its hinges. Let's just say that I didn't sleep too well that night, not too well at all.

By dawn, the situation had worsened.

In fact, it was downright ugly.

Tuck woke me up and when I got out there Jimmy was already there and so was Diane. Outside the fence the numbers had doubled again. They were not holding back now: they had pressed up to the fence and the voltage didn't seem to be bothering them at all. They were beating on it and clawing it, mulling and active and wanting in. I sensed a desperation to them I hadn't seen before.

"I think we better lay the rest of those Claymores," Tuck told me. "If they make it this far, I want to thin them as much as possible."

"Need my help?" Jimmy said.

"No," Tuck told him. "I want you right here with the spotting scope. We're taking the walkie-talkies. Keep us posted." He turned to Diane. "Go wake Ricki and tell her the situation. Tell her we might need to move out at a moment's notice if things get bad. We'll need to start getting things together just in case."

We went down to the crib, gathered up the Claymores and ringed them around the tower for maximum effect. We wired them together, preparing for the very worst. Before hooking them up to the clacker we went and out to the barn and got the Jeep and a similarly-armored Chevy Tahoe. I left Castleberry's suburban there. It was of no use now. We gassed the vehicles up and filled extra cans with fuel and made them ready in case we got overrun.

Back in the tower, everyone was chipping in and packing food and weapons and provisions in case the worse came to worse. Maria was helping, too, her eyes red and puffy from crying. I knew that my world had changed immensely in the past month but I had to wonder what it was like for her. Young, fragile...her parents dead, her brother dead. Now she was stuck with a bunch of strangers that looked like they were preparing for D-Day.

We were in good shape by noon.

That's when the first helicopters showed. I saw a Blackhawk and two Kiowas. They passed over the zombies but made no runs at them. Things were getting tense. Between the zombies massing out there and the military taking an interest in them, things were getting decidedly dicey. We made sure we were well-fed, prepared, and dressed for a run.

Tuck had a radio and got on it, trying to raise somebody, anybody, but he wasn't getting through. Then, a few minutes before two, the first sorties came. F/A-18 Hornets came screaming over the trees and dropped clusterbombs that went off in rapid succession blanketing the road and the zombies with explosions that made the tower shake. Out by the fence there was fire and smoke and flying debris. The next sortie dropped more clusterbombs and it would have been all right if they had stopped there. The zombie masses were obliterated but further sorties destroyed the fence, blowing off the gates and tearing big holes everywhere when it didn't knock it right down.

It wasn't good.

Because after the Hornets were long gone, the zombies were regrouping again. Maybe not hundreds as before, but waves of twenty and thirty at a time that had survived the bombing. They pushed forward, swarming, crossing the fence and spreading out over the compound. Tuck flooded the trench with fuel oil and fired an incendiary into it and it went up with a resounding *WHRUMP!* pushing a wave of heat back at us. It further slowed the progress of the dead. Many were coming down the road, but others were trying to wade through the oil and were incinerated and still others went up in blazing pyres, wandering around, flaming. Others pushed into the minefields and the mines went up one after the other: *THUMP! THUMP! THUMP!* They did not kill the zombies. They just mutilated them...tearing open legs and feet, slowing them down but hardly stopping them.

"They're still coming!" Ricki said, watching them approach with her spotting scope. She was out on the walkway with Diane and Jimmy.

"Hell yes, they're everywhere now," Jimmy said.

Diane scanned the fields with binoculars. "I'm counting at least fifty or sixty coming in from the north," she reported. "Heavy weather ahead, man."

I went out there and it was chaos. The fence line was destroyed, of course, the landscape pitted from the clusterbombing. Black smoke was roiling in the air from the bombs and from the burning fuel oil that blazed with a greasy stink that seared my nostrils.

Tuck flooded the secondary trench and lit it up.

It ignited with a rushing, whooshing sort of sound and, again, the heat rolled at us. I didn't think firing the secondary was a good idea because it was already bad enough out there with the smoke and fire and heat. From the walkway it looked like a boiling, steaming witch's cauldron. We had to shut the hatch after a few minutes because the air was so hot and so thick with smoke. But what I saw before we did was the very thing I'd always been worried about: the blazing fuel oil had lit up the surrounding dry, uncultivated fields and now they were burning, too. I think the compound was about as close to Hell as I could have imagined.

"We're going to have to get out of here," Tuck said. "At least for awhile until it burns itself out."

"That fire is going to destroy our crops," Diane said, very pointedly. She'd mothered those fields, she nurtured them with blood, sweat, and tears. She didn't get pissed off easily. But right then, she was as hot as the fields beyond the tower. "It's going to destroy everything. Did you have to light that oil on fire? That was fucking stupid, man, just plain fucking stupid."

"I'm trying to save our asses!" Tuck shouted at her.

Diane just shook her head. "Yeah, well I hope your escape plan isn't a clusterfuck like this."

Tuck just stared at her, trying to intimidate her but it did no good. She stared right back at him.

"Diane, knock it off," Ricki told her. "He's done everything for us. We're alive because of him."

"Shut up, Polyanna."

"Don't you call me that!"

Diane rolled her eyes. "Lookit me I'm Sandra Dee."

Ricki boiled.

"Okay, that's enough," I said, getting in-between them. "We've got enough problems without bickering."

This was a really, really stupid time to start picking at each other. Realistically? I agreed with Diane. I thought the minefield and the Claymores were a good idea. But I never liked the idea of the fuel oil. The chances of collateral damage were too high. That fire would burn everything. It would roast the zombies like marshmallows but at the same time it would leave us with a barren compound.

I told Tuck we needed to get down to the crib to wire the Claymores to the clacker but he was in a foul mood by then. "I'll do it," he told me. "I'll blow a hole through them and then I'll get the trucks over here."

"I'll come with."

"Suit yourself."

That was one thing about Tuck. I loved the guy and respected him but he had a stripe of pride running through him a mile wide. He did not like his efforts questioned even when they didn't work out so good. He'd brood for awhile, I knew, but he'd get over it. We were in the shit now. I thought it could not get any worse but I was wrong, very wrong. Tuck was in his element now and I could see that. He lived for combat and for many years he'd had none save an occasional bar fight. He was probably more alive now with the zombie pandemic than he'd been since the Vietnam War.

We got down to the crib.

The dead were out there. We could hear them pounding on the security door. Scratching and clawing at it. Tuck had cut gunports on all sides of the crib and we could see that there were probably only eight or ten zombies hanging around outside the tower. The real menace were the dozens moving in from the fields. The haze of dust and smoke out there was a thick pall, but the wind moved it away from time to time enough so that I could see the numbers coming at us.

"What do you got?" Tuck called out to me.

"I got at least twenty to the north and maybe ten or more from the west," I told him.

"Got three times that many coming down the road, another thirty to the south. Let's draw them in."

Tuck wired the Claymores to the clacker and got ready.

I kept an eye out the gunports. They were massing now. I watched them coming. Many were battle-scarred: burnt and blasted, missing limbs or with gaping wounds from the bombing. But it did not slow their steady inexorable march.

I got on the walkie-talkie. "Ricki," I said. "Get everyone and everything down to the second level. When we move we're going to have to move fast."

"Got ya," she said.

The throng of the dead were within ten feet of the Claymore line now.

"Get ready," Tuck said.

I turned away from the gunport, sweat running down my face, my shirt stuck to my back. I waited. It seemed to take forever and then, "HAVE A TASTE!" Tuck screamed and fired the Claymores. There was a resounding boom and when I looked out the gunport there was more smoke and flames, the stink of burnt ordinance. But the wall of zombies was just…gone.

"ALL RIGHT!" Tuck said. "LET'S MOVE!"

"Get down into the crib!" I called over the walkie-talkie.

Tuck keyed open the door and we charged out, knocking three or four zombies out of our way. Before they could recover, we capped them in the heads with our CAR-15s. We saw a few stragglers and dropped them, too. The smoke and heat of the advancing fire was unbelievable, absolutely disorienting. I wasn't sure in which direction to move. We tied neckerchiefs over our mouths so we didn't breathe in those caustic fumes. Tuck seemed to know which way to go and I followed him. I saw one zombie and Tuck took it out with a fast, perfect killshot.

We hadn't made it more than fifteen feet from the tower when we heard the sound of the F/A-18 Hornets coming in for another airstrike. I couldn't imagine why. It made no sense. We heard them dropping more clusterbombs in the distance. *WHAP! WHAP! WHAP-WHAP-WHAP!* The ground shook and more debris was sent airborne. The shock waves cleared the smoke long enough for us to see a missile come screaming through the air and hit one of the pole buildings. Tuck knocked me down as the building collapsed and fiery bits of sheet metal flew through the air like shrapnel. There was a concussive *WHAM-WHAM-WHAM!* as the drums of gasoline stored inside went up, a rolling fire cloud rising above the wreckage.

"THEY'RE TAREGETING US!" Tuck cried over the noise. "THEY'RE ATTACKING THE COMPOUND! WE GOTTA MOVE!"

We climbed to our feet and started running towards the barn before it, too, got hit. The good thing was that we saw no more zombies. The bad thing was that the barn was burning and there were kerosene and fuel oil stores in it. Fighting through the heat and black clouds of smoke, coughing and gagging, we found the vehicles, got in and were rolling.

Tuck was in the Jeep and I was in the Tahoe.

I followed the Jeep through the haze, calling out on the walkie-talkie for everyone to get ready. Behind us there was a series of rolling concussions that made the Tahoe bounce on its springs. I couldn't be sure, but I thought a Hornet had just targeted the barn and the other pole building. I wasn't naïve enough to think that the tower wouldn't be hit within the next few moments.

We pulled in front and the door opened and out came Jimmy leading the troops. And as they came out, the zombies moved in. There was so much smoke drifting around that by the time they emerged from it, they were scarce feet away. I opened up on full auto and I heard the others doing the same. I drove them back, dropped four of them with headshots as another took me from behind. I felt its cold slimy arms ring around my throat and I acted instinctively: I jabbed my elbow back and felt it sink into something soft. Then I reached back and flipped my attacker over my shoulder as we'd been taught in infantry school.

It was a man and I popped him in the head.

The others moved in for the kill.

I blew the face off another man and shattered the head of a little girl and then two women were on me. Their faces were like white pulp. One of them grabbed me and I gave her the stock of the CAR-15 in the face. It was like hitting a water balloon. Her face seemed to splash off the bone beneath in a spray of rot. The other woman had my arm and as she made to bite it, I lashed out and stomped her knee with my boot. It cracked and she fell backwards. A man rushed in and I put a round right between his eyes, a purely lucky shot.

There were more explosions in the distance and they were getting closer all the time. A wave of heat knocked me off my feet and lit the hair of a zombie woman on fire.

The others were having it no better.

I saw Jimmy shooting into an approaching pack as Diane and Ricki got the kids into the Tahoe. Tuck was a wild man. He was shooting, using his weapon like a club. Kicking zombies, smashing through their numbers, hitting them, and stomping them. I saw him grab a man and throw him into three others and they all went over like bowling pins.

But I had no time to watch.

The women I had put down were on me again. The one I'd smashed in the face came at me, clawing for my eyes and I jabbed out with the barrel of the CAR-15. As luck would have it, I stuck the barrel right in her mouth. I gave her a quick three-round burst and her head flew apart. At the same moment, the other woman grabbed my ankle and I saw her teeth going for my leg. Too late. She would have had me, but she bit my combat boot. I smashed her head to sauce with the butt of the CAR-15.

I turned and dropped two more.

I saw Diane kill a couple zombies and Ricki start climbing into the Jeep and it was at that point that twenty or thirty of the dead rushed in out of the smoke. I saw them go after Diane. Jimmy dropped a few and so did she. I knocked a few stragglers out of my way, shooting and kicking my way to the Jeep. I killed three, then four and five. They were dropping everywhere and I wasn't watching where I was going. I tripped over a corpse and saw Jimmy jump into the Jeep, calling to me. Tuck got into the thick of it and drove off a pack that were closing on Diane.

Then...then as Ricki tried to get in, five or six of them grabbed her and started to drag her off.

I heard her screaming.

I launched myself forward, shooting and clubbing but they had her and they were biting into her. I screamed myself as the dead hemmed me in and I heard my CAR-15 click on an empty chamber. I used it like a club and then hands were pulling me back and away. It was Tuck. He was trying to pull me into the Jeep. I saw Paul crying and fighting in there, Diane holding tight onto him. Tuck pulled at me. I swung at him. I hit him and made to go after my wife and then I heard his voice say something like, *"I'm sorry, my brother, I'm so sorry."* Then something hit me in the back of the neck and I went down, lost in a dark haze.

And that was the last time I saw my wife.

RUN FOR THE HILLS

I came to about ten minutes later as Jimmy pulled the Jeep out onto the cratered main road, everyone bumping and jumping and being thrown around. I saw the tower through the haze. I saw it take a direct hit from an air-to-surface missile and collapse into itself.

But Ricki was gone.

I had the desire, the *need,* to go completely haywire and start shouting and screaming and raising a stink. But I controlled myself because I knew I had to. Tuck had hit me. He had knocked me out to save me. He knew I would have committed suicide trying to save my wife. Maybe he thought that one parent for Paul was better than no parent at all. I wasn't sure whether to thank him or hate him. I was in the backseat with Paul. Diane was holding him. He was pale and shaking, tears running down his face. I took hold of him and he started fighting and shouting, *"MY MOTHER'S DEAD! YOU LET MY MOTHER DIE! YOU LET HER! YOU LET THEM KILL MY MOM YOU DID YOU DID YOU DID—"*

I held him until he collapsed against me, worn and trembling and limp.

Guilt?

Oh yes, there was guilt. Oceans of guilt. Universes of it. From a rational perspective I knew I had done all that I could…yet, I was tortured by the idea that I could have done more, a lot more. If I hadn't tripped over that corpse I would have reached her in time. If I hadn't have brought us to the goddamn tower she'd probably still be alive. If I'd been more concerned with protecting my family and less with playing perimeter guard she would still be alive. Paul would have a mother. I would have a wife. We would not both be ripped open and bleeding. I would not be seeing my wife's screaming face as she was engulfed by the living dead.

I tried to hold onto that rational perspective, to cancel out all the guilt, but grief does not understand rationality. It deals in loss. It deals in pain. Its politics are those of suffering. So I suffered. God knows, I suffered. And God? Well, if my faith was shaky before it was now a black void of emptiness. I believed in nothing.

I wanted to fall into a depressed heap. I wanted to seize up and retreat into myself. But I did not have that luxury. When you have a child and you lose your spouse you cannot afford to be anything less than the solid rock that child needs to cling to. So I was a rock. I shut myself down and felt nothing. I only cared about my son. He slept on my lap for nearly two hours and when he came awake he looked up at me and said, "I didn't dream it, did I?"

"No," I said.

He nodded, gathering himself, trying to be tough like I was. A boy feels that he has to do two things in life: protect his mother and garner his father's respect. He had lost the one and he would not sacrifice the other. I wanted to tell him that it wasn't important, that we would grieve together, that pain was okay…but I couldn't. And I couldn't because I knew how much he needed right then to be a man in my eyes. It was important to him. It was all he had and I couldn't take it away from him.

He patted my arm and said, "It'll be okay, Dad…I think it'll be okay. I just hope they didn't…" he took a deep breath "…hurt her too much."

"It went fast," Jimmy told him. "I'm sure it went fast."

But we didn't believe that. Being torn apart is not painless and it does not go fast. I just hoped they rendered her to nothing. I don't want to think that she might be walking around out there somewhere with them, *as* them. I don't think she would have made a very good zombie. It just wasn't in her.

Diane was watching both Paul and I very closely. I guess I had forgotten that she had just lost her kid sister, too. Our eyes met, pain acknowledged and shared. We both looked away. She was holding Maria on her lap. Maria was sucking her thumb. She looked shattered. So much loss, so much despair, so much tragedy. I was worried that we would not survive this one.

I heard Jimmy and Tuck discussing what to do and I knew right then that good old Tuck had no back-up plan and he was not a guy who liked to be caught with his pants down. But, honestly, there had been no need for a back-up plan. The compound should have been the end. The perfect secure location. I couldn't even really, truly blame the zombies for destroying our shelter.

They had the minds of animals.

They knew only prey and feeding.

The ones to blame were the assholes in the F/A-18 Hornets. Why in the Christ did they attack us? Why did they ignore Tuck's distress call? Why did they have to flatten everything? Why? Why? *Why?*

As if reading my mind, Paul said, "Why did those jets want to blow us up, Dad?"

I had no answers but Jimmy did. "Son, I been mulling that over and I have a funny feeling that we were attacked by mistake. I think the Air Force or Air Guard or the Navy or whoever the hell that was were given a bombing mission. Those helicopters scouted us out and the fighter pilots were just carrying out their orders. Somebody out there thought we were a threat. So we were targeted."

"If I ever get my hands on those flyboys," Tuck said.

We drove around without any direction for hours. We saw the state of our world and it was not very reassuring. There were small towns that were either burning or burnt out, nothing but collections of blackened buildings and rubble. We saw craters from bombings. Abandoned vehicles on the sides of the roads. Corpses in the fields that were being fed on by dogs and crows. And zombies, of course. They were walking everywhere, watching us as we drove by or simply ignoring us. The smell of death was on the wind. In the distance we could see plumes of black smoke like smudges of charcoal against the pale blue sky.

Finally, about ten miles east of Scarsdale, we found an abandoned airfield. It looked like it had been closed up a long time. It wasn't much. A couple old runways with weeds growing from the cracks, a few rusting hangars, and Quonset huts. It was enclosed by a chain link fence which was good. Tuck blew the lock off and we went in. The hangars had huge holes in their roofs and pigeons roosting in the rafters. One of the Quonsets was piled with rusting machine parts. The other had no door and was full of birds. Then we found a little office with a garage hooked to it. The garage had no windows. It was locked but we found the key in the office which Tuck got into it after forcing a window. The garage was mostly empty save for a few old drums of fuel and hydraulic grease. It was a little dusty, but not bad. We set about cleaning it up the best we could and then fortifying the office so nothing could get at us. Jimmy and Tuck found some lumber and nailed it over the windows.

It was a start.

Over the next few days we settled in. There was no zombie activity and that was a good thing. We laid our sleeping bags on the floor. Jimmy found a rolled carpet in the office and we spread that out. It was a little musty-smelling but it was better than sleeping on the concrete. We missed our fresh vegetables from Tuck's gardens and his variety of frozen meats. We ate mostly MREs which are all right now and again—much better than the old C-Rations, I'm told—but I'd gotten very sick of them in Iraq where we were in the field. Paul thought they were the coolest thing in the world and Maria loved how the ration heater cooked up the spaghetti and meat sauce when you pulled the tab.

Paul and Maria amazed me.

Even with the loss they'd both suffered, they did not retreat into themselves. They worked hard and I was impressed. We all worked hard. For the time being this was home. We made it as livable and safe as possible. Paul and I mourned together. The others left us alone save for Diane. One day Maria saw me brooding. She went outside with Jimmy and returned with a daisy.

She handed it to me. "This will make you feel better," she said.

And you know what? It really did.

Once we were safe, we explored the other buildings to see what we could scavenge. We didn't find much. Our fourth day there, it poured buckets and we took advantage of this by going out there and soaping up...Maria and Diane did theirs privately, of course. It felt good to be clean. My mother used to say, *"Never underestimate the power of a good shower."* She was right as always. Being clean made us all feel a little more human.

The next day, Diane and I searched one of the hangars and, suddenly, out of pure impulse I took hold of her and started kissing her. She responded at first and then pushed me away.

"No," she said.

I didn't know what came over me. "I'm sorry. I'm losing my mind."

"Grief will do that to you."

"I'm not like that," I said. "I don't know why I did it."

"Grief."

She told me a story about some teenage pal of hers who was shattered by her father's death when she was sixteen. She ended up getting high out in the alley behind the funeral home with her best friend's boyfriend. They ended up in the backseat of his car. She did not know why. She did not understand why. It just happened. Good story and relevant, but it didn't make me feel any less of a heel. What would have happened if Diane hadn't stopped it? Would we have ended up doing it right there on the dusty floor? Would I have even been able to perform? I was an absolute fucking mess. It seemed like the world was spinning so fast I couldn't get back on.

We didn't talk about it again.

What was there to say? I told myself it was grief. I was trying to escape it. I was trying to shield myself from it. Was that what it was? I just didn't know and it gave me something else to feel like shit about.

When I made to leave, Diane made me sit on a pile of lumber. "I have a confession to make," she said.

"Oh?"

She nodded. "I'm out of dope. I'm out of pills. I don't have anything and my brain is starting to act funny."

I was tempted to tell her that, *no,* your brain is just functioning normally for the first time in years. But I couldn't say that.

"I had a dream last night," she said.

Now let me preface this by saying that Diane very often had dreams and she loved to talk about them. She was into things like prophetic dreaming, lots of weird New Age shit that made absolutely no sense to a hard-headed Agnostic like me.

"You know me," she said. "I've always had some strange dreams and sometimes I wonder if that's why I like to get stoned and drunk as if, you know, there's something in my brain that I need to *tone* down. Something I need to keep sluggish and sedated. Does that make sense? Probably not. Fuck it. Now here's something you don't know: this weird dreaming thing runs in the family. It really does. I bet Ricki never told you about that. She didn't have it, so she rejected it. But I have it and so did our mom. Here's something else you don't know, something else Ricki didn't tell you: a week before you two hooked up, Della had a dream that you would come. She never said if it was your face she saw, but she dreamed that a man came into Ricki's life and gave her the security she needed because, you know, Ricki was a basket case. I loved her, man, but she was a basket case."

No, Ricki had never mentioned any of that and if she did I imagine my reaction would be pretty similar to the one I was having now.

"There's other things, too, but they're not important. Not right now. Let's just say that Della dreamed that Ricki was pregnant a month before Ricki knew and Della saw the face of her grandchild. We'll leave it at that." Diane lit a cigarette and blew out a column of smoke. "My dreams have been getting very weird and intense since I ran out of stash. Last night—this one's freaky—last night I dreamed of Cadillacs and God. *Really.* I saw Cadillacs lined-up like in one of those deserts where they bury the rich guys in their cars. I saw that, rows and rows and rows of them and I saw myself there and then...*wow*...I saw the eye of God looking at me from the horizon: it was bright orange and red and burning, sending out plumes of yellow light. It was an eye of hate, an eye that was opening and when it did it would scorch the world with its heat. I woke up, thinking: *hey, maybe that's not the eye of God but maybe the Devil or maybe something like the Devil.* That was my dream and you probably think I'm nuts but I'll tell you one thing, Steve: I'm not. What I saw will come to pass next week or next year, who knows?"

"That's pretty heavy shit," I said. On one hand, being the rational guy, I dismissed it, of course. But if I'd learned anything since the dark box of Necrophage was kicked open, it was that rationality didn't seem quite so *rational* anymore. I wasn't as ready to dismiss what she said as I might have been before this all started.

"I dreamed something else, too," she said and she was even more serious. She was so serious that she got about three inches from my face and I thought she was going to kiss me or something. "I dreamed that you and I were doing it, you know, making love or fucking or whatever you want to call it. And that was the beginning of the end."

"Us having sex?"

"In some way it was."

"That's way too mystical for me," I said.

"Me, too," she admitted.

We never spoke of her dreams, not for a long time, but I was always wondering about them. And, more so, I was wondering about things that Ricki might not have told me.

What I remember most about our new digs was one night when we settled in. Paul and I whispered about Ricki a little bit, trying, always trying to put it all in some sort of perspective. Right before I fell asleep, Paul said, "I'm going to kill them, Dad. The zombies. I'm going to kill every last one of them."

PANIC LIST

1. Okay. We seem to be in okay shape.
2. We're alive. We have weapons. Supplies are in good shape.
3. I feel vulnerable as hell here.
4. I tell myself every morning to put on a bright face for Paul, but it isn't always so easy. Ricki's face is in my mind. I hear her voice. I sometimes think I can almost feel her touch.
5. Enough. I have to get my shit together.
6. How long before the dead find us again?

SCAVENGERS

I realized something over the next week or so as we hid out in the garage and secured our position as much as possible. I realized something about the human mind and how it works: just surviving is not enough. It was enough for animals and it had been enough for our ancestors, but with our modern mindset we needed more. We needed something to reach for, to aspire to, a light at the end of the tunnel. When we were at the tower, we had that, I thought. Our plan was to wait for a few months and then start waging war on the dead and taking back what was ours. It was the carrot at the end of the stick. It unified us and made us whole.

Now we lacked that.

We were just rats surviving.

Although war is never a good thing, a popular war like World War II can unify everyone and give them a common enemy. It was kind of like that after 9/11. It didn't last, of course, and before long it was back to the same infighting and bickering. But for a while there, we were unified. Our little group, on the other hand, had unity to stay alive, but we lacked something bigger than mere survival. Somehow, some way we had to find that.

We had to find something.

We needed the carrot.

I told that to Jimmy. "You're right," he said. "We need that. We're all getting shack happy, we've all got cabin fever. We all feel the need to do *something* but I don't think we know what it is."

"I hope we find it."

"We will."

The only real pastime we had besides staying alive was scavenging. We made regular raids into Scarsdale, avoiding the dead whenever possible and searching out food, weapons, ammo, anything that might be of use to us. We all took turns. Even Paul got to go. Trust me, I didn't want to put him in harm's way but the first time Tuck and I went out on scavenging trip, Paul had a real fit and we had to take him along. Paul wasn't a bratty kid, he did not throw temper tantrums. This was something else. This was separation anxiety. He'd lost his mother and he was afraid of losing me.

We recognized that, even Tuck.

So Paul got to come.

I didn't care for the idea and it made me nervous as hell…yet, I had to admit the kid was a born scavenger. He had an uncanny sense of where to find hidden stashes of things. Each of our scavenging trips was successful. We came back with canned goods and dry goods, lanterns and batteries, gasoline. We raided an Army/Navy surplus store and, although somebody had already emptied the knife case, we found lots of work boots, raingear, and a positive stockpile of British DPM clothing, which is Disruptive Pattern Material, the UK version of camouflage. We all took to wearing it. It was comfortable and practical. We looked like a squad of Royal Marines. All we lacked were the berets.

Our trips into the city were not entirely scavenging missions, they were reconnaissance as well: we needed to know where the dead were and how many there were. We discovered that it was worse than we had imagined. There had been something like 18,000 people in Scarsdale before Necrophage and it was my rough guess that more than half of them were in the streets as the undead. You would find block after block of deserted neighborhoods, then you'd wing around a corner and there'd been fifty of them bearing down on you.

The zombies were bad enough, of course, but we began to see something else that was equally disturbing: armed bands of men in pick-ups and SUVs. They were dressed in camo fatigues and carried a variety of weapons, mostly semi-automatics. One afternoon we were entering the city and a truck bore down on us. Our first thought was great, here's some survivors, but then they closed in and started shooting at us. We led them a merry chase through the streets with me at the wheel and finally lost them. A few days later we were at a hardware store getting some chain and six trucks rolled on by. Luckily, we had the Jeep parked out back or they'd would have probably come after us.

It was scary.

Weren't things bad enough without survivors fighting one another?

Although I wouldn't say they were organized to a military level, there was no doubt they were part of some militia. They'd probably been waiting for something like this so they could run wild without the risk of the police kicking their asses. Regardless, they were trouble and we all knew it.

"The question is," Tuck said that night. "Do we just run and hide from them or do we smoke their asses? That's the question."

"Might be a good idea not to tangle with them if we don't have to," Diane pointed out. "Every stone thrown in every pool casts ripples."

Jimmy lifted an eyebrow. "Sure. Makes sense, but just because we leave them alone don't mean they'll do the same for us," he said.

I had to agree with that. "They didn't look like the types to live and let live."

"Wannabes," Tuck said. "That's all they are. Any real force would cut 'em in half. They're weekenders, little boys playing soldier. They got the numbers so they think they're badass. They're used to pushing people around and not being pushed back. Bullies. All the militias are the same. You start shooting back and killing them, they'll start pissing their pants and running."

I hoped he was right.

RILEY

Between the zombies and the militia, we only went into Scarsdale when we had to. Even at the airfield we took to hiding the Jeep in one of the hangars so it couldn't be spotted from the road. The last thing we needed were a bunch of drunken cowboys coming in shooting. We had to be careful in every way. We knew we couldn't make the garage our permanent HQ, but for the time being it would have to do.

We thought we were pretty secure.

We thought no one could sneak around in there without us knowing it.

Then one afternoon I was out in the hangar with Jimmy and Diane. They were selecting useable boards from a stack of lumber and I was doing some work on the Jeep. I replaced the old stock Autolite four-barrel with a Holley Truck Avenger carb kit to crank up performance and horsepower. I wasn't paying much attention to Jimmy and Diane. I had the Jeep running and I was adjusting the float level on the carb. Sounded smooth. I shut the Jeep off and stepped out and that's when I realized someone was right behind me.

"Turn around, real slow," a woman's voice said.

I did as I was told. I found myself looking at a forty-something African-American woman. She was dirty, face scratched and bruised. She had a gun in my face and it was mine. While I was working on the Jeep, I took off my Sig-Sauer 9mm and left it sitting on the bench in its holster. My bad. Now she had it in my face.

"Listen," I said. "We're friendly, we're not—"

"Shut the fuck up," she told me, looking around and slowly backing away from me, keeping a clear field of fire between us. Just by the way she held the gun I could see she knew what she was doing and she'd been trained. She was dressed in what looked like mechanic's coveralls and they were dirty with greasy stains and what might have been old blood. The sleeves were ragged, holes torn in the seat and shoulders. The name sewn at the left breast said her name was *ED*.

"Where are your friends at?" she asked me.

"I don't know. They were here."

"Don't fuck with me!"

"Take it easy," I said. "Nobody's fucking with you. They were hauling lumber. They must be outside."

"I want the keys to that Jeep."

"Why?"

"Because I need a ride, asshole. There's somewhere I got to go. Some people that need help and I plan to see that they get it," she explained. "That's something you militia pukes can't understand: there's people out there, *real* people. People just trying to get by. Trying to survive. Not like animals, but like *people.*"

"Wait a minute. I'm not—"

"Shut up before I blow your face off," she instructed me. She turned towards the darkness at the back of the hangar. "Jilly? Jilly, get out here. It's safe." She turned to me. "Now give me those goddamn keys or I'll kill you."

I believed her.

I could see by looking in her eyes that she had been through the shit. Used and abused and roughly-handled. She was desperate. She would kill. There was no doubt of it. The problem was that we needed the Jeep. We would not survive without it.

"I'm not with any militia," I said.

"Mmm-hmm, I bet you're not. You just dress like that because you're a law-abiding citizen," she said. "Now I ask for the third time: gimme the keys." She raised the Sig so that it was eye level with me. *"Now."*

A girl came running out of the shadows. She was maybe fourteen or fifteen, Asian, with huge dark eyes and long beautiful hair. She was a pretty thing, but like the other woman, dirty and bruised and scratched.

I took the keys out of my pocket because I didn't see where I had much of a choice.

That's when Diane stepped out of the shadows with her CAR-15. "Drop that gun, bitch, or I cap twenty rounds into you," she said, calmly and resolutely.

For the first time there was indecision in the woman's eyes. She saw the CAR-15 staring down at her and she knew she was beaten. But something in her wanted to fight on and I could plainly see that.

"Do it!" Diane told her. "Don't make me fuck up my Karma by killing you!"

The woman let out a sigh that was pure defeat. She let the gun drop from her hand and without being asked, as if she'd done this before, she kicked it over to me.

I picked it up.

The girl was crying and the woman held her.

"All right," I said. "We're not the militia. You can both relax."

"You serious?" the woman said.

"Very."

To make a long story short we got them inside, explained who and what we were and how we happened to be at the airfield. The woman said her name was Riley—not *ED*—and the girl's name was Jilly. Then she told us a story that was sickening to the extreme. The militia we had seen around was called the American Resistance Movement (ARM). They'd been small-time before Necrophage, maybe thirty or forty extremists, but now their numbers had swollen into the hundreds. They had fought a few minor battles with the Army and National Guard, but mostly steered clear of open confrontation and concentrated on guerrilla warfare. Riley said they were nothing but hoodlums. Animals. They had numbers and they had weapons and they specialized in murder, rape, and robbery. They took what they wanted and anyone who challenged that was killed. One faction of them had set up in Kingsbridge Heights in the Bronx, just down from the old Medieval-looking armory in a former Catholic school complex there. It was ideal because it was surrounded by a high chain link fence and was defensible against the hordes of the living dead. Riley said she had been a cop with the 50th Precinct. When word reached them that women and girls were being snatched off the streets, something had to be done.

"We were in bad shape at the Fiftieth," she explained. "Between the dead and the pandemic, our force was down like sixty percent. But we had to do something. Word reached us that the abducted were being taken to an abandoned school. I went there with five other cops."

She was the only survivor.

The others were gunned down by ARM as they tried to get out of their cars. Riley fought back until she ran out of ammo and then they took her. They locked her in the basement with twenty other women who had been brought there for one express purpose.

"A rape camp," Jimmy said.

"Those motherfuckers," Tuck said.

She nodded. I was glad Diane had taken Maria and Paul out of earshot so they could get to know Jilly. "That's exactly what it was. I was there for two weeks. I'm not going to tell you what was done to me and done to Jilly or the others. You can use your imagination. I'll just say that we were first beaten into submission and then…well, you get the picture."

By my figuring it had been roughly two months now since The Awakening. Two months, maybe not even. Time had lost meaning for the most part. Regardless, in that short span of time the world had changed and not for the good. The zombies were one thing. Like disease germs invading a body, you couldn't hate them really, you couldn't personalize them anymore than you could a virus that makes you sick or a snake that bites you. But ARM was something else entirely. They had taken advantage of a bad situation and shown their true colors. Nothing but outlaws and predators.

"Jilly and I escaped," Riley said, "using an old steam tunnel that leads out into the alley beyond. Other women and girls had tried to escape and the militia killed them. Only Jilly would come with me when I decided to try and get out. See, at the Precinct, we had the old plans for the school and if we found out that the rumors were true, a SWAT team was going to use the steam tunnels to get in there and get the abductees out."

"When you went missing…did the Precinct send anyone after you?" I asked.

She shook her head. "That's what I hoped for. Then they brought in another woman and she said the Precinct was overrun by the dead. There was no more Fiftieth. So we were forgotten. That's when I decided to make a run, using the tunnels."

"But the others wouldn't go?"

"They were terrified. Others were not in their right minds from the abuse," Riley said, getting emotional for a minute and wiping her eyes. "There are women there that I think were going to try if we made it out alive. A lot of them are ready and willing to fight. Maybe some of them got out. I don't know."

She said that Jilly and she ran and ran. The Northwest Bronx had been hit by numerous airstrikes and it looked worse than ever. Like London after the Blitz. It was hard to find your way, the landscape had been completely altered. But they got out. In Yonkers they stole a car and made it to Scarsdale. ARM was there, too, and they were attacked, their car destroyed. They barely made it out of the city. That's when they found the airfield. They hid in the woods across the road, watching us coming and going. Today they made their move.

"So you wanted the Jeep to go back in and free the women?"

"If I could. Jilly and I were willing to die trying."

"Sounds like suicide," Tuck said. "The militia would shoot you down."

She shook her head. "You don't understand. When we escaped, the militia was gone. The entire neighborhood was overrun by zombies. ARM did what they do best: turned tail and ran. There were hundreds of zombies. We barely made it. But there was one thing for sure: there was no way I could get back to the steam tunnels to lead the others out. The dead were swarming."

"At least we know why the tower was hit," Jimmy said. "They must have thought we were a militia outpost."

"But now you want to make a run to the school with a Jeep?" I asked her.

"I have to do something. It's been four days. Those women are trapped in there. If the dead are as thick as they were, they'll never get out."

"How many were still alive when you left?" Jimmy asked.

"Fourteen or fifteen."

"I don't think you'd make it in," Tuck said.

"Not alone," she said and I knew we had suddenly become part of her rescue team. "If I can reach those tunnels, and if I have some back-up to keep the maggot-heads away from me, I think it can be done."

We discussed it then. There was never a moment of hesitation where one of us said, *no way, that's suicide, we're not risking our necks.* We started planning with her on how it could happen and how it couldn't. In retrospect, it's amazing how we went for it. A big part of it, of course, was that we were not a militia. We were compassionate human beings who still had morals and ethics and a well-balanced sense of right and wrong. Those ladies had been through hell. They needed help. We were going to help them.

"The problem is the zombies," Tuck said. "That damn many, we just don't have the firepower to secure a corridor for you to get in and out. We need heavier artillery."

Riley nodded, undaunted. "You're right. What if I told you I know where there are some armored cars with machine guns?"

We all looked at her.

"APCs?" Tuck said.

"Yes, they belonged to a National Guard unit. They're in a garage near the Precinct."

"What sort of APCs?" I asked, warming to the idea.

Riley shook her head. "Listen, I wasn't in the Army or anything and one pretty much looks like another."

But I had a feeling. "Describe them to me."

She did.

I smiled. "Those are Strykers," I said.

BLUEPRINT

In any operation there are countless maybes and what ifs, dozens of small little details that you cannot plan for. And this one was worse than most. First off, the zombies. Were they still there (at the school)? Were there more or less of them now? The militia. Had they returned? Had they tried to take back the school? The neighborhood. Was it still there or had it been bombed to rubble? The Precinct. Ditto. Was it still standing? How about the garage with the Strykers? Had it been bombed? Had the Strykers been taken away? Without them, there was no hope of success. Everything depended on that. The plan we threw together spun on them.

That night after a round of MREs for everyone, and after Jilly and Riley had cleaned up and we outfitted them in some DPMs, we got down to it. We drew a map of the school. It was not just a single schoolhouse, but a complex of sort. Behind the fence, there was a wide courtyard you drove into that was sort of a quadrangle with the schoolhouse in the center (three stories, brick), another building on the left, a sort of convent where the nuns had lived, and to the right a chapel (falling apart) with a clock tower up on top of it and, above that, an open belfry that had once housed a bell.

Our plan was to block off the alley with a Stryker (God, I hoped they were Strykers), then one of us would go with Riley into the steam tunnels to get the women out. Once we had them in the alley we could drop the rear gate and get them in back and then get the hell out. That was our basic plan. We had some back-up ideas, but that was the gist. It all depended on luck, timing, and more luck.

"You know this is fucking suicide, don't you?" I said to Tuck.

He laughed. "It sure is, isn't it?"

Same old Tuck. Looking for a fight and having found one, he was excited like a kid on Christmas morning. I had said earlier that surviving wasn't quite enough, that we needed something to aspire to, something to unify us in a common cause. Well, I thought we had found it. This was the carrot at the end of the stick. Getting to it would not be easy. Not easy at all, but we were all excited, I think. Riley told us there were four APCs in the garage near the Precinct house. If they were Strykers we would need a minimum of two people in each: a driver and someone to man the .50-cal machine guns. The beauty of the Stryker is the Remote Weapons Station where you can operate the .50-cal remotely without having to stick your head out of the vehicle. The more I thought about it, the more it sounded more realistic to take only one Styker. I mean, I could give Tuck and the others a crash course on the vehicle, but if anything went wrong—with me in the second Stryker and zombies in-between—there wouldn't be much I could do to help them without exposing myself to an ugly death.

No, one vehicle.

Generally what you had in a Stryker was a driver and the TC, Truck Commander, up front. In the back there were eight soldiers and a squad leader. So you were talking eleven people without crowding. On this op, it would the four of us and ten or twelve others, maybe more. We'd be a little crowded but at least we'd be together in case something happened.

I knew right from the onset that Paul would not be coming on this one and I didn't care how much of a fuss he threw. I pulled him aside and talked to him about it once we had decided that Tuck, Diane, Riley, and I would be going. Jimmy would stay behind with the kids and he was okay with that, deciding he'd had enough action for awhile.

"I can't go, can I?" Paul said.

"Not this time."

He brooded.

"Listen," I said to him. "I've let you come on a lot of runs now. I've allowed you to do things your mother would not have approved of. But this time you can't come. I need you here. I need you to be strong. I need you to set a good example for the girls— we all have a job to do and if we don't do it, we won't survive. That's the way it is. I need you here with Jimmy. I need you to keep Maria and Jilly safe. They've both been through a lot. They're both fragile in different ways. They both need a friend. I want you to be that friend. That's what I need of you. I need to know that if I go into the city that things are safe here. I'll have enough to worry about. Can you help me?"

I took a cue from Diane and I did not treat him as a child. I talked with him the way one man would talk with another. He looked at me and smiled. "You can count on me, Dad."

I have to say that I felt an immense welling of pride at that moment. It was all I could do not to hug the kid and tell him how proud I was of him. Because you know what? I *was* proud of him. He'd been through the mill, he'd lost his mother, but he was adapting to it. It was something that neither he nor I would ever really get past, but we were honoring her memory, I thought, by going on and being strong and taking care of ourselves. That's what Ricki would have wanted. Paul was pulling through and though he was only ten years old, I was beginning to see less of the kid and more of the man he was to become.

Later, after we had cleaned and oiled our weapons with Tuck and packed everything in the Jeep we thought we would need, I pulled Diane aside. "How do you feel about all this?" I asked her.

She pulled her long hair back and put it in a ponytail ring. "I feel like we're doing the right thing."

"You want to go?"

"Yes."

"Good. We need you. If you didn't want to, Jimmy would have to come."

"Jimmy needs a break, man. I think he's feeling his years."

I sat down by her. I smiled.

"What?" she said.

I laughed. "I had this real strange scenario in my mind when we went to the tower. I was certain that you and Tuck would hook up. Opposites attracting and all that."

"Matchmaking, eh?"

"I guess."

"No, I like Tuck, and maybe we would have gotten together if things were different. I was wild in the old days. Sex, drugs, and rock-n-roll, man." She shook her head. "But I've had to kind of reassess who and what I was. Things have changed. *I've* changed. I'm not the same person I was before. Are you?"

"No," I admitted. "And I never will be again."

The next morning before we left, Jimmy came over to me and said, "I don't want you worrying about anything here, Steve. I got the reins. I won't let go of them. You got my word on that."

"I know," I said. "I have complete faith in you."

"Good. I wanted to hear you say that."

We said our good-byes and Paul stood strong even when Maria broke down and started crying. Jilly and Paul kept her between them and she hung on tight. Jilly still wasn't talking much, but I could see in her eyes that she felt she was part of us now and it gave her strength and made us stronger. It was all good.

"Be careful out there," Jimmy said as I climbed into the Jeep.

We pulled away and he waved to us.

CEMETERY

We came into the Bronx on Broadway, creeping our way past Van Cortlant Park which looked like it had become some sort of immense tent city. We slowed down to see if we could see any life out there, but all we saw were the dead walking around. There were National Guard trucks parked and a few of them looked like they'd been hit by heavy fire, maybe artillery, but we saw no one living over there. Just the dead mulling about in packs. There were upwards of a hundred from what I could see at the park's outer edge.

The deeper we got into the city, the more it began to stink.

We were moving deeper into what had to be one of North America's biggest graveyards and it smelled like it. The air was hot and fusty, moist with the stench of putrefaction. It's hard to describe what that odor was like. Certainly it was overpowering and nauseating, but the combined stink of thousands, *millions*, of decomposing, unburied bodies was unimaginable and nearly indescribable. It was a fog of death, fuming and thick, a dirty, profane, *mean* smell of carrion boiled green in the hot sun, of husks bursting with maggots, human flesh gone to a liquid ooze of rot. Like some immense black cauldron of steaming, hot putrefaction boiling and bubbling and releasing a pandemic reek of simmering death.

We all smelled it and we recoiled from it.

We knew the smell of death by that point. Tuck had been a combat Marine in a jungle war. Riley was an inner city cop. I was an Iraq vet. We knew death. We knew its scent. And since Necrophage we'd come to know that scent on a very personal, almost intimate level...but this, Jesus, it was enough to put you to your knees and all I could think about was all those corpses, both walking and inanimate, and all the germs that must have been brewing. I thought that even if we completed our mission and got those poor women out of that awful place we'd be damned lucky to escape the city again without an infectious disease or a certain particularly nasty virus.

Tuck had cranked up the AC but it did little good. The air in the Jeep still smelled like spoiled pork only now it was cooler. I looked at all the tenements and high-rises and apartment buildings around us and imagined what it must have been like in them. The dead sequestered in them, slow-cooked in the ovens of those hotbox rooms. Some of them would never move, but others would. Others were moving right now. And we could see them. They were on the sidewalks and in the streets, shambling out of alleys and down steps, swarming in parks and vacant lots.

I saw packs of wild dogs running at our approach in lethal wolf packs. I saw a cat chewing on the face of a dead woman sprawled over a curb. That was bad enough in itself, but two children were gnawing on the woman's legs. I saw a man whose face had mostly rotted away, leaving him eyeless, look in our direction as we passed…then dip his head back into an abandoned baby carriage to feed on what was also abandoned in there. A little boy who was so mildewed it looked like he was wearing a fuzzy green T-shirt was squatting on the corpse of a man, trying to yank something free. As we passed he succeeded and shoved it into his mouth: the man's tongue. I saw a woman standing there, her face white and expressionless, staring off in the distance as the little girl standing next to her gnawed at her wrist. And I saw the immense and bloated corpse of man leaking a foul black fluid that a teenage girl lapped up like a dog. When we passed, she looked up and her face was a mass of feeding flies.

These are the things we saw.

The things we came to know and bury deep within ourselves where they would haunt us forever, I imagined.

"Was it this bad when you escaped?" I asked Riley.

"Yeah. It was this bad." She looked out the windshield at two of the dead dragging a legless corpse behind them. "I don't know…I hate to say it, but it might even be worse and I didn't think that was possible."

Tuck moved us forward, taking it slow because zombies were in the streets and they had no fear or understanding that the Jeep would smash them down.

"Did you have any family?" I asked her.

"Yes. I had a husband. He got the virus right away," she told me. "By then I knew what was happening, so I had him taken away to be incinerated. He wasn't even dead twenty minutes. I couldn't bear the idea of…"

"I know."

"How about you?"

I swallowed. They always said that it was good to talk about loss, to share your pain, but I wasn't so sure. Riley watched me with moist dark eyes that held leagues of pain and leagues of understanding. So I told her about Ricki. I spoke in low tones so as not to make Tuck and Diane uncomfortable in the front seat. I'm sure they were anyway. But I told Riley all there was to tell and somewhere during the process she reached out and took my hand and held it in her own, gripped it as if she were trying to infuse me with some of her own strength, and I could almost feel it running into me. She held my hand for a long time after my tale was told and I looked at her brown hand holding my white one and I thought of all the black/white racial bullshit that had come down for so many years. It was only now as the world we knew was trembling on the edge of the pit that I could see it with true clarity and recognize the absurdity of it all.

She looked at our hands, too, then she looked at me and I think she was thinking the same thing.

Tuck slowed down and it wasn't for the zombies but for the wrecks. Broadway was a sea of cabs, trucks, buses, and cars. They were bumper to bumper, all jammed together in a silent train of mangled metal and chipped paint. There was a path cut through them and cars had been heaped on top of other cars and I wondered if maybe somebody had come through here with a big front-end loader and cleared the way. Many of the cars were blackened from fire. Some were twisted or flipped over, hoods crumpled and windshields shattered. I saw bodies in those cars, all of them withered down to husks and skeletons with wide screaming jaws. Birds—crows and ravens and buzzards—were perched atop cabs and peering from the missing windows of trucks. Some were feeding on what was inside.

At the intersections it was often much worse—rivers of cars smashed into other rivers of cars. It was like some mass exodus had occurred (I didn't doubt that), everyone trying to escape at the same time and I could just imagine what it must have been like: the flaring tempers, the road rage, the fighting and battles waged amongst the auto graveyard. A lot of those people would have been infected. Many would have been stark raving mad. Some of them might have even been trying to smuggle their dead loved ones from city so the authorities did not burn them. A lot of those loved ones would have reanimated in backseats and trunks. And zombies, of course, would have pushed in from every direction when they realized people were trapped, that there was no escape from the madhouse for them.

Hearses, that's what we were seeing.

The world's largest collection of hearses locked in a traffic jam of immense proportions.

"It's worse in Manhattan," Riley told me. "A lot worse from what I've been hearing. I can't even imagine what it must be like there."

"And the militias and the Army have been fighting over…*this?*" Tuck said. "Bomb it flat. Burn it. That's what I say. Fuck yes. This ain't nothing but an open grave, man."

He was right. And once we got the women out, they could do just that as far as I was concerned.

I watched the cars as we passed. Windshields were threaded with cracks, many of them splattered and stained with old blood. Corpses hung out of windows. Some were headless and others chewed right down to the vertebrae. I wondered if some mop-up crew had passed through, wasting the dead as they fed. I saw a minivan with a spiderwebbed driver's side window. There was a corpse on the other side of it that had apparently impacted with the window at considerable velocity because it looked like its head had exploded behind the glass like a very ripe and very wet honeydew melon.

"Kingsbridge Ave is coming up," Riley said.

Tuck was watching for it, guiding the jeep through that narrow avenue of Detroit steel. Now and again a few of the dead would see us and come over, beating their hands against the steel plating.

"How are you doing?" I asked Diane.

She looked back at me and what was in her eyes told me all I really had to know. She was doing about as good as I was doing which wasn't very good at all. Even though we were probing deeper into the wormy carcass of the city and were no doubt in incredible danger, I was worried about Paul. And Maria. And Jilly. And Jimmy. Had we made the right decision leaving them behind? I thought so…yet I was nagged by guilt.

All I could think of was seeing my boy again. Nothing else remotely mattered and I knew right then I'd claw my way through a million rotting zombies to get to him if I had to.

IN THE STREETS OF THE DEAD

We got lucky when Tuck cut over on West 236th to Kingsbridge Ave. There were wrecks and pile-ups everywhere, but there was still a passable lane down the middle of the street and the farther we went the fewer vehicles we saw. But, on the other hand, the farther we went the more of the walking dead there were. And nearly all of them paused in what they were doing to watch us drive on by. Two of them decided to meet the Jeep head-on and Tuck ran them down. It was amazing (and maybe even a little disturbing) how desensitized we were all becoming. We didn't even cringe at such a thing anymore.

Tuck took his time getting us down the Ave so we didn't smash into any abandoned or wrecked vehicles, yet he maintained enough speed that the deadheads didn't pay too much attention and mount some organized attack. As we drove I noticed something that I had not seen before: the zombies were armed. No, not with guns or anything, but some were carrying clubs and sticks, lengths of rebar. I saw one of them with a baseball bat. We were still talking rudimentary weapons that any jungle ape could use, but I hadn't seen that before and I didn't like it.

Leave it to urban zombies to arm themselves.

I mentioned it to Riley but she'd seen it before.

We came upon the Precinct house and there were zombies everywhere. They were in the streets and on the sidewalks, clustering in parking lots. I didn't like the idea of getting out of the Jeep in a situation like that. Tuck kept driving until we found what looked like an old public service garage set just back from the road.

"That's it," Riley said. "That's where they are."

"Let's cross our fingers that nobody took them," Diane said.

Tuck pulled into the drive before the doors and Riley and I jumped out with our CAR-15s. There were zombies out in the street, seven or eight of them, but they hadn't picked up on what we were doing yet. We had to move fast and I knew it. It was dangerous as hell and I figured we'd get our asses smoked at any time. We sidled alongside the building and down a narrow passage between it and the building next door. Once we got in there, the dead came.

First it was one or two and we shot them down.

Then a dozen came striding in to meet us. We put down four of them before the others got too close for comfort. Three of them were cops and from the way Riley gasped, I had a pretty good idea that she had known them in life. When they came at us, hands raised like claws...she hesitated. I shoved her out of the way and dropped two of them with nice headshots and most of the others immediately dropped and began to feed on them, tearing open their bellies and stuffing themselves with the entrails that spilled out.

The third cop kept coming.

I shot him in the face, but it wasn't a good shot. His lower jaw was blasted away and it was a ghoulish sight to see him coming on in his filthy, gore-clotted blues, nothing below his upper jaw but a squirming black tongue. With the second shot I dropped him.

"Sorry," Riley said, then she opened up on the others and we made them all into cold, unmoving corpses again.

We leaped over them and got to the side door.

Locked.

"You don't have a key do you?"

Riley almost smiled, blowing the lock off with her CAR-15. As she did so, I saw another four zombies coming at us. And if we had waited five minutes, the four would have become fourteen and the fourteen would have become thirty. It was insane. But they would just keep coming and coming and I knew it. They would drown the world in their numbers.

We got through the door, shut it, shoved a huge metal desk covered with dust and papers against it to keep the dead out.

"What now?" I said.

"In here," Riley told me, going through an archway and into the garage itself which was huge and almost Romanesque with its high vaulted ceiling. It smelled of ancient gasoline and grease.

There were dark oil stains on the concrete. I saw two pick-up trucks...and on the other side, the four Strykers. They were still there and what a sight they were. I stood silently, just admiring them, a hundred memories of the war flooding through me and making me almost dopy, a silly sort of half-grin on my face.

"Are these the ones you wanted?"

"Oh yeah," I said. "If they're in good shape, we're golden."

Stryker Vehicle
Type: Armored Fighting Vehicle
Weight: 19 tons
Length: 22 feet
Operational Range: 312 miles
Armor: 14.5 mm

I approached them, noticing that three of them had their .50-cal machine guns and grenade launchers mounted. Both the .50-cals had ammo belts hanging from them and they were ready to rock. That's exactly what I wanted to see. The fourth vehicle was the Stryker ATGM (Anti-Tank Guided Missile) variant. The launchers were armed with TOW missiles. That was more firepower than we needed.

"If they turn over and we've got fuel, plenty of ammo, then there's nowhere in the city we couldn't go."

"Great," Riley said, sighing, relieved that we had a chance of success now.

"Do you know why they're here?"

"Not sure," she said. "But I heard a rumor that if it got bad, that they would use these to put down the unfriendlies with."

TOW missiles? Apparently they were expecting real trouble.

She shrugged. "That was one story. Another was that the military were hiding vehicles and ordinance around the city for emergencies."

It was kind of a surreal moment for me hooking back up with Strykers again. I remember when my ETS (Estimated Time of Separation) came around in Iraq. I'd ended up there for nearly eighteen months because of the Pentagon's Stop-Loss program which wouldn't let guys like me go home like they were supposed to—we called it the Back-Door Draft. But when that day finally came and my ETS was not changed for what felt like the fifth time, I remember feeling naked when they took my weapons from me, and oddly lonely when I was separated from my platoon and our Strykers.

These are the things that ran through my head and if I hadn't been daydreaming and maybe paying attention to my surroundings as I was trained to do, I would not have been caught unprepared when I was attacked. One of them had gotten in there and I didn't know how, but he charged out at me from around the back of the second Stryker.

He was on me before I could even hope to draw my weapon.

It happened very fast.

It took both Riley and I by surprise. It was a little boy, naked, his flesh ulcerated with gaping holes that his bones stuck through. His face was a pallid mask, his eyes like white marbles. He dove at me and I went down with him on top of me. He was hissing and gnashing his jaws, wanting nothing more than to sink his teeth in me. I held him away from me by the shoulders, his lips gone like so many of the others, his teeth bared, his head snapping from side to side. He wasn't very strong, but he was motivated to feed on me and that added a little something extra…just a deranged, starving animal.

Riley didn't dare shoot with us being in such close proximity.

Instead, she kicked him in the side of the head and he rolled off me. By the time I got to my knees and Riley drew her weapon he was already on me. He clawed at me and snapped at me. I sidestepped his lunge and caught him off balance. Before he could recover, I grabbed the hair on the back of his head and drove him into the armored plating of the Stryker again and again and again until his skull came apart, loose and sloppy under my fist, gore and brain matter leaking from his head.

Then I got away from him and Riley drilled him with three rounds point blank and that finished him.

"Thanks," I said, panting.

I heard Tuck yelling over the walkie-talkie and I got on there and told him it was cool, to get ready to drive in.

"We got maybe fifteen of them out here circling around us," he said. "Be ready to bust caps."

We went over to the big garage door. I unlocked it. "Ready?" I said.

Riley had her weapon up in a shooting stance. She nodded.

I gripped the hand-pull on the garage door and pushed it up with everything I had. It rode on tension springs so it did most of the work itself. The Jeep was a couple feet from the door. I gave it room and Tuck pulled it in. Riley and I dropped six zombies and hobbled a couple more, then I grabbed the rope and shut the door. And locked it. Safe and sound. For now.

Tuck pulled the Jeep over by the pick-ups and Diane and he stepped out.

I climbed up on the first Stryker and checked it out. It had power and a full tank of fuel so we were in good shape. In the back where an infantry squad of nine men would wait until it was time to deploy, I found more goodies. Six boxes of .50-cal ammo, an M240 Bravo 7.62mm machine gun and six boxes of ammo for it. I was glad to see the ammo boxes stored back there because in Iraq they were bolted to the outside of the vehicle and it meant you had to retrieve them under fire sometimes. I found some more MREs, probably left there by the crew, water, rain ponchos and tarps. I unwrapped the M240 and it was in nice shape. I was glad of that. It was intended as a squad gun that could be mounted outside at the back air guard hatch to provide covering fire for the troops when they deployed off the ramp. I had no intention of mounting it. We would use the .50-cal which could be operated from the Remote Weapons Station at the commander's chair. That way we could keep a very low pro to and from the school.

I went up front to the gunner's station where the TC, Truck Commander, would sit. I turned on the screens and we still had satellite because the video mapping system was operational. Using the gunner's screen, you could swing the .50-cal above in a 360° arc. There were also ten periscopes that would allow you to see in any direction. And if that failed, you could always stick your head up out of the TC hatch. I checked the .50-cal above. I did a complete inventory and systems check on the second, third, and fourth vehicles and we were in good shape. As an added incentive, I found that they all had AT4 anti-tank weapons. That gave us serious artillery if needed.

"Well?" Tuck said.

I smiled. "We're ready to rock. Come aboard."

I dropped the ramp in the back of the first Stryker and gave my "squad" a guided tour.

MOVEMENT TO CONTACT

We rolled out thirty minutes later when I had drilled everyone on what they would need to do. I made sure everyone could drive the Stryker and use the .50-cal on the gunner's screen and access the grenade launcher. There wasn't that much to it, really. Like everything else in the Army, the Strykers were designed so that anyone could pretty much operate them. I took the driver's seat and Tuck and Riley were at the gunner's station, familiarizing themselves with it. She knew the way over to the school very well but she navigated me using the mapping system which I think she got a kick out of. Generally, the TC was the commander, the senior guy and he sat at the gunner's station, but we were real liberal as far as rank went.

I pulled the Stryker out of the garage, stopping so the back end was only a foot or so from the garage door. Tuck climbed up out of the back air guard hatch, grabbed the bottom of the door and pulled it down. The springs did the rest, slamming it into place. We had already locked it so the deadheads didn't get in there and mess with the other Strykers or the Jeep. We had every intention of coming back for them.

The dead pushed in from the streets as I roared out there. I told Tuck and Riley not to waste ammo until we had to. Twenty or thirty zombies got in my way and I knocked them aside or rolled right over the top of them.

The Strykers were really something and if you surfed the internet back in the Before Times (as I was now mentally referring to the good old pre-zombie days) then you would have seen plenty of trash being talked about how the Strykers were no good and the Army was wasting money on them. But for us, the guys who used them in the Sandbox, we had absolute faith in them. I'd seen Strykers get hit by IEDs. Sometimes they flew up in the air and sometimes they rolled, but the crews were usually intact outside of a few cuts and bruises. I always felt sorry for the guys in Humvees because those things were nothing but death traps. When an IED was detonated under them, it was a massacre. You'd find nothing but a burning frame and some blackened skeletons that had once been human beings. The Strykers, on the other hand, could usually take IEDs and hits from RPGs and still keep rolling. They had a steel shell surrounded by Kevlar with ceramic plates on the outside. The plates would take the blast and shatter and that was the beauty of it because the plates were replaceable. A couple hours after a good hit, the mechs would put new plates in place and you'd be rolling. The Stryker was eight-wheeled, four-wheel drive with eight-wheel drive optional. There wasn't much they couldn't go through.

I knew the zombies never stood a chance.

The real danger would be when we dropped the back ramp or climbed through one of the hatches and exposed ourselves. Other than that and barring an airstrike, our shit was pretty safe.

We saw zombies everywhere. I was beginning to think there probably wasn't a more dangerous place on earth than New York City, as far as the undead were concerned. I didn't imagine LA or Chicago was any better and maybe there were worse cities, but what we saw was plenty. There were car pile-ups and wrecks, traffic jams of dead yellow cabs, lots of corpses and parts of them. Most of the wrecks we just plowed right through with the Stryker, but there were a few we had to go around. I saw entire neighborhoods that were bombed to rubble, others that were burned down to skeletal frameworks. Certain streets were riddled with bomb craters. I saw blackened LMTV deuce-and-a-half trucks and Humvees riddled with bullet holes. There had been battles fought and some of them must have been pretty damn intense.

On West 225th, a zombie army filled the street and I was estimating that there were well over a hundred of them. They shambled right at the Stryker and I called out to Tuck that we were about to take contact.

"Light their asses up," I said.

He got the zombies in the crosshairs on the screen and opened up with the .50-cal. The dead were torn literally in half and we drove straight through their wriggling remains and just kept going. Right before we hit the Major Deegan Expressway, two Humvees with mounted M240 Bravo squad guns came at us, opening up on us and, again, Tuck put the crosshairs on them and torn them apart. They were both smoldering with dead men hanging out of them as we passed. There's nothing more devastating than the fifty.

"What'd you make of that?" Tuck said.

"It wasn't the Army," I said. "They wouldn't come after a Stryker with nothing but a Bravo. They didn't even have a recoilless on them. My guess is that they're militia pukes."

"Roger that," he said.

West 225th became West Kingsbridge Road and then East Kingsbridge and I was pretty sure my crew was feeling what I was feeling by then: a mixture of fear and excitement and anxiety. I think if it hadn't been for the fact that I had a son out there to take care of, it would have been pure adrenaline-charged excitement. As we neared our target, I found myself falling into old habits, reaching for my caffeine pills to give me the edge for combat just as I had in the old days.

But we weren't in the Sunni Triangle and this wasn't Ambush Alley.

Our enemies weren't foreign insurgents or crazy Hajjis with AKs.

This was a different sort of war. I had to keep that in mind and not fall into old patterns. I focused my mind and became increasingly aware of my surroundings. More of the same. Shattered buildings, burned neighborhoods, wrecked cars and sprawled corpses chewed down to skeletons. Wild dogs, carrion birds, zombies, and the stink of open graves. Same old, same old.

I saw the armory in the distance and, like always, I thought it looked like something plucked from a European city with its spires and battlements. I saw twenty or thirty deadheads wandering around by it. Riley told me to hang a left and less than a minute later we passed the school. We went by it real slow so we could scope it out properly. I saw no signs that any of the ARM dipshits were hanging around. I saw a couple wrecked pick-ups in the courtyard but that was about it. The layout was exactly as she described it to us. The front gates were wide open and nearly torn from their hinges.

There were zombies everywhere.

I noticed with a passing chill that while most of them looked like they'd been just your average Joes and Janes in life, several were wearing camo fatigues and had probably been militia members.

"There's the alley on the right," Riley said and the excitement in her voice was almost palpable.

I guess I felt it, too.

Sitting around in a defensive position all the time is not a good thing. It's better to be on the offensive regardless of who—or *what*—your enemy is. Zombies got in the way and I knocked them down and aside, then, just as we'd planned, I brought the Stryker to a stop and backed into the alley so when we came out with the women we'd have a clear shot to the back ramp. We were about fifteen feet down from the entrance which would give Tuck a clear killzone. Right away, some of the dead came to investigate and he cut them down, giving the others something to chew on. It had already been decided that Riley and I would go after the women, so we got ready.

We put fresh magazines in our CAR-15s, grabbed flashlights and taped them to the barrels with duct tape, and waited at the air guard hatch. We each carried a satchel around our shoulders with MREs, water, extra CAR-15 mags, and some basic first aid items. Ten or twelve zombies were coming down the alley and Tuck swung the .50-cal around and chopped them down.

It was time to go.

Diane wished us luck and we climbed out of the rear air guard hatch and hit the alley running. The trapdoor to the steam tunnels was just ahead and we had to wade through the gore of the zombie carcasses that Tuck had blasted apart.

We got to the trapdoor which was iron rusted orange and we both began tugging on the ringbolt to lift the trap. It took some effort but we got it open just as six or seven of the dead moved in at us. Some of them were carrying crude clubs.

"Get your ass down already, dude," I heard Diane say over the walkie-talkie.

Clicking on our lights, we descended into the darkness.

TUNNEL RATS

Once Riley was down the metal rungs, I joined her and let the trapdoor slam down. The thing weighed over a hundred pounds and when it clattered shut it echoed through the tunnel system. There was a latch on the inside, but we lacked a peg to put through the ring.

Riley started searching around with her flashlight. "There's a piece of metal here somewhere," she said. "I had to work it free when we escaped."

Up in the alley I could hear the .50-cal barking. Several zombies thudded as they hit the top of the trapdoor.

"Got it!" Riley said, holding up a piece of iron about the size of a pencil.

I slid it through the loops, jamming it in place.

Between it and the fifty, we had some security. Now on to phase two. The tunnel was unbelievably claustrophobic. It smelled dank and dusty. I could hear water dripping somewhere and the occasional furtive scratching of rats. As we moved forward, Riley in the lead, our lights threw distorted shadows of us against the crumbling brick walls. A thin stream of water ran down the center of the floor and it smelled like rust and buried things.

"We're still under the alley," Riley said. "The tunnel is like an L, it'll cut to the right in minute or so."

She was right. We came to the bend in the L and made it around the corner. I had been smelling something a little bit worse than old brickwork and standing water and now we saw why: a corpse. No, two…then three corpses. They were sprawled on the floor and one was leaning against the wall in a sitting position. All of them wore the fatigues of the militia which were not US-issue or UK like ours but more like four-color Russian shadow camouflage with bands of black, indigo, and light blue. Probably military surplus like ours. I couldn't be sure what had killed them, not at first, but they were green with mold, their eyes rotted from their skulls.

"We're they here before?"

Riley shook her head.

"That means that the militia must have figured out the steam tunnels, too," I said. "They must have come for the women."

"But something got them."

The closer we looked we could see that they had been horribly chewed upon. Their throats and bellies were hollowed out. One of them was missing an arm. Some of that would have been the rats, but not all of it. I was trying to put together a scenario in my mind where these men had come after the women and been killed by zombies. But if that was the case…where were the zombies?

Riley looked tense. "You notice something?" she said, panning her light around. "No weapons. I can't believe they came in here unarmed. Somebody must have taken them."

I hoped it was the women, I dearly hoped so.

We moved on down the tunnel, our lights bobbing, fingers sweaty on the triggers of our CAR-15s. Side by side, pushing a wall of light before us we moved closer to our destination. Scenarios of what might have happened played through my mind again and again. I hoped we were not going to find something particularly ugly ahead. I didn't want all our efforts to end in disappointment or disaster. I hoped those women were all well…or as well as they could be locked in a cellar without food for all these days. The possibility of a grim discovery was very real and we both feared it as I think we had right from the beginning.

Our light found eyes.

Dozens and dozens of glittering pink-red eyes. Rats. There had to have been three or four dozen of them and they watched us coming on. They had no fear of us. Not immediately. The sight of all of them made my skin crawl. I began entertaining thoughts of them all attacking at once like in a paperback book by James Herbert or one of those guys.

But if I felt fear of them, Riley did not.

She was an inner city cop and to her rats were no more alarming than squirrels or horseflies were to a country boy. "Rats!" she said. *"Skit! Skit!"*

I don't know if it was the tone of her voice or her motions, but they took off squeaking at a good pace, running off somewhere in the depths of the network. We saw soon enough why they hadn't been so willing to leave: more corpses. I had a feeling these were the zombies that got the militia boys. The interesting thing was that they'd all been put down with heavy blows to their skulls. Their heads were split right open and pounded to hamburger. I counted six of them. They had been dead for weeks, I was guessing, but only recently had they stopped moving.

I had a new and optimistic scenario in my head.

The militia boys came down here to retrieve "their" women and some zombies followed. There was a battle. The militia lost. The dead fed upon them. The women beat the zombies to death with pipes or clubs. They took the guns with them and retreated to the cellar.

I was guessing that Riley was thinking the same thing because she grabbed me by the hand and towed me along at a pretty good clip. Either way, I figured she wanted this done with. If those ladies were dying or in rough shape we needed to get to them; if they were dead, we needed closure on this whole thing because we still had to fight our way free of the city.

"There it is," she said.

If this had been a steam tunnel back in the day then what we should have found was a grill or a mesh but what we were looking at was a circular iron hatch rusted just as orange as the trapdoor. Riley approached it carefully and I was right at her side, one ear perked up for sounds of life from the other side and the other ear listening for any unfriendlies behind us. I thought I heard something back there but I couldn't be sure.

"Help me," Riley said.

We gripped the edge of the hatch and tried to pull it but it wasn't moving. All we got for our efforts was orange dust on our fingers.

"There's a latch on the inside," she told me. "Somebody must have locked it."

Which made perfect sense, I suppose. Why leave it wide open?

Using the barrel of her CAR-15, Riley tapped on the door. *Boom, boom, boom,* it echoed through the tunnels like a metallic beating heart. "Hey! In there! It's me! It's Riley!" she called out, her mouth very close to the hatch. "I've come to get your asses out of there! Hey! Hey!" She pounded again and again and the noise echoed through the tunnels. She kept at it for over five minutes and with each passing second my heart sank. Even if the women were simply too weak to open the hatch, there was no way we could get to them. Just no way. We'd never get the damn thing open and we sure as hell couldn't shoot through it with 5.56mm.

"I hate to say it, but—"

"*Listen,*" Riley said.

I listened…and, yes, I could hear something on the other side. I was almost sure it was the whispering of several voices.

"Hey! In there!" Riley said, pounding on the door. "It's me Riley! Open up! I got a way out!"

"Riley?" said a voice through the hatch.

"Yes!"

There were voices from the other side and I felt relief sweep through me. As the latch was worked from within, and by the grunting and creaking I heard it was no easy bit, I began to hear other sounds. They were distant but echoing. I thought it was the .50-cal firing nonstop punctuated by the booming of grenades.

I got on the walkie-talkie. "Hell's going on?" I said.

The connection was rough, filled with static. I could barely hear Tuck: *"They're all over the damn place,"* he said. *"Hundreds…I mean fucking hundreds of 'em…"*

"Hang tight," I said. "They can't get inside the Stryker. Don't waste ammo."

"You take…all the fun out of life," came the reply.

Then Diane got on the box: *"They're everywhere in the alley,"* she said. *"We must…we must have dropped sixty or seventy of them and they're still coming. Don't try coming out yet…let me know when you do…they're fucking everywhere…"*

"Let 'em be everywhere," I told her. "Don't waste ammo."

The women were having trouble on the other side and whether that was from their weakened condition or just a real peckerwood of a bolt I did not know. But I did not like the idea of waiting in that tunnel. I just had the worst feeling about it.

And then:

"Watch it down there!" I heard Diane say over the walkie-talkie. *"They're tearing that trapdoor off. We're dropping 'em but they keep coming."*

"Just sit still and wait it out," I told her. "We'll be okay."

If they ran out of ammo, they'd have to go topside on the Stryker to reload the fifty and I didn't want either of them to attempt something like that. Tuck would know how to do it quickly, but it wasn't worth the risk. When the Strykers are closed up you could beat yourself bloody against the hatches and they still wouldn't open. It's how they were designed.

But we had our own trouble.

Diane came over the box and told me they were coming down, but I already heard the tell-tale clanging of the trapdoor. Within minutes and probably less, they would be swarming down here.

"If they don't get that fucking hatch open," I told Riley, "we're toast."

"They're doing their best!"

The seconds ticked by. I was tense from my toes to my scalp. I got down in a firing position behind Riley and waited. Sweat ran down my temples. I could hear them coming. At first it was the dragging footsteps of one or two but then it became the sound of an advancing army. I would see them anytime now, I knew.

Then I did.

The first few were men. One of them was a militia puke whose fatigues were black and brown with some kind of morbid drainage. The second was a barefoot man in a business suit with some kind of fungus on his face that was eating it away. I clicked the CAR-15 on semi-auto and put both of them down with nice economical headshots. They fell on top of each other twitching. Four more showed, then a pack of a dozen or more behind them. Their mouths were open, teeth gnashing, eyes the lusterless white of the bellies of dead fish.

I stood up.

No fancy trick shooting now.

Full auto rock 'n' roll. I fired three-round bursts in the directions of their heads and skulls came apart like rotting pumpkins. The dead fell over each other, but they still poured forward, greedy for flesh, driven by that most basic of primal instincts: the need to feed. I must have dropped ten of them when the hatch opened and then Riley was pulling me in while I kept dropping them. Then a tidal wave of the dead surged forward with a sharp, gagging stench of putrescence. They would have buried me alive in their numbers.

Inside, we swung the hatch closed just as countless bodies hit it from the other side. It swung back. Riley, me, and three or four other women threw everything we had against it while another lady tried to get the bolt through the latch. It was a battle. The door would swing in and then we would push it back. We gave inches and we took them. Dead white hands clawed around the edge of the hatch. We hit it with everything we had and those hands were smashed to paste, fingers severed and the door shut. The bolt was slid in place and not a fraction of a second before they hit it again with such force it shook on its hinges and brick dust fell from the ceiling.

We were safe.

For a time.

I turned and looked at who we'd come to rescue and I saw maybe a dozen women standing there by the light of a lantern. They wore ragged, filthy clothes. Their faces were dirty and bruised, seamed with scratches and cuts, their eyes huge and empty, cheeks hollow.

Riley said, "Steve, meet the girls."

And they swept forward.

THE BARRICADED

I hate to say it, but when those poor creatures came at me I pulled back because I was honestly afraid. They did not smile. They did not emote. They came at me like mannequins. They looked barely human. I was looking into faces that were a catalog of human suffering. Their eyes were stark and fixed and I thought for one crazy moment that I had been led into some kind of crazy trap. Those faces…dear God…they took my breath away and made me feel weak in the knees. These were the faces you saw peering through chainlink fences during World War II at places like Auschwitz and Mauthausen. That's how they looked: like survivors from a death camp.

Then they took hold of me and Riley as she explained we were there to get them out. They took hold of us and held onto us and would not let go. Many of them were sobbing. It was singularly the most touching and despairing moment of my life.

ARM.

The American Resistance Movement.

They'd done this.

They'd kept these women like animals.

They'd caged them and abused them, violated and degraded them. I swore to myself at that moment they would fucking pay for this. That I would not distinguish between the walking dead and those animals who pretended to be human beings. I would slaughter them all. At least the zombies had an excuse.

That fucking militia had none.

Rounds of introductions were made. There were so many names and faces it became a blur in my mind. Some of them were as old as forty and others were only twelve or thirteen. Only eleven of them were still alive. The others had died from disease and infection and were buried beneath the dirt floor of the next room. The disgust and anger and horror I felt was limitless and the pity I felt for these poor ladies was boundless. The one woman who really stood out was a tough scrappy Latino named Sabelia Cortez. She had choppy black hair and huge dark eyes. She had a beautiful face that was marred by nicks and contusions and what looked like a knife scar that ran across the bridge of her nose to one cheekbone.

She walked right up to me when the others had parted. She had not been part of the welcoming committee. She got in so close I thought she was going to hug me, but instead she took my hands in her own and said, "You are a soldier that has come to fight. I will fight with you. I will die by your side."

Then she pulled back, but after that she never really did leave my side. For some reason, she connected with me immediately and had adopted me and she was Robin to my Batman or the other way around.

The zombies continued to beat on the hatch, but it was holding.

We opened our packs of MREs and fed the girls and gave them water. I had never seen anyone in my life enjoy food as much as those ladies did. At first they chewed and swallowed without tasting, but after a few minutes they slowed down and savored every bite. And I swear by the time they were done—and they ate every scrap we'd brought with us—they all looked better. Something human came back into their faces and their eyes softened.

One of them, a tall blonde whose face was dark with ground-in dirt, scraped and swollen, came up to me and threw herself on me. I wasn't sure if she was attacking me or being romantic. When she tried to get her tongue in my mouth I knew it was the latter. The others pulled her away and she broke down crying.

"Stop it," Sabelia told her.

Katherine, a tall regal-looking redhead who seemed to be the leader, said, "That's Anna. She's not right since…since what they did to her. They broke her in so many ways. I don't know if she'll ever be right again."

"She thinks you'll take care of her and protect her if she…you know," Sabelia said.

It was heartbreaking. There was no other word to describe the defilement of Anna and the others. It made me sick to my stomach. I wanted to go to each and every one of them and tell them that it would be okay now, that I would never let them be hurt again…but

I couldn't. I couldn't promise them anything like that much as I wanted to. I mean, who was I kidding here? We were in a real fix, a real bind. We were stuck smack dab in the center of the mother of all clusterfucks. We couldn't slip out through the tunnel. And from what I had seen of the school courtyard, there was just no way we'd make it through hundreds of those dead things.

Katherine filled us in on a few things. As far as she knew the militia pukes were all dead. Most had been slaughtered out in the courtyard (she figured) but she had heard a helicopter so some of them might have been plucked off the roof. A few tried to get in the other day but the zombies got them. They heard them screaming in the tunnel. Katherine, Sabelia, and a few others went out and found the militia men dead and the zombies feeding on them. They broke their heads open with pipes and chair legs. They had their guns now—three bolt-action Rugers and a pair of AK-47s, a couple .45s—but they hadn't tried to get upstairs. Not yet. That had been next on the agenda for they were in a position by the time we arrived that they simply couldn't afford to wait anymore, zombies or no zombies.

"Are the dead up there?" I said. "Are they inside?"

"We can hear them walking around now and again."

I heard Tuck on the walkie-talkie. "We're okay," I told him. "We found the women and they're alive—" I hesitated to say *they're fine* because I knew better "—but there's no way we can get back through the tunnel."

"Roger that. What's your plan?"

"Not sure yet. What's your situation?"

There was silence for a moment. Then a crackle of static. *"We got shit-eaters thick as flies. They can't get at us but I don't think we can get at you either. I'm open to suggestions."*

"I'll get back to you," I told him.

I pulled Riley over with Katherine, Sabelia, and a couple others. I told them that the only thing we could do was try to get up there. Go through the school, kill the deadheads, and see if we could get ourselves in some room maybe up on the second floor where we could do some shooting. Maybe thin the herds and then call in the Stryker, evac our asses out the back door.

I saw no other alternatives.

We then shared the plan with the others. They were all for it. Anna didn't really understand, but that was okay. A couple others were out of their heads, too, but we'd just point them in the right direction. First off, it was a matter of which girls would be armed. Sabelia and another woman named Carrie took the AKs. I had the feeling they were both urban girls who'd come up hard in the wrong neighborhoods. Katherine took one of the .45s and a plucky teenager named Ginny took the other. They'd both used guns before. The bolt-action Rugers were given to three others—Susan, Mia, and Dorian. The latter had grown up on a farm and hunted with her brothers, the other two were country girls and rifles were nothing new to them. The problems were that while the .45s had full clips, only one of the Rugers had a full magazine of five rounds. One of them had three and the other only had two. Not good. The AKs had thirty rounds in their mags when they were full, but both only had half that. I instructed the girls to fire only on semi-auto. Headshots.

"All right," I said. "Let's do this."

The women made ready and I don't think I ever saw a more determined squad. I led them up the stairs to the door. We all got real quiet then, listening. We couldn't hear a thing, but the stink of the dead was heavy.

I pulled out my Sig-Sauer and blew the lock and faceplate off the door.

I looked back and Sabelia was grinning. She was ready for a good fight.

I didn't think she was going to be disappointed.

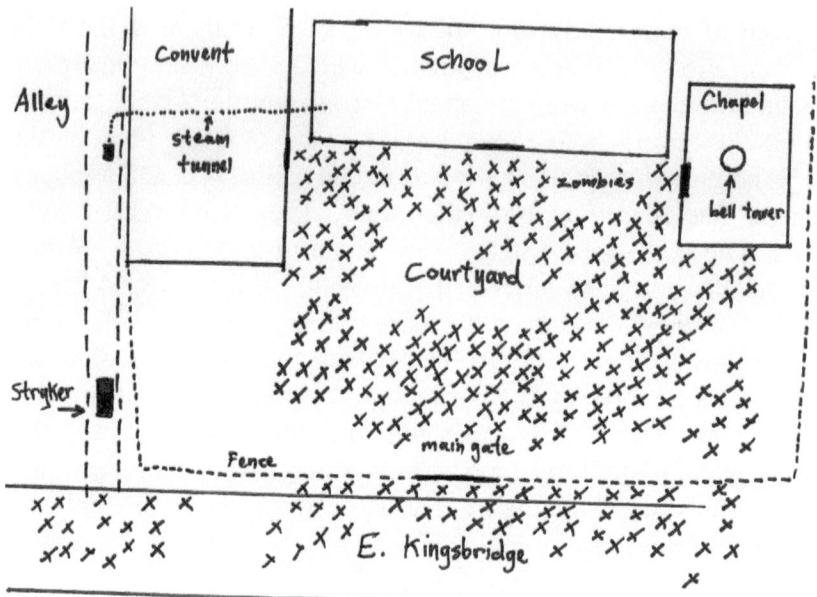

BREAKOUT

It was calm when we got upstairs. I saw nothing or no one. We found a few cadavers that were nearly stripped to skeletons. They had been militia pukes. There were bulletholes in the walls and doors. We found another AK but it had been used to beat off attackers and was pretty mangled. The good thing was we found three full magazines in an ammo pouch.

I led the girls down the corridor that Katherine told me led to the entrance hall and the old office wing. The school had closed down about five years before Necrophage and had sat empty all that time. As we walked I could hear pigeons cooing somewhere above us and I saw little piles of rat droppings in corners. What we were facing I knew was pretty much insurmountable but we had little choice. The dead had the numbers and all we had was reasoning. It would have to do.

I came to the end of the corridor and Riley told everyone not to bunch-up together too much. We might need fighting room. I was in the front with Sabelia and Katherine, Riley was in the back with the other armed women. Those who were too out of it to fight or didn't have weapons other than pipes or chair legs were in the middle: Anna and Leslie, Kasey and Brittany.

The door was ajar.

We stopped and listened.

I came forward and pushed the door open gently, deciding against a dramatic kick. Silence was important.

The door opened and I went through it and a zombie was standing there like he'd been waiting for me and maybe he was. My stomach jumped.

He was a big guy, utterly naked, gnawing on the gristle of a bone. He saw me and came at me, tossing the bone aside now that he had something better. He was barely four feet from me and there was no time to aim. I opened up and drove him back with a three-round burst to the belly that split him right open and made his intestines come snaking out. He stumbled back, groping at his own guts and wondering maybe if they were tasty.

I shot him in the head.

Anna made a whimpering sound.

Sabelia told her to shut up.

We moved into the entrance hall and I saw that the front door was half-open and then it opened all the way as a group of the dead came to investigate the sounds. We spread out and fired, putting them down, but six or seven more crowded in and I could see that there were dozens more coming up the steps.

Dorian cried, "Look out!" as several more came down the opposite corridor. Sabelia fired, pushing them back, correcting her aim and dropping two of them. I got the third. Dorian shot another coming down the steps from the second floor and it was a perfect shot. The zombie rolled down the stairs.

And then things got real hairy.

We had them pouring in from the front door and coming down the other corridor. A pair of them came out of the offices. We started shooting. Some of the girls bunched in the middle were freaking out. Anna was screaming. The entire thing lasted about fifteen seconds, I'll bet, but it was a very frightening and tense fifteen seconds and we spent a lot of ammo. When you're in the middle of the shit, going at it hot and heavy in a firefight, there's no time to account for everything that goes on around you. The lead is flying and you're trying to cover your sector and hoping like hell everyone does the same. I drilled a woman who was carrying a butch knife right in the forehead, spraying her brains onto three more who were not bothered by it at all. I dropped a mammoth guy that looked like some kind of biker, two elderly women, and a teenage girl still wearing a hospital johnnie.

And as I was shooting, I nearly got bitten by a little girl who came crawling on all fours through the legs of the adults. She was about two feet away when I punched her ticket.

Like I said, a wild fifteen seconds.

When it was over, there were corpses all around us.

One of the younger girls let out a cry and ran for the door. She got past me before I could stop her.

"TERESA!" Katherine called.

Too late. In her hysteria she threw herself out the door right into a pack of ten hungry ghouls. And maybe that act saved us. I don't know. But there were forty or fifty more coming and the feeding slowed them.

"GET TO THE STAIRS!" I shouted.

Katherine and Riley got them moving and Dorian dropped another zombie that came down the other corridor.

They started up and two more came down for them.

Mia and Susan drilled them. One of them rolled down the stairs dead, but the other came down with its throat split open, biting and snapping. Katherine shot it in the head.

And I say *it* here because they were both so badly decayed it was really hard to tell whether they were animal or vegetable, let alone man or woman.

Riley led the girls up the stairs past the corpses and at the top a little girl stood there with a hatchet in one hand. She was dressed in the shredded remains of a nightgown that was filthy with the stains of what she'd been feeding upon. She was deathly white, almost phosphorescent it seemed, something accentuated by the red gore staining the hatchet and splattered right up her arm to her elbow. Her lips were chewed away. She hissed through blood-caked teeth.

Riley fired a single round at her.

Her head exploded with gouts of fluids and tissues and she was tossed back by the impact.

Riley was telling everyone to get up the stairs, *"HURRY! HURRY! GET THE FUCK UP HERE!"* Katherine was forcing them from the bottom, pushing and shouting at them until they were moving at a good pace. Sabelia and I, of course, had made the cardinal error of turning away from the door for a moment and that's when Ginny came at us with the .45 raised.

I thought she was going to shoot me.

Then she fired and a zombie dropped dead behind me.

They started pouring through the doorway.

Sabelia and I raced up the stairs as the zombies flooded in. I don't know how many of them there were, but it was enough to give me the cold sweats. Thirty? Forty? Fifty? They flooded the entrance hall and just kept coming and coming. I dropped five or six of them to tangle some bodies up at the bottom of the steps and it worked long enough for us to join the others in the corridor above.

Which was full of more zombies.

While Katherine and a couple others got most of the women into a classroom that was clean of the dead, the rest of us opened up with everything we had. We dropped a dozen and a dozen more surged at us. The bolt-action rifles were emptied and as a zombie came forward, Dorian split its head with the stock of her rile. Carrie covered her, dropping three more and then it was pretty much a rear guard action as we backed into the classroom, Sabelia and I providing cover for the others.

That's when Leslie (whose mind was pretty much gone) slipped past me, trying to break free. I watched a zombie grab her. He broke her over his knee and bit right into her throat. I hesitated, but Sabelia did not—she opened up and killed both of them.

I fired to the left and to the right and when Sabelia tried to come out and fight with me, I shoved her back in. "GET INSIDE! GO!" I cried and dropped a few more until my mag was empty. Then I jumped through the door and it was slammed shut and locked. Thank God, it had a lock. To reinforce it, we pushed a few desks in front of it. There were half a dozen stored in there.

At first, the dead amused themselves by fighting over the remains of their fallen comrades. While they were so entertained, I went over to the windows that looked out over the courtyard. Riley was already there. She looked positively gray.

Jesus.

I looked out and there were hundreds of zombies down there. It looked like the crowds at a rock concert. And all of them seemed to be pushing towards the doors below.

We had to have a plan and we had to have one now.

But I was fresh out of ideas.

Then the dead began pounding on the door.

HIGH-WIRE ACT

I made myself calm down and think.

The only edge we had on them was our brains and we had to use them. That was the important thing and sometimes the very hardest thing to do. In any contest of survival, it's the guy or gal that uses their head that's going to come out on top and prevail. I'd pretty much learned that in Iraq and I'd been learning it only too well since Necrophage. The problem was in a survival situation the tendency to freak out and panic becomes overwhelming at times.

"They get through that door and we're cooked," Dorian said.

"I'll kill 'em," Susan said. "I'll kill 'em with my bare fucking hands if I have to."

I liked her gumption. Sometimes raw attitude will shift the insurmountable in your favor.

"There's got to be something we can do," Katherine said.

Tuck came over the walkie-talkie: *"You still in one piece, bro?"*

"So far."

"You come up with anything?"

"Not yet."

Sabelia then called me over to the window. "There's a way out," she said. "But it's risky."

She slid the window open and I looked out of it with her, both sticking our heads out, trying not to look at the crowds of mulling zombies below. I knew what she was talking about right away. The ledge that ran beneath the window was a good one as far as ledges went. It was about two-feet wide, plenty to stand up on and hold your balance. When I was a kid in Yonkers my buddies and I used to sleep out in tents in backyards and go over to our school and climb up to the second story ledge and walk around the building. It was stupid and suicidal, but that ledge had been maybe a foot and this thing was twice as wide.

"We get out there," Sabelia said. "We might make that roof over there."

I craned my head out as much as I dared and saw what she was talking about. The ledge fronted the building for about thirty feet and ended at the brick face of a flat-roofed addition that came pretty close to the roof of the chapel. I saw something down there. Something red spanning the addition roof and the chapel roof. I couldn't see exactly what it was from that angle. A pipe? I couldn't say. But if we could get down there and shimmy across...

"I'm going down there," I said.

"I'll come," Sabelia said.

"You don't have to."

"I want to."

I explained things quickly to Katherine and the others and I could see they weren't crazy about our plan. It was like walking the tight-rope over a crocodile pit. But it was our only chance and they knew it.

I got on the box. "Hang tight," I told Tuck. "We might have a plan."

"About fucking time," he said.

I handed Sabelia my CAR-15 and eased myself out on the ledge. For a second there I experienced terrible vertigo but I forced it from my head. If this was a two foot plank laying on somebody's lawn I knew I'd have no problem walking it, so why should I have a problem with it out here? I tried to keep that in my mind. I knew from ledge-walking in my youth that there was only one "safe" way to do it: you put your back against the wall and arched it slightly so you were just leaning back a bit. That threw your center of gravity at the wall and not out into space.

Okay.

It was a typical inner city ledge: stained with pigeon shit and a few stray feathers. I saw cracks running through it and I prayed it would hold. I shimmied over away from the window and Sabelia handed me out my weapon and her AK-47. She climbed out and with such ease I figured she was part ape.

"We used to do this kind of shit all the time when we were kids," she told me and I laughed.

"Me, too," I said.

The most important thing in ledge-walking besides shifting your gravity against the building is not looking down. Isn't that a time-worn saying? How many old movies have you heard that on? *Whatever you do, pal, don't look down,* the heroic cop always tells the kid or the jumper he rescues. Looking down under any circumstances inspires vertigo. And looking down into a nest of swarming, flesh-eating zombies will inspire sheer terror…the kind that will make you fall.

"Well, let's go already," Sabelia said.

I had been hesitating, talking myself through the whole thing. Okay.

I sidled along the wall and at first I was moving at a snail's pace until I got my rhythm, then I started to move faster. In about five minutes we were at the addition. The roofline was about four-feet above the level of the ledge so I had to turn and face it, toss my rifle over, and pull myself up and over to join it. Easy. Sabelia did the same and we found ourselves on an ordinary rooftop with heating vents and an air conditioner, lots of stained pigeon shit. We walked over to the far side that ran parallel to the chapel roof.

A ladder.

The red thing I'd seen was a ladder.

One of those old wooden red firemen's ladders. It was about twenty feet long. There was a span of about fifteen feet between the two rooftops and somebody had laid it across there no doubt to escape with.

"The militia," I said.

Sabelia nodded.

"Some of them might be in the chapel," she said.

"Could be."

"Or it could be the other way around—maybe they'd used it to cross *from* the chapel."

Regardless, this was our way out. It was risky but it could be done. I walked back to where we'd climbed onto the rooftop. From there I could easily see the front of the chapel. The front doors were closed. They were huge, about fifteen feet high with massive brass hinges. Sabelia and I threw together a quick plan of action then I got on the box and told Tuck what I had in mind. He liked it. It was daring and crazy so, of course, he was all for it. And it meant plenty of action on his end.

"When I give you the call," I told him, "cut a path to us."

"Roger that shit, Booky."

Sabelia told me to stay on the rooftop. She would begin bringing the ladies over. She clambered over the wall and went back down the ledge in half the time it had taken me. I could hear them discussing it over there and there was a certain amount of swearing and arguing. Then Dorian came out followed by Susan then Mia and Carrie. I could see they weren't crazy about any of it. When Dorian got near to the wall, I took her rifle and pulled her over.

"Thanks," she said. "Hell of a time to mention it, but I'm terrified of heights."

"You did good."

"Something about zombies eating my ass inspired me," she admitted.

We helped the others onto the rooftop. Riley came next with Katherine. Anna was between them and they were each holding one of her hands which I didn't like at all because if she went, they went. I sweated it out the whole time until I pulled Riley over and got my hands on Anna. But she made it and so did Katherine. Then came Kasey and Brittany who were friends of some sort and held hands. Neither of them had spoken since we showed up in the cellar. I got them up and over and then Sabelia scrambled onto the rooftop.

There. We got that far.

The women all stood there looking at the ladder.

"I don't know about this," Dorian said. "I mean, shit, lookit 'em down there."

Yes, the zombies were everywhere. If one of us fell during the crossing we wouldn't even hit pavement there were so many of them. We'd be absorbed into their ranks. No, it was not a pleasant thought. But staying on that rooftop wasn't an option.

"Don't look down and you won't know they're there," Sabelia said.

Words of wisdom. I was studying the bell tower on the chapel. What we didn't need was for some crazy militia asshole to open up on us while we were crossing. I saw nothing up there and I hoped our luck would hold.

I handed my CAR-15 to Sabelia. "Here goes nothing, as they say."

I got on the ladder while it was held by Sabelia and Dorian. I gripped both handrails and kneeled on it, then I just sort of scooted myself across without ever once looking down. I made the other roof and wiped sweat from my face. Dorian, afraid of heights or not, came next. She came slower than I but she made it. Next came Carrie and Susan followed by Mia and Katherine. Kasey and Brittany came together, of course. Then it was just Sabelia and Riley over there with Anna.

"Come on, honey," Katherine coaxed her. "It'll be fine. I'll meet you half way."

I didn't care much for it but Katherine went back out there and even though Anna kept shaking her head, Riley managed to get her on the ladder. She crawled along right behind her. It was going to work. It was all going smoothly, I thought, and it was going to work.

Those thoughts barely crossed my mind when Anna fell.

She went over the side and hung by one hand, screaming and drawing the attention of those below. Riley got a hand on her, but she dropped away…right into that sea of zombies. We all saw them get her. Like meat in a piranha tank she was torn apart, split and ripped and dismembered until she was nothing but a huge clot of gore that disappeared in the zombie ranks.

There was nothing anyone could do.

We could say it was an accident in our minds, but was it? I was of the mind that she threw herself over and then, like many suicides, thought better of it at the last moment when it was just too damn late. Katherine and Riley got back over and Sabelia came across after tossing us our weapons.

I think we all took a deep breath at that moment and let it out slowly.

The rooftop of the chapel was flat, too, which was very much in our favor. The problem was the bell tower rose up twenty- or twenty-five feet above it.

Forming a chain, each holding onto the other's waist to give us strength and balance, I reached out and grabbed the ladder. When I yanked it free of the other roof it swung down and probably would have taken me with it if not for the girls holding onto me. We all pulled together and got the ladder over.

Then it was time to do some climbing.

OUT THROUGH THE IN DOOR

We brought the ladder up to the bell tower and stood it up at a slight cant against it. I went up first. I took my CAR-15 with me because honestly I didn't know what we were getting into. I went up the ladder slowly, amazed at the view I had up there. The ladder did not reach all the way to the belfry so I knew I was going to have to stand on the top rung and pull myself up and in. But after the ledge and the crossing…hell, it sounded like a piece of cake.

Riley and Sabelia stood below holding the ladder.

Near the top, I looked down and waved to them.

"Just get your ass up there, Sunshine," Riley told me.

Sabelia laughed as did some of the others.

I slung my CAR-15 by the strap over my shoulder and climbed up to the uppermost rungs. It was doable. I would get up there and then help the girls in. Simple enough. I took the CAR-15 and tossed it up into the belfry. I heard it clatter. I reached up in a delicate act of balance and gripped the outer ledge of the belfry.

And that's when I heard a sound.

The sound of the bolt being drawn back on my own rifle.

I was pretty much fucked.

One of the militia pukes looked over the edge and I was looking right down the barrel of my CAR-15. He was grinning. He was going to kill me. After all I'd been through, this weekend warrior goddamn amateur was going to kill me with my own weapon and the absolutely ironic thing was that I had given it to him.

I heard a *c-rack* sort of sound and I thought he had just blown me away but then I saw his head explode in an eruption of gore and he fell back into the chapel.

I looked down and Dorian pulled the rifle away from her chin. "My last bullet," she said. Maybe that girl had no true sniper training, but she knew the basics all right and was one hell of a shot. Growing up in the country will do that to you. But it was a natural talent, I knew. You could give twenty grunts rifles and drill them every day for a month and they still wouldn't be the kind of shot Dorian was.

"Thanks," I said.

She shrugged, *shucks, 'tweren't nothing.* I pulled myself up into the belfry and almost slid on the gore up there. A .30-06 full-metal-jacketed round really takes a head apart and was the bullet of choice for Marine snipers in Vietnam. I looked back down and watched the women coming up. When they got near the top they threw me their rifles and I set them aside. Dorian, Sabelia, Katherine, and Carrie were easy because they were very tall so you didn't have to reach down too far to get a hold of them. Brittany and Casey were both petite types and we had to practically dangle out in space to get a hold of them.

But we did it. We got everyone up there in one piece.

"We better go easy now," Katherine said. "If there's one militiaman here, there's bound to be others."

Warning to the wise.

There was no stairway leading to the belfry but a series of ladders that led down to the second floor. After what we'd been through it was no big deal. We heard or saw nothing on our way down. We gathered together in a little room at the bottom. I went over to the door and listened. It was quiet out there. I didn't hear a thing.

I turned off the walkie-talkie because stealth was going to be important now.

Sabelia threw open the door and I went out there in a crouch.

Nothing.

Just an empty hallway.

We started down it. At the end was a window and we could see the living dead down there. It seemed like there were more than ever. Sabelia led us down to the far end. We came around a corner and another empty corridor greeted us. We crept down it, thinking we were being very quiet and quite unseen. And that was our first mistake. Seeing the empty corridors I think we all relaxed a little too much. The first rule in a combat zone is to pay attention to your surroundings, scope out ambush sites and possible killzones, find places to hide in case the lead starts flying.

I knew that.

I'd been trained to do that.

I had survived the war by following those rules.

So I should have seen the partially opened door at the end and I should have seen the gun barrel poking out. But, God help me, I didn't. There was the report of a weapon and we all hit the floor. Katherine did, too, only she never got up again because she'd taken a slug right through the left eye.

Two more shots rang out, punching into the walls.

I saw where they came from and fired a three-round burst and with some accuracy because a man cried out. We put a few more rounds into the door. Sabelia, Carrie, and I crept over there. Without telling them a thing about tactics they both knew what to do. While Sabelia and I crouched down and made ready, Carrie kicked in the door the rest of the way.

I went in fast, scoping the room out in a split second.

There was a man in those Russian fatigues up against a wall radiator. He was hit in the chest. His fatigue shirt had gone red.

"Doctor," he said. "I need a doctor…please…"

His weapon, a Colt .357 was on the floor, forgotten now in his agony. I knew right then this guy was a fucking amateur like all the others. No matter how bad your wound was, if you were conscious you held onto your weapon. It was the only thing that stood between you and death sometimes.

"That's Tanner," Sabelia said with venom in her voice.

"Piece of shit," Carrie said.

The others had arrived and I could see by the looks on their faces that they all knew him and I knew without a doubt he was one of the animals that ran the little rape factory in the school.

"He was one of them," Dorian said.

I saw those women all staring at him, seething with hate, positively rabid with the need for vengeance. I'm glad they weren't directing it at me. They looked like animals ready to feed. This is the place in some crappy old war movie where the hero defends the bad guy against those he has treated like shit and put through hell. *We can't do that! It'll make us no better than him.* Shit. I'm no hero and I'll be the first to admit it.

I looked at the girls. "Wreak your vengeance," I said and stepped from the room.

I don't know what happened in there exactly and I didn't go back for a second look, but I heard that asshole scream. I heard him screaming his lungs out the way a lot of his victims must have and I felt no pity for him. What goes around comes around, as they say. After he had gone silent they were still kicking and stomping him in there until Sabelia said, *"Enough. He can't get any fucking deader."*

They came out and I asked no questions or made no judgments: what they had done was necessary. It was no more a crime than stepping on a spider that sank its fangs into your toe or a zombie that tries to tear out your throat. They had killed a parasite. Now they had closure of sorts and that was important for them and I could see it in their eyes: like after they had eaten, putting down that animal had mellowed something in them and let something else stretch and relax. That was good. All victims need this sort of catharsis and so few ever get it.

We found the stairs okay and we descended them unopposed. We saw no militiamen or zombies. The chapel was quiet as a chapel should be. While the main body of my little force waited near the steps with gunners in defensive posture, I took a walk over to the front doors. They were double doors, as I said, of good stout oak two inches thick with heavy locks in place. No wonder the zombies had never gotten in. They could have beat their fists to pulp without putting so much as a dent in the wood. Set up high to either side were narrow stained glass windows. I got on a little table and boosted myself up. The zombies were still there, so damn many of them. Through panes of yellow, blue, and red glass it was made all that much worse. But from what I could see none of the dead were near the chapel steps.

That was good.

I got on the walkie-talkie. "Okay, we're in place. Do your thing."

"Hell, yeah!" Tuck cried.

I got back up on the table. I wanted to see it happen…or what of it that I could. I heard the Stryker roar into life. I could only see a little bit of the street out in front of the school compound and there were zombies everywhere. The .50-cal started hammering and zombies started falling, torn into pieces. Then the grenades started dropping and there were a series of booming explosions that rattle the stained glass. I saw zombies blasted into rains of flesh and blood and then the Stryker was nearing the gates. The .50-cal barked again and two dozen zombies just inside the gates were pulverized and then more grenades landed in the compound. These were incendiaries and roaring blankets of flames burst engulfing the dead. Countless zombies were trying to escape, many of them burning.

Tuck drove right through curtains of fire, rolling over burning zombies, swinging around and pointing the nose of the Stryker right at the chapel doors. He was beginning his run. I jumped down and opened the locks on the doors and then dove out of the way. Seconds later the Stryker burst right through them. One of the doors was slammed inward and the other came right off its hinges. The Stryker pulled right into the entry of the chapel which was as big as a garage. Tuck swung it around so the nose was facing out and dropped the rear ramp.

"GET INSIDE!" I shouted. "GET INSIDE! GET INSIDE!"

My squad knew when freedom was at hand and they scrambled inside and I was making for the ramp myself, Sabelia waiting there for me. Diane stuck her head out and said, "The fifty's jammed, Steve!"

Shit!

I climbed up onto the Stryker just as the zombies began coming up the steps in waves.

"GET THAT RAMP UP!"

I heard it close and saw Sabelia climbing up onto the Stryker with me and I knew there was no way I could talk her out of it. She got up there with her AK and started busting rounds, trying to drive the zombies back. It worked with the first wave. She dropped six of them and the others either fell over them or stopped to feed on them. But there were more, wave upon wave of the dead coming at us. By then Tuck had poked out of the driver's hatch with his CAR-15 and was dropping the dead, too. Pieces of zombie anatomy were flying like rice at a wedding.

"TUCK! ROLL US OUT!"

He dropped a few more then disappeared back inside while Sabelia emptied the last rounds of her AK, tossed it, grabbed up my CAR-15 and started putting them down again.

"HANG ON!" I told her when the Stryker began to move.

I figured sitting there was the most dangerous thing we could do. The Stryker moved forward, knocking the dead out of the way and bouncing down the steps into the courtyard. Sabelia and I hung on tight. I went to the fifty and saw the problem immediately: one of the links had caught and jammed the gun. I pulled back the bolt and freed it. The entire operation probably took thirty seconds. It would have taken less, but the Stryker was bulling its way forward, rolling over dozens of zombies and I had a hell of a time hanging on.

As we cleared the gates, the vehicle mowed down a pack and rolled right over them and I lost my balance. I slid towards the edge and felt my legs dangling out in mid-air. And all around us, converging from every side were the dead, hundreds of them. I felt hands grip my ankles and pull me and I hung onto the .50-cal mount for dear life. The Stryker was still moving and some of the zombies let go only to be replaced by more and more of them.

Sabelia rose up, screamed something, and emptied the clip of the CAR-15 into a cluster of heads and then I was loose. She pulled me up and more zombies reached for me. I kicked out, my boots smashing into soft rotten faces and then I was safe, but the zombies were everywhere. We were like a ship caught in a sea of thrashing, biting sharks.

I knocked on the gunner's hatch and Diane opened it.

Sabelia got in and then I followed her. I locked down the hatch and jumped in the gunner's seat. We had made it.

DEAD ZONE

I knew our problems were hardly over, though.

The Stryker is a powerful vehicle and Tuck was jamming it forward through the bodies in eight-wheel drive, but the more they piled up the more trouble we were going to have. It would literally become a bog of putrescence out there and I didn't care for the idea of us becoming mired in it.

I opened up with the .50-cal, cutting a path through their ranks. I followed this with a patterned barrage from the grenade launcher: high explosive, incendiary, HE, incendiary. Ranks of zombies were obliterated in explosions of blood and meat that rose up in boiling red mists. They were incinerated and pulverized, but there were more, always many more. I zeroed in on them with the crosshair on my screen and dropped row after row of them and it was no easy bit with the Stryker jumping and bucking as we rolled over heaps of corpses. I fired off more grenades and blasted a path…and then we saw daylight.

The dead were not congregating now.

We'd made it through the main force and we were going to make it.

We were really going to make it.

Tuck steered the Stryker through the last zombie groups and we plowed aside a wrecked car and we were really rolling, really on our way.

That's when we heard the chopper.

It zipped right over our heads.

I caught sight of it on the screen and it was a Kiowa scout helicopter armed with Hellfire anti-tank missiles. We got hit by one of those and we were done. It zipped over us again and I got on the radio and tried to hail them, telling them we friendly, we were not a militia, that I was a soldier formerly with a Stryker Cavalry Brigade and I was evacuating people from the city. I thought if they were the Army it would work. But if they were listening, they ignored me. Which told me one thing: barring communications failure, these guys were members of ARM. And I had just told them we were not part of their forces. I knew they had a chopper. Katherine had told me so, but I had no idea they had something like this…a freaking Kiowa armed to the teeth.

Jesus.

Out in the streets we were sitting ducks. The Hellfire missiles were laser-guided and we had no maneuverability in those avenues with wrecked cars and overturned busses everywhere.

"I don't like this," Tuck said as he pushed the Stryker forward.

On my screen I saw the Kiowa coming in again and I didn't think he was just going to buzz us this time. I was pretty sure he meant business. I looked around and all I could see were huge ramparts of mangled cars and trucks that had been pushed aside by someone to clear the streets. It was our only option.

"GET US AROUND THAT PILE OF CARS!" I called out to Tuck. "TWO 'O CLOCK!"

Tuck jammed the Stryker forward, and cut to the right just as the Hellfires came screaming through the sky. They missed us by mere feet, striking the rampart of cars with resounding explosions that threw the Stryker off its wheels and threw all of us around. The Hellfires obliterated the heaped cars and a rain of burning metal and vehicle parts slammed into the outside of the Stryker and I knew one of them had hit the .50-cal above which was our only true defense against the Kiowa.

We were in a real world of shit.

Then I remembered the AT4 anti-tank weapon. It would do in a pinch and it was our only chance. I told Tuck to jig us around a bit and zig zag so they couldn't target us so easily and I went into the rear and grabbed the AT4. I had just got it out when Tuck plowed through some cars and I hit the floor of the vehicle and I heard another Hellfire detonate. Like before, the Stryker jumped into the air and came down with a concussion that threw us all over the place. I ended up in a tangle with Susan, Sabelia, Riley, and Mia. More wrecked cars and pieces of them struck the outside of the Stryker.

AT4 Anti-Tank Weapon
Type: Disposable Rocket Launcher
Kill Range: 900 feet
Warhead: 84 mm High explosive Anti-Armor

"TUCK!" I cried out as I disentangled myself. "STOP US DEAD!"

He did.

Carrying the AT4 I went over to my screen at the gunner's station. We were right in the middle of the Hellfire blast area. There were burning remains of cars everywhere. Plumes of black smoke rose up into a dark haze above us. One flaming car was standing on its hood and leaning right up against us. We were nicely camouflaged by burning wreckage. There was no way the Kiowa crew could know if it was the Stryker burning or the wrecks.

And that's exactly what I wanted.

I popped the gunner's hatch after warning Sabelia in no uncertain terms that she was not allowed to follow me or try to retrieve my ass if the shit hit the fan. I got out there and it was hard to see in the smoke. The fire around us was so hot it was like being downwind from a blast furnace. I heard the Kiowa flying over the tops of the buildings.

Strictly recon now: he thought he'd hit us.

The driver's hatch opened and Tuck stuck his head out. "We got company," he said, then went back inside.

Of course we did.

The zombies were coming again from behind us. Like sharks that sense a ship has gone down in mid-ocean, the dead realized that something was happening and it might mean meat in the offing. They were about a half a block away and closing. Whenever the smoke cleared, I saw them. First forty or fifty and then twice that number. Things were getting dicey. The Kiowa started its run from the opposite end of the street. Unless I was wrong, I didn't think he'd waste Hellfires on us when it probably appeared from the air that we were already hit and immobile.

The zombies kept coming.

The Kiowa zoomed in. We were sandwiched now between them.

It was time.

The smoke in my eyes and fire singing my hair, I wiped sweat from my face and took up the AT4. The AT4 is a fire-and-forget-it weapon meaning that it's disposable after you shoot it. I pulled the safety pin at the back of the tube. I got into firing position and removed the first safety. Then I sighted in on the chopper as it came down at us. It was still a good distance away but definitely in range of the AT4. I held down the red safety lever and it was armed. I zeroed in on the chopper and pressed the red firing button.

The missile took off with a thundering jolt, spewing a cloud of back-blast flames and at that distance, the Kiowa was helpless. The pilot tried to bank it to the right and the missile went right into the chopper's underbelly and the explosion was deafening. The chopper went up into an immense fireball and its forward momentum carried it right over us, dumping over a ton of burning metal and debris right on top of the zombies and scattering fiery wreckage in every direction. A chunk of blazing metal seared my forearm and another lit my hair on fire.

I patted my head out and slid back down into the gunner's seat and I got a round of cheers from everyone and Sabelia came over and kissed me full on the mouth. Diane did the same.

Then we were rolling again.

Really rolling.

And by then there was nothing left to stop us.

PRELUDE TO WAR

I was never so happy as to be free of the city.

We didn't head directly back to the airfield, of course. There was no way we were leaving those three other Strykers behind. I drove one, Riley drove another, and Diane drove the one with the TOW missile launch platform. Sabelia jumped into the Jeep with Dorian and away we rolled. We danced with some zombies in the streets when we got to the garage and we had to break a window to get in because I'd locked the big door. There was some shooting, a few moments of anxiety, but we got it done.

When we rolled into the airfield I was nervous.

Nervous because no one came out to greet us.

Then they must have seen the Jeep and Jimmy came out followed by Paul, Jilly and Maria who were holding hands. I held my son, the weight of everything pressing down upon me, and I could barely stand. I got inside and it was still on my shoulders. Everything that had happened since the Necrophage/Necrovirus outbreak was rolling through my mind and I was thinking about my wife and my neighbors and the tower and what happened to Davis and all the rest. It made me want to cry but I knew that there was a place and time for that, but it wasn't now. Yet…I couldn't stop thinking about Ricki. I hoped to God that she was not walking around out there. I remembered the day it started for me and how I was wiring the damn air conditioner and planning on grilling a few steaks that night.

How in the hell had all this happened?

I still had so damn many questions.

And no good answers.

Introductions were made between Jimmy and the kids and the ladies from the school. It became very apparent to us that the garage simply wasn't going to work any longer—there were too many of us.

"There's an Air Guard Station over near Pelham," Sabelia pointed out.

"That's right," Riley put in. "My brother was stationed there."

We held a council of war—as Tuck called it—and discussed our options. We definitely needed somewhere big enough for all of us to operate out of. Because there was one thing for sure and one thing we all agreed upon: we were not going to hide like rats in a hole. We were going to take the fight to the streets now that we had the Strykers. We were going to kick zombie ass. It was the only thing we really could do: if you've got a threat to you and yours, you exterminate it. And that's exactly what we were going to do. Put the dead back where they belonged and if we bagged a few members of ARM along the way then that was just fine.

We all agreed to make our run in the morning.

It was just getting dark when we got back from the city and that night I sat by myself under the stars and did some thinking. I was thinking about our little group and particularly the kids. What kind of world was it they were poised to inherit? Something had happened that caused Necrophage to run rampant. I'd seen a foreshadowing of it in Iraq, but that was localized. This time it was global. And still I had no idea—nor did anyone else, apparently—on how it could spread so goddamned fast. It happened overnight, more or less. What was the vector? What could it possibly be? And even if there was some super-fast vector to spread it globally within a matter of hours…what about those that were already dead when it started? Because a great many of the zombies out there had died *before* the virus showed up. And that made no sense. Even if we had our hypothetical super-fast vector, would the virus—or any virus for that matter—target corpses intentionally? And if it did, how in the fuck did it get inside coffins and down in graves?

There were answers. Somewhere out there were answers. And I wanted them. I think we all did. Maybe if we knew we might be able to stop it from happening again if and when we ever got civilization rolling. And that worried me. That worried me to no end. That brought me back to the kids. Paul and Maria and Jilly. Jesus, we had to do something to straighten this out. We couldn't leave them to inherit a graveyard. We had to strike back and we had to strike back hard. It would begin as a guerrilla war but before it was over it would become a very nasty, very ugly war of extermination.

But there was no choice. None at all.

I heard someone coming and I knew it was Paul. "Dad…what are you doing?"

"Just thinking, son."

"About what?"

"About what we're going to do next."

He nodded and stared up at the stars with me, maybe wondering like I was what sort of dramas might be playing out up there and if maybe there was some race out there seeing our star and saying, that's a pretty one, never realizing the horror that was coming down on its third planet.

"Dad," Paul said. "Things are going to be okay, aren't they?"

"Damn right they are," I told him. "I wouldn't have it any other way."

And I meant it.

The dead had taken the world from us and now we were going to take it back.

—The End—

www.severedpress.com

NECROPHOBIA

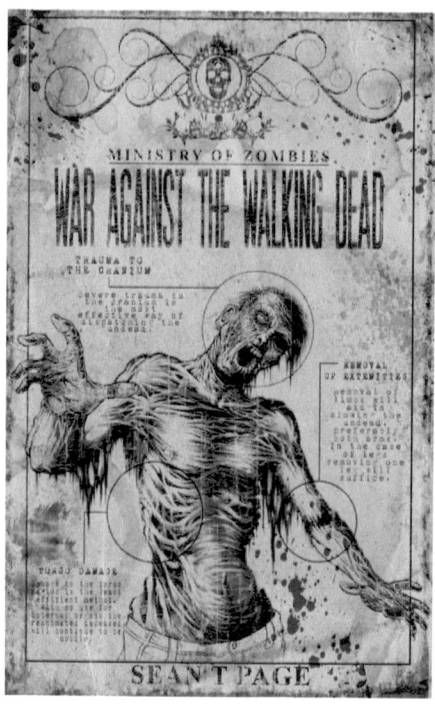

More than 63% of people now believe that there will be a global zombie apocalypse before 2050...

So, you've got your survival guide, you've lived through the first chaotic months of the crisis, what next?
Employing real science and pioneering field work, War against the Walking Dead provides a complete blueprint for taking back your country from the rotting clutches of the dead after a zombie apocalypse.

* A glimpse inside the mind of the zombie using a team of top psychics - what do the walking dead think about? What lessons can we learn to help us defeat this pervading menace?
* Detailed guidelines on how to galvanise a band of scared survivors into a fighting force capable of defeating the zombies and dealing with emerging groups such as end of the world cults, raiders and even cannibals!
* Features insights from real zombie fighting organisations across the world, from America to the Philippines, Australia to China - the experts offer advice in every aspect of fighting the walking dead.
Packed with crucial zombie war information and advice, from how to build a city of the living in a land of the dead to tactics on how to use a survivor army to liberate your country from the zombies - War against the Walking Dead may be humanity's last chance.

Remember, dying is not an option!

Available at www.severedpress.com, Amazon and most online bookstores

RESURRECTION
By Tim Curran
www.corpseking.com

The rain is falling and the dead are rising. It began at an ultra-secret government laboratory. Experiments in limb regeneration-an unspeakable union of Medieval alchemy and cutting edge genetics result in the very germ of horror itself: a gene trigger that will reanimate dead tissue...any dead tissue. Now it's loose. It's gone viral. It's in the rain. And the rain has not stopped falling for weeks. As the country floods and corpses float in the streets, as cities are submerged, the evil dead are rising. And they are hungry.

"I REALLY love this book...Curran is a wonderful storyteller who really should be unleashed upon the general horror reading public sooner rather than leter." – DREAD CENTRAL

Available at www.severedpress.com, Amazon and most online bookstores

THE DEVIL NEXT DOOR

Cannibalism. Murder. Rape. Absolute brutality. When civilizations ends...when the human race begins to revert to ancient, predatory savagery...when the world descends into a bloodthirsty hell...there is only survival. But for one man and one woman, survival means becoming something less than human. Something from the primeval dawn of the race.

"Shocking and brutal, The Devil Next Door will hit you like a baseball bat to the face. Curran seems to have it in for the world ... and he's ending it as horrifyingly as he can." - *Tim Lebbon, author of Bar None*

"The Devil Next Door is dynamite! Visceral, violent, and disturbing!." *Brian Keene, author of Castaways and Dark Hollow*

"The Devil Next Door is a horror fans delight...who love extreme horror fiction, and to those that just enjoy watching the world go to hell in a hand basket" – *HORROR WORLD*

Available at www.severedpress.com, Amazon and most online bookstores

Dead Bait

"If you don't already suffer from bathophobia and/or ichthyophobia, you probably will after reading this amazingly wonderful horrific collection of short stories about what lurks beneath the waters of the world" – *DREAD CENTRAL*

A husband hell-bent on revenge hunts a Wereshark...A Russian mail order bride with a fishy secret...Crabs with a collective consciousness...A vampire who transforms into a Candiru...Zombie piranha...Bait that will have you crawling out of your skin and more. Drawing on horror, humor with a helping of dark fantasy and a touch of deviance, these 19 contemporary stories pay homage to the monsters that lurk in the murky waters of our imaginations. *If you thought it was safe to go back in the water...Think Again!*

"Severed Press has the cojones to publish THE most outrageous, nasty and downright wonderfully disgusting horror that I've seen in quite a while." – *DREAD CENTRAL*

Available at www.severedpress.com, Amazon and most online bookstores

DEMONMACHY
Brant Danay

As the universe slowly dies, all demonkind is at war in a tournament of genocide. The prize? Nirvana. The Necrodelic, a death addict who smokes the flesh of his victims as a drug, is determined to win this afterlife for himself. His quest has taken him to the planet Grystiawa, and into a duel with a dream-devouring snake demon who is more than he seems. Grystiawa has also been chosen as the final battleground in the ancient spider-serpent wars. As armies of arachnid monstrosities and ophidian gladiators converge upon the planet, the Necrodelic is forced to choose sides in a cataclysmic combat that could well prove his demise. Beyond Grystiawa, a Siamese twin incubus and succubus, a brain-raping nightmare fetishist, a gargantuan insect queen, and an entire universe of genocidal demons are forming battle plans of their own. Observing the apocalyptic carnage all the while is Satan himself, watching voyeuristically from the very Hell in which all those who fail will be damned to eternal torment. Who will emerge victorious from this cosmic armageddon? And what awaits the victor beyond the blood-drenched end of time? The battle begins in Demonmachy. Twisting Satanic mythologies and Eastern religions into an ultraviolent grotesque nightmare, the Messiah of Death Saga will rip your eyeballs right out of your skull. Addicted to its psychedelic darkness, you'll immediately sew and screw and staple and weld them back into their sockets so you can read more. It's an intergalactic, interdimensional harrowing that you'll never forget...and may never recover from.

Available at www.severedpress.com, Amazon and most online bookstores

ZOMBIE ZOOLOGY
Unnatural History:

Severed Press has assembled a truly original anthology of never before published stories of living dead beasts. Inside you will find tales of prehistoric creatures rising from the Bog, a survivalist taking on a troop of rotting baboons, a NASA experiment going Ape, A hunter going a Moose too far and many more undead creatures from Hell. The crawling, buzzing, flying abominations of mother nature have risen and they are hungry.

> "Clever and engaging a reanimated rarity"
> **FANGORIA**

> "I loved this very unique anthology and highly recommend it"
> **Monster Librarian**

Available at www.severedpress.com, Amazon and most online bookstores

BIOHAZARD
Tim Curran

The day after tomorrow: Nuclear fallout. Mutations. Deadly pandemics. Corpse wagons. Body pits. Empty cities. The human race trembling on the edge of extinction. Only the desperate survive. One of them is Rick Nash. But there is a price for survival: communion with a ravenous evil born from the furnace of radioactive waste. It demands sacrifice. Only it can keep Nash one step ahead of the nightmare that stalks him-a sentient, seething plague-entity that stalks its chosen prey: the last of the human race. To accept it is a living death. To defy it, a hell beyond imagining

"kick back and enjoy some the most violent and genuinely scary apocalyptic horror written by one of the finest dark fiction authors plying his trade today" HORRORWORLD

Available at www.severedpress.com, Amazon and most online bookstores